BETRAYAL

ALSO BY PHILLIP MARGOLIN

Heartstone

The Last Innocent Man

Gone, But Not Forgotten

After Dark

The Burning Man

The Undertaker's Widow

The Associate

Sleeping Beauty

Lost Lake

Worthy Brown's Daughter

Woman with a Gun

Vanishing Acts (with Ami Margolin Rome)

Amanda Jaffe Novels

Wild Justice

Ties That Bind

Proof Positive

Fugitive

Violent Crimes

Dana Cutler Novels

Executive Privilege

Supreme Justice

Capitol Murder

Sleight of Hand

Robin Lockwood Novels

The Third Victim

The Perfect Alibi

A Reasonable Doubt

A Matter of Life and Death

The Darkest Place

Murder at Black Oaks

BETRAYAL

A ROBIN LOCKWOOD NOVEL

Phillip Margolin

MINOTAUR
BOOKS
NEW YORK

First published in the United States by Minotaur Books, an imprint of St. Martin's Publishing Group

BETRAYAL. Copyright © 2023 by Phillip Margolin. All rights reserved. Printed in the United States of America. For information, address St. Martin's Publishing Group, 120 Broadway, New York, NY 10271.

www.minotaurbooks.com

Designed by Omar Chapa

Library of Congress Cataloging-in-Publication Data

Names: Margolin, Phillip, author.
Title: Betrayal / Phillip Margolin.
Description: First edition. | New York : Minotaur Books, 2023. |
   Series: A Robin Lockwood novel ; 7
Identifiers: LCCN 2023027935 | ISBN 9781250885791 (hardcover) |
   ISBN 9781250885807 (ebook)
Subjects: LCSH: Lockwood, Robin (Fictitious character)—Fiction. |
   LCGFT: Legal fiction (Literature) | Novels.
Classification: LCC PS3563.A649 B48 2023 | DDC 813/.54—dc23/eng/20230703
LC record available at https://lccn.loc.gov/2023027935

Our books may be purchased in bulk for promotional, educational, or business use. Please contact your local bookseller or the Macmillan Corporate and Premium Sales Department at 1-800-221-7945, extension 5442, or by email at MacmillanSpecialMarkets@macmillan.com.

First Edition: 2023

10 9 8 7 6 5 4 3 2 1

Betrayal *is my twenty-seventh novel, and I am dedicating it to Jean Naggar and Jennifer Weltz, my brilliant agents who made it possible for me to have a career doing something I love*

PART ONE

911

THE PRESENT

CHAPTER ONE

Shortly before Megan Radcliffe's favorite show started, a very odd event occurred that was followed by a horrifying event.

The show started at 8:00, so Megan walked to her kitchen at 7:50 to make a snack. To get to the kitchen, she passed a window that looked across the street at the home of Margaret and Nathan Finch and their two children, Annie and Ryan. Megan saw a woman pounding on the Finches' front door. She was shouting, but Megan couldn't hear what the woman was saying.

Megan watched for a moment. Then she went to the kitchen, fixed some cheese and crackers, and headed back to the living room. She had taped the show, so she wasn't worried about missing any of it. At some time between 8:05 and 8:10, she passed the window again and saw the woman leave the porch and walk away from the Finches' house. That was the odd event. Megan's show paused for a commercial at 8:15, and she looked out the window in her living room that faced the Finch house. The light from the Finches' living room illuminated the porch, but no one was on it. At 8:30, when her show ended, Megan heard a car stop across the street. She recognized Arthur Proctor, who taught English at Marie Curie Middle School, walking to the Finches' front door. She saw him ring the bell, then she saw him go inside. She had finished her snack, and then took her plate to the kitchen. When she returned to the living room, she saw Proctor bolt out of the Finch house, leaving the front door wide open.

Megan opened her front door and walked toward the teacher. He looked horrified.

"What happened?" Megan shouted. Proctor waved her away. He had his phone out and was shouting into it. This is what Megan heard:

"911. What is your emergency?"

"They're all dead."

"Sir, who am I speaking with?"

"Sorry, I'm just . . . I'm Annie's teacher, Arthur Proctor. I came to the house to talk about Annie's scholarship, and I found them."

"Found who?"

"Everyone. The Finch family. They're all dead."

The Folly of Youth

TEN YEARS EARLIER

CHAPTER TWO

Robin Lockwood's first-year contracts class at Yale University's law school was held in a large classroom where six rows of desks curved in a graceful arc from one side of the room to the other in front of the professor's podium. Robin tried to hide from the professor by sitting three seats in from one end in the last row. Despite her best efforts at camouflage, Professor Dawkins found her on the second day of class and posed a hypothetical question that presented facts that were similar to the case she had read the night before, but added an unsettling twist.

Having a really good memory had made life easy in college, but Robin had discovered that law school required much more than just memorizing facts. You had to be able to solve puzzles, because the professors were always challenging you with problems that made it impossible for you to put a square-peg fact in a round-hole situation.

When the professor zeroed in on Robin, Robin's stomach

clenched the same way it did at the beginning of a fight in the Octagon. Robin could solve problems in a cage fight with an arm bar or a
right cross, but she suspected that she would be thrown out of Yale if
she coldcocked her professor. So, she took a deep breath, thought for
a moment, and gave an answer that made Professor Dawkins smile.

"Very good, Miss Lockwood," Dawkins said just as class ended.

"Great answer," said the woman seated next to Robin.

"Thanks. I was really sweating," Robin answered as she shut her
laptop and stowed it in the duffel bag that contained her workout
gear.

"Samantha Jefferson, but everyone calls me Sam," the woman
said as she held out her hand.

"Robin Lockwood," Robin said as she shook it.

"I'm in a study group that's meeting in an hour," Sam said as
they headed for the door. "Do you want to join us?"

"I'd love to, but I'm in training, and I've got to get to the gym."

The woman's brow furrowed. "Training for what?"

Robin blushed. "I'm a professional fighter, MMA. I have a fight
in Las Vegas coming up in a month."

"No shit?"

Robin laughed. "Yeah, shit. The only good news is that fighting
isn't nearly as scary as these law school classes."

"Is this fight on TV?"

Robin blushed again and nodded.

"Wow. How does a law student get into MMA?"

"It's the other way around. Fighting got me into law school."

Sam looked puzzled. Robin smiled.

"My dad and my three brothers were all championship wrestlers in high school, so I wanted to be on the high school team. Some
of the parents panicked when they found out their sons would be in

close physical contact with a girl. They lobbied the school board, and I was told I couldn't be on the team. But Lockwoods are fighters, and my dad hired a lawyer. We sued and we won. That's when I decided that I wanted to be a lawyer when I grew up."

"You wrestled against boys?"

"Yup. And I did okay. I actually placed third in my conference my senior year. Then I went to a college that had a ranked Division I team. I didn't even think about trying out, but I still liked combat sports, so I found a gym that taught mixed martial arts, and the rest is history."

"Well, I'm impressed, and I'll warn everyone not to piss you off."

Robin laughed.

"And the offer to join the study group is open when you don't have a conflict. We can use a brain who can get a smile out of Professor Dawkins."

When they were outside the Sterling Law Building, Robin and Sam swapped phone numbers and chatted for a few minutes more. Then Robin headed for the gym that she'd found in her first week in New Haven.

Robin was five foot eight with a wiry build, blue eyes, high cheekbones, blond hair that molded to her oval face, and a straight nose that had never been broken—a tribute to her defensive skills as a cage fighter. As she ran, she wondered how she was going to balance law school and her fighting career. It hadn't been that difficult in college, where she'd majored in physics, a subject that came easily to her. But the amount of reading her law school professors assigned had her burning the midnight oil and rising groggy and bleary-eyed every morning. Add in several hours of intense physical training and the end result was a body and brain left gasping for air every day.

Twenty minutes after saying goodbye to her new friend, Robin stopped in front of a building that could not have been more different from the Sterling Law Building. That Gothic-style edifice was modeled on the English Inns of Court and embellished with stone sculptures, wood carvings, and stained glass. Robin's gym was on the ground floor in a corner storefront that advertised training in boxing, karate, and other martial arts and let passersby look through plate glass windows at wrestlers grappling on mats, fighters working the heavy bag, and muscular men and women hoisting weights or running on treadmills.

Robin went inside and started for the locker room when she saw her manager, Bruce Dowling, walking in her direction. Dowling was thick and wide, with thinning brown hair and a face that displayed scar tissue built up during his days as a professional boxer.

Robin was always glad to see Dowling, but she was surprised to see him in her gym this morning. The last she'd heard, Dowling was in Manhattan working on contracts for his other fighters. Robin smiled, but Dowling looked serious.

"What brings you to New Haven?" Robin asked.

"Business. We need to discuss something that's just come up."

"Oh?"

"You know who Mandy Kerrigan is?"

"Of course. Next month, I'm on the undercard of her fight in Vegas."

Dowling nodded. "Kerrigan is the number two contender in your weight class, and she was supposed to fight Angelina Mendes in the co-main event, winner to fight for the championship. Yesterday, Angelina broke her ankle during a training run. They need a ranked contender to step in so they won't have to cancel the fight. You're ranked ninth, and you're on the card."

Robin felt a rush of adrenaline, and she lit up like a Christmas tree. Then she noticed that Dowling looked grim.

"Why the long face?" Robin asked. "This could be a huge break."

Dowling nodded. "It's a good payday, and you'll get national exposure, but I don't know if you're ready for someone like Kerrigan."

"Hey, Bruce, aren't you supposed to give me the *Rocky* pep talk?"

"No. I'm supposed to tell you the facts of life. You haven't lost yet, and you have a ton of potential, but you've been knocking off opponents who have nowhere near what Kerrigan can bring. In baseball terms, you're Double-A and you're ready to jump to Triple-A, but Kerrigan is in the big leagues."

Robin reached out and touched Dowling's forearm. "I know you're looking out for me, and I appreciate it, but I have to take this fight to see how good I am. I won't be fighting when I finish law school. This might be my only chance to be in line to fight for a championship."

"You're sure you want to do this?"

"I have to, Bruce."

"Okay, then. I'll make the call."

Robin squeezed Dowling's arm. "Cheer up, Mr. Dowling. Think about the big fee you're going to get."

Dowling shook his head. "I just hope it doesn't all go to doctor's bills."

Bruce Dowling had hired several sparring partners for Robin, and she spent part of her workout grappling and part on improving her boxing skills. After a quick shower, Robin walked around the corner to a local Italian restaurant. Over lunch, she and Bruce discussed the contract for the Kerrigan fight. Robin had leverage because the show was coming up soon and Dowling had gotten her the best payday of her career.

After lunch, Bruce returned to New York, and Robin walked to her apartment, which was halfway between the gym and the law school. Robin had no time for entertaining. All she did was study and train. The apartment was perfect for her Spartan existence. It had one compact bedroom, a small kitchen with a table for dining, and a living room wide enough for a sofa, a television, and the desk where Robin studied.

She had her torts class in an hour. She parked herself at the desk and started reading a case the professor was going to discuss, but she found it difficult to concentrate. She couldn't believe everything that had happened to her in the five years since graduating from high school in Elk Grove, the small midwestern town where she'd grown up. She'd had a stellar college career that had led to acceptance at an elite law school, she'd become a nationally ranked MMA star who fought on internationally televised fight cards, and she had hobnobbed at parties in Las Vegas, New York, and LA with celebrities from the movie, sports, and music industries. Now, she was on the verge of a shot at a world championship.

Robin wondered what she would do if she became a world champion. She had always assumed that she would stop fighting when she graduated from law school, but she might put off her legal career if she could become financially secure by fighting.

She laughed at herself. *One step at a time,* she thought. That world title was only a vague possibility. Professor Gupta's torts class was very real and, now, less than an hour away.

CHAPTER THREE

The lights in the arena dimmed, the announcer called out her name, and Robin walked toward the Octagon bathed in the spotlight that accompanied her down the aisle between thousands of screaming spectators. The loudspeaker was blaring her walk-in music, Bobby Day's "Rockin' Robin," and her fans belted out, "Old Rockin' Robin is really gonna rock tonight," as she passed by. Robin knew her mom, brothers, their wives, and some of her classmates were in the audience, but all she could see was the entrance to the cage.

Once inside the Octagon, her trainer rubbed her shoulders and whispered encouragement in her ear. Robin was always nervous before a fight started, but this was the first time she'd felt fear. She'd experienced her first moment of doubt when she'd come face-to-face with Mandy Kerrigan at the weigh-in. Robin treated her fights as sport and never hated her opponents. Out of the ring, she got on well with most of them, and she didn't let the women who were angry or unfriendly bother her. Mandy Kerrigan was different.

There was the difference in their physiques. Kerrigan was a rippling muscle, with a body constructed out of accentuated abs, thick, corded biceps, and tree-stump legs. And Kerrigan was different in another way. Robin never took the stare-down that was a traditional part of a weigh-in seriously. Robin and her opponents always put on their game faces when the cameras were rolling. Then most of them eased up when the weigh-in was over. Robin had never faced an opponent who radiated so much menace. Kerrigan looked like she was fueled by rage and could barely wait to close the distance between her and the woman she saw as an obstacle to be demolished and destroyed. When Robin tried to speak to her when the cameras shut off, Kerrigan had turned her back and walked away without saying a word.

Robin was facing away from Kerrigan when her opponent entered the cage. Then the referee called Robin and Kerrigan to the center of the Octagon. Robin turned and faced the woman who stood in the way of a championship fight. The referee gave them last-minute instructions, then gave the signal for the fight to start.

The crowd roared, and Kerrigan shot across the ring, throwing wild punches. Robin had watched tape of her opponent, so the manic assault didn't surprise her. What did surprise her was the power behind the punches. She blocked most of them and rolled with the ones she didn't block, but she couldn't avoid the hammer-like impact on her arms and shoulders.

Robin tied up Kerrigan and used her wrestling skills to turn Kerrigan against the side of the cage. Kerrigan laced a leg behind Robin and tried to tip her onto her back. Robin kept her balance and pushed off.

Now that the first punches had been thrown, Robin was no longer nervous. The two women circled, keeping their distance as they looked for openings. Robin's strength was wrestling, and she calculated the distance between her and Kerrigan's legs. Getting to them without absorbing too much punishment would be a challenge, and once she was in on Kerrigan, there was no guarantee she could take her to the ground. Kerrigan's strength was boxing, but Robin had watched videos of Kerrigan's bouts. Other opponents who had gotten in on her legs had found her so strong that they'd been unable to take her down.

Robin decided to jab her way in and hope that Kerrigan would make a mistake. She threw a stiff jab, expecting Kerrigan to back away, but Kerrigan blocked the jab and charged. Robin hadn't expected the move. She threw a punch, but she was off balance, and it bounced off the top of Kerrigan's head without slowing her down. Suddenly, Robin was being crushed against the side of the cage, and Kerrigan was landing punches. Kerrigan drove a knee into Robin's stomach. Robin grabbed it and bulled her way forward. Kerrigan's leg was like iron, and she extended it backward, breaking Robin's hold.

Robin scrambled away from Kerrigan. Both women got to their feet. Kerrigan feinted with a left, distracting Robin, who lost focus for a second and did not see the foot that came out of nowhere and smashed into her temple.

Bruce Dowling waited to go into Robin's hospital room until Robin's mother and brothers had left.

"How are you feeling?" Dowling asked as he walked to the side of Robin's bed.

Robin flashed a game smile. "I'll live. The doctor says I've got a concussion, so they're keeping me overnight for observation, but he told me I can probably go back to school soon."

"That's good."

Robin's smile disappeared. "I've got short-term memory loss, Bruce." She shook her head slowly. "I don't remember anything about the fight."

Dowling smiled. "That's a good thing. You'll see what I mean when you look at the tape."

"It's that bad?"

"It ain't good."

Robin sighed. "I gave it the old college try, but you were right."

"I didn't want to say anything to you once you decided to take the fight, but you know I boxed professionally."

Robin nodded.

"I was twelve and two with eight consecutive knockouts when I went up in class and fought a top contender. It wasn't even close. He was so fast that I couldn't protect myself. That night, I learned that there was a whole different level of boxer, and I wasn't on it. After that fight, I accepted the fact that I was never going to be a champion, so I became a manager and trainer."

Dowling put his hand on Robin's shoulder. "You've got a bright future. You're gonna do great things, but you're gonna do them as a lawyer and not in the Octagon."

PART TWO

Meet the Finches

TEN YEARS LATER

CHAPTER FOUR

Lloyd Standish was as American as apple pie, if the pie was moldy and inedible. The black sheep in a family whose ancestors had come over on the *Mayflower*, Lloyd had blond hair, a Roman nose, and blue eyes that screamed WASP, and he didn't contain a single strand of DNA linking him to any state in the disbanded USSR. That, and a sociopathic personality, were the reasons that Jack Kovalev, who ran the Russian mob in Oregon, had made Lloyd his right-hand man. Standish could mingle with a class of people who would never associate with a Slavic mobster. He also had no qualms about getting his hands very dirty. In truth, Lloyd enjoyed tasks that involved violence.

Tonight, Lloyd was watching a torrential rain inundate a supermarket parking lot as he waited to send a prize piece of trailer trash on a mission that would net his boss several thousand dollars. Twenty minutes after he was supposed to arrive, Otis Truax parked his car on the edge of the lot. Lloyd raised his umbrella and walked through a row of cars to the driver's window. Truax was a scrawny, unemployed nobody with mousy brown hair, watery brown eyes, and outstanding debts to loan sharks, which made him the perfect recruit for the mob's staged auto accident insurance scam.

Truax lowered the driver's-side window a crack, leaning away from the drops that the unruly wind swept into his car. Lloyd stared at Truax until Truax looked away.

"You're late, Otis," Standish said, his tone reeking of menace.

"Sorry. Traffic," Truax mumbled.

"I do not appreciate having to stand outside in a fucking downpour for twenty minutes because you can't tell time. And I definitely do not like people who apologize for fucking up. Are you weak, Otis? Are you a fuckup?"

"No," Truax said.

"Speak up, Otis. Are you someone I can count on? Because you are being entrusted with a very important mission. If you accomplish this mission, your debt to certain vicious degenerates will be taken care of. Are you going to complete your mission and get your reward, or do you want to beg off and have many bones in your body broken?"

Despite the chill in the air, Truax was sweating. "You can count on me, Mr. Standish," Truax said.

Lloyd smiled. "Of course I can. You're my man, Otis. I wouldn't have selected you if I didn't have complete faith in you. So, are you ready to go?"

"Yeah, but are you sure about this?"

"Of course. It'll be a piece of cake. We have it down to a science. There's a spotter. He'll tell you when the mark is headed into the intersection. Then you smash into the side of the vehicle. We have a doctor who'll say you're injured, a lawyer who deals with the insurance company, and an insurance agent who's in our pocket. You just crash the car, and we'll take care of you."

"What if the cops don't believe me?"

"Not a problem. Didn't I tell you that we supply witnesses who'll claim our mark was speeding or ran a red light?"

"Yeah, that's what you said. But what if I really get hurt? This rain is coming down hard."

"Hey, Otis, you know how to drive a car, right?"

"Yeah," Truax answered hesitantly.

"Then fasten your seat belt, and let's get you a payday."

Alan Chen decided that he would call out, "Free at last, Lord, free at last," when he walked in the door. He was sure that would get a laugh out of Susan. And it was completely true. They had a two-week vacation at an all-inclusive resort in Mexico, and he planned to spend every waking hour sipping piña coladas on the beach and not looking at anything that had a number in it.

Alan pulled into the driveway and was surprised that the house was dark. Susan was usually home before he got in, but he wasn't worried. His wife worked as a trial assistant at a law firm and might have had things to wrap up before she could leave on their vacation.

Alan took off his shoes when he entered the house. Then he went into the bedroom and put on a T-shirt and sweatpants. After he changed, he walked into the living room and looked out at the front of the house to see if Susan had come home yet. When he didn't see her car, Alan walked into the kitchen and started to fix dinner.

He enjoyed his job as a CPA, but he had been working long hours and he couldn't wait to unwind in Cabo. They'd bought a New York steak to celebrate, and Alan took it out of the freezer. While he waited for it to thaw, he prepared their salad.

Susan still wasn't home when he started working on the baked potatoes. Alan checked his watch. It was almost six. He frowned. What could be keeping her? He took out his phone and called Susan. The call went to voice mail, so he dialed her office. She didn't pick up, so he dialed her best friend at the office, hoping that she was still in.

"Hi, Tina," he said when he was connected. "Is Susan still working?"

"No. She left around five, Alan."

"Did she say she was going somewhere other than home?"

Tina laughed. "She was definitely headed home. All she's been talking about is your vacation."

Tina suddenly understood why Alan was calling, and her light tone changed to concern.

"Isn't she home yet?"

"No."

"She probably stopped off to get some sunscreen," Tina said.

Alan laughed, but he was worried. And his anxiety increased with each passing minute. Alan tried Susan's cell phone again, with the same result. Then he peered through the drops beating on the living room window, willing her car to appear. It didn't, so he went back to the kitchen. He was putting the baked potatoes in the oven when the doorbell rang.

Alan hurried to the front door and opened it. Two men were standing on the welcome mat. One man was wearing a yellow slicker over a policeman's uniform, and the other man was tall, thin, and balding and he was wearing a raincoat over a brown suit.

"Yes?" Alan asked, afraid of what he might hear.

"I'm Chet Marx," the man in plainclothes said as he held up his identification. "I'm a detective with the Portland police. This is Ronald Jefferson. Can we come in?"

Alan had been oblivious to the rain that was pounding on the two men until they asked to enter his house. He stepped back.

"Of course. Come in," he said.

"Are you related to Susan Chen?" Detective Marx asked.

"I'm her husband, Alan."

Marx looked at the living room. "I think you should sit down," he said.

"Why? What's this about?"

"We have some very bad news, sir. It would be better if you were sitting when you heard it."

"Is this . . . Is it Susan?"

Marx nodded, and Alan collapsed on the nearest chair. The detective took a seat opposite Alan. Jefferson stood off to one side.

"Your wife was in a traffic accident," Marx said.

"Is she in the hospital?" Alan asked, hoping that the detective would say she was.

"I'm afraid she passed," Marx said.

Alan stared at Marx for a second. Then his chest heaved, and he began to cry. The detective waited until Alan stopped sobbing.

"There's something else you need to know," Marx said. "We think that the accident that killed your wife was staged as part of an insurance scam."

Alan's head jerked up. "What?"

"There are organized groups who stage accidents to collect insurance money. It's unusual for there to be a fatality, but this time . . ."

Marx let the sentence hang.

"Someone murdered Susan?" Alan asked.

"We think so. We have the driver of the other car in custody, and I want to assure you that we are going to make the people responsible for your wife's death pay."

Alan didn't respond. He had stopped crying, and he was looking past the policemen.

"The district attorney may contact you. He might need you as a witness. But it's too early to tell. Meanwhile, we need you to come with us to identify your wife. Do you feel up to it?"

Alan nodded.

"I'm sorry to put you through this," Marx apologized.

"I understand. Let me change."

"Of course."

Alan headed for the bedroom, and Jefferson shook his head.

"Poor bastard."

Marx sighed. "I don't know how many times I've done this. It never gets easier."

CHAPTER FIVE

Margaret Finch, attorney-at-law, was almost six feet tall, with cheerleader hair she dyed blond, blue eyes that were made bluer by contacts, and a slender, toned body that had been manufactured by personal trainers in upscale gyms and maintained by a vegetarian diet. She might have been more attractive if her face was a little fuller, but plastic surgery had given it a pinched appearance that struck people as a little bit off. Margaret also put people off because she rarely smiled. That was a product of being under constant stress, because of the work she did and the people who paid her for this work.

Lloyd Standish had summoned Margaret to a meeting a little before midnight. Meetings with the mobster outside normal office hours rarely involved anything good, but given the size of the retainer Jack Kovalev paid her, she had no choice but to get dressed and drive downtown in the dark in the middle of an unsettling downpour.

What was as unsettling as the manic rain and having to meet Standish, who gave her the creeps, was having to meet him in a seedy bar owned by Kovalev. The usual place for a meeting with Standish was one of the upscale restaurants where he preferred to dine.

Three things occurred to Margaret as soon as she entered the bar. First, Standish, who usually dressed like a banker, was wearing jeans, a dark baseball cap, and a gray sweatshirt under a black raincoat. Second, he was sitting in a booth in the back of the bar, where the lighting was dim. Three, he had summoned Margaret to a meeting in the middle of the night. It didn't take Sherlock Holmes to deduce that something had gone horribly wrong. That didn't keep Margaret from being annoyed.

"Why the cloak-and-dagger scenario, Lloyd?" Margaret asked as she slipped onto the seat across from Standish. "Is there some reason we couldn't meet during office hours like civilized people?"

"I'm in no mood for impertinence, Margaret. You're paid to do what we tell you to do, when we tell you. So, stow the attitude. There was a very bad screwup tonight. One of our drivers killed a woman."

"Jesus!"

"The man's name is Otis Truax. He's in custody, and he is spineless. You are going to go to the jail right now and shut him up before he cuts a deal to save his worthless skin."

"What happened? I need some background before I see him."

"I wasn't at the scene, but one of our people told me Truax was going way too fast. The roadway was slick, he went into a skid, and he may have hit the accelerator instead of the brake. He T-boned the other car. Hit it right in the driver's door. The car was totaled, and the driver died at the scene."

"What about Truax? Why is he in jail instead of the hospital?"

Standish laughed. "If the asshole had died, it would have saved me a lot of trouble, but all he walked away with were a few bruises."

"I told you this insurance scam was risky," Margaret said.

"Maybe you were right, but we're not going to be Monday-morning quarterbacks right now. What you are going to do is damage control. Shut up Truax and bail him out."

"Then what? There was a death. The DA is going to have Truax over a barrel. They'll know he was a tool, and they'll offer him a sweetheart deal to get him to roll over. How am I going to keep him from talking after I get him out?"

The look Standish gave her made Margaret's stomach roll.

"Let me worry about that problem. You take care of business right now."

Standish slapped a twenty on the table and left. Margaret waited to leave so they wouldn't be seen together. While she waited, she wished she'd ordered a stiff drink. Even the crap they probably served in this dump would have helped calm her down and kept her from thinking about the future Otis Truax faced once he was free and unprotected by steel bars and jail guards.

Margaret drove to the Multnomah County Justice Center, an eighteen-story, concrete-and-glass building in downtown Portland. The building was home to the central precinct of the Portland Police Bureau, a branch of the Multnomah County District Attorney's Office, several courtrooms, and the Multnomah County Jail, which occupied the fourth through tenth floors.

The jail reception area was on the second floor. At this hour, there was almost no one around. Margaret walked through the building's vaulted lobby, past curving stairs that led to the courtrooms, and through a glass door. She showed her ID to the duty officer and went through a metal detector before taking an elevator to the floor where attorneys met their clients.

Margaret walked out of the elevator into a narrow, concrete hallway whose walls were painted pastel yellow. There was a thick metal door at one end. She pressed the button on the intercom and announced her presence. Moments later, she heard the electronic locks snap, and a guard opened the door and escorted her down another narrow hallway that ran in front of three contact visiting rooms. She could see into the rooms through large windows outfitted with shatterproof glass.

The guard stopped in front of a solid metal door that opened into the first visiting room. Molded plastic chairs stood on either side of a metal table that was bolted to the floor. Moments after the guard shut the door to the hallway, a second door in the room's other wall opened and Otis Truax shuffled into the visiting room.

The first words that sprang into Margaret's mind when she saw her client were *pathetic* and *pitiful.* Truax swam in his orange jail-issued jumpsuit. His shoulders were hunched, and, when he raised his eyes from the floor, Margaret could see that they were red-rimmed from crying.

"My name is Margaret Finch, and I'm going to represent you."

"I ain't got any money, Mrs. Finch."

Margaret smiled in a way that she hoped would gain Truax's confidence.

"That's not a problem. You have friends who are going to take care of you."

"You mean—"

Margaret raised her hand to cut him off. "No need to mention names when we don't know if anyone is listening to our conversation, is there?"

"No, ma'am."

"Good. Tomorrow, I'm going to be by your side in court, and I'm going to ask the judge to set bail for you. You don't have to worry; bail will be posted for you, no matter how much the court requires. So, you'll be out of here sometime tomorrow."

"Thank you."

"Until then, there's only one thing you have to do. Do you know what that is?"

Truax's brow furrowed, and Margaret could almost see the rusted wheels in his tiny brain turning slowly. After a few moments, Truax gave up.

"I don't know the answer," he confessed.

Margaret smiled warmly. "It's something you'll be able to do easily, Otis. May I call you Otis?"

"Yeah."

"What you have to do is nothing. And by that I mean, you have to keep your mouth shut. No talking to guards, inmates, or anyone else about what happened last night. If anyone tries to talk to you, you will say these simple words: 'I will only talk when my attorney is with me.' Do you think you can remember that sentence?"

Truax's head bobbed up and down.

"Good," Margaret said. "Why don't you repeat it back to me. I'm a guard and I say, 'Hey, Mr. Truax, what happened in that accident?' What do you say?"

"I ain't saying a word unless my attorney is with me."

Margaret beamed. "Excellent."

"Uh, I did have a question."

"Yes, Otis?"

"When they arrested me, there was this detective. He said I could be charged with murder and go to jail for the rest of my life.

But he also said that I could make a deal that might keep me out of jail if I told them who told me to make the accident."

Margaret struggled to keep the smile on her face. "What did you say to that?"

"What Mr.—"

Margaret held up her hand.

"Yeah, right," Truax said as he nodded up and down rapidly. "I said I wanted to talk to a lawyer."

"That's great, Otis. You did the right thing."

"Sure, but I don't want to get charged with murder. So, do you think I should take the deal?"

"That's a complicated question to answer, Otis, because we don't know the details of the deal. So, my suggestion, as your attorney, is that we get you out of jail first. When you're out of here, I'll talk to the DA and get the details of the deal. Then we can discuss it in my office, after you've gotten a good night's sleep. How does that sound?"

"It makes sense."

"Do you have any other questions?"

"Not right now."

"Good." Margaret stood up and pressed the button that summoned the guard. "You hang tight, and I'll see you in court real soon."

CHAPTER SIX

Nathan Finch shoveled a forkful of eggs and hash browns into his mouth without looking up from the betting line on the Colts-Rams game. Finch was six foot one, rail thin with the flabby, washed-out look of a man who never exercised or spent much time out of doors, and he studied the information on the game through thick-lensed glasses that magnified his watery, nearsighted eyes.

Finch absentmindedly ran a hand through his thinning grayish-black hair as he reached for his coffee with his other hand. The Rams' left tackle was out with an ankle injury, and the Colts had two of the best linebackers in the NFL. But the Colts' best wide receiver had suffered an ACL tear in his last game and was out indefinitely. What to do, what to do? He was concentrating all his energy on his betting dilemma, so he didn't hear the door to the café open or notice the two large men who walked in.

Nathan looked up when the men's shadows cast a dark cloud over the sports page. One of the men had shoulders that seemed as wide as the booth, a massive bald head, a cauliflower ear, and a nose that showed signs of multiple breaks. The other man was even bigger and meaner looking. Nathan's appetite disappeared, and a bead of sweat formed on his forehead.

"Hi, Rick," Nathan said to the man with the cauliflower ear.

"How's the breakfast here?" Rick asked.

"Good. You haven't eaten here?" Nathan said, pretending that this would be a normal conversation.

"No, but you've been a little hard to find, and we heard you do, most mornings."

Nathan forced a smile. "You came to the right spot. They make great hash browns."

"Good to know," Rick said as he slid onto the bench across from Finch. His companion stayed on his feet and continued to cast a shadow over Nathan.

"I'd go with the Rams, Nathan," Rick said.

"Their left tackle is out."

"Yeah, but McCabe can read a defense as fast as anyone, and he gets the ball out quick."

"Thanks, Rick. I'll follow your advice."

"That's good, because Mario sent us to advise you that you need to make good on your obligations if you want to avoid serious consequences."

"About that. I was going to make a payment, but I had some trouble at work and . . ." Nathan flashed a sickly grin. "There's no way to sugarcoat it. They fired me. I haven't even told Margaret yet. She still thinks I'm going to King Pharmaceuticals every day."

"Sorry about the job, Nathan, but Mario doesn't handle excuses well. Just between you and me, I think the guy has trouble feeling compassion. I read somewhere that an inability to empathize is a trait common in psychopaths. I'm not saying Mario is one, but I've seen how he deals with people who welch on bets. It ain't pretty."

Nathan's forehead was starting to resemble Niagara Falls.

"Hey, I get it, but I'm going to need some time before I can get you the next payment. As soon as I get a new job, you're on top of my list."

"You have a week, Nathan, and a wife who makes a good living."

"I can't ask Margaret for the money, but I do have another source of income. Tell Mario he doesn't have to worry. I was always on time before I got canned, wasn't I?"

"One week," Rick repeated as he stood up to walk out of the booth. "Enjoy your breakfast. I hope you'll be able to enjoy many more."

Rick and his fellow goon walked out of the café. Nathan felt as if he might throw up. He squeezed his eyes shut and took several deep breaths, but it didn't help. Nathan had heard stories about some of the things Mario had done to bettors who didn't pay up, and he knew that he had to make good on the debt he'd built up with a string of can't-miss bets that had missed.

Margaret was making good money, but she'd made it crystal clear after the last time she'd helped him make good on a gambling debt that she wasn't going to bail him out again. Now, everything depended on Ryan.

CHAPTER SEVEN

When she arrived at her law firm, Margaret Finch told the firm's receptionist that she didn't want to be disturbed while she prepared for Otis Truax's bail hearing. Margaret had just opened Truax's file when the receptionist buzzed.

"Yes, Stacey?" Margaret said, clearly annoyed by the interruption.

"There's a Mr. Claypool in reception. He wants to see you. I told him you were busy, but he says he's your brother."

Margaret swore silently. Then she closed her eyes and took the deep, calming breaths her yoga instructor recommended when dealing with stressful situations.

"Show him in," Margaret said.

Moments later, the door opened and a handsome man with broad shoulders and a weight lifter's chest walked into Margaret's office. Harry Claypool was clean shaven, his dirty-blond hair was slicked back, he was dressed in a suit that looked a little frayed, and he was wearing a tie that didn't go well with his suit. The impression he gave was of a man who was down on his luck but trying to make a good impression.

As soon as the receptionist closed the door behind him, Claypool flashed an ingratiating smile.

"Hey, Margie. It looks like you're doing great."

Margaret didn't return the smile. "When did you get out?"

"A few months ago."

"I thought you were doing ten years for armed robbery. If you got out this year, you only did four."

Claypool shrugged. "Good behavior, overcrowding in the prison. The new governor made a big point about that in his campaign. And I made a great impression at my parole hearing."

"I bet you did. You always were a terrific bullshitter."

"No, honest, I'm reformed, Margie."

"I have to be in court, and I'm very busy. What do you want?"

Claypool forced himself to keep the smile on his face. "That's my big sister. You were never one for small talk. Even when we were kids, you always wanted to get straight to the point."

Margaret looked at the designer watch that encircled her wrist. "The clock's ticking, Harry. Get to it or get out."

Claypool held up a hand. "Whoa, okay. I know you're busy, which is great. I'm happy you're such a success."

"You've got one more minute."

"Okay. Slow down. I'll get right to it. You represent people who've done time. You know how hard it is for an ex-con to get a job. I've been making the effort, honest, but no one's hiring, and I'm in a bit of a jam."

"How much do you want?"

"I'm not after money, Margie. That's not why I'm here. You know how tough it can be inside. I can hold my own, but I'm not the toughest guy. Anyway, it helped a lot when the other inmates learned that you were my sister. The guys inside know your name and your connections. And I was wondering, you know, if you could hook me up. Maybe get me a job at a club."

"You want me to vouch for you?"

"Hey, I'm your brother."

"You're a fuckup, Harry. You've always been a fuckup. These connections you're talking about are my clients. My reputation is very important to me. So, no, I won't hook you up."

Margaret kept petty cash in a drawer in her desk. She opened it, took out two hundred dollars, and pushed the bills across her desk. Claypool's smile faded, and he glared at Margaret as he scooped up the cash.

"Thanks for nothing."

"Get out, Harry, and don't come back."

"You're gonna regret this, you bitch," Claypool said as he opened the door. "You've always treated me like dirt, and I'm sick of it."

Claypool stomped out of Margaret's office, slamming the door behind him. Margaret buzzed her receptionist.

"If Mr. Claypool comes here again, call security and have him thrown out."

The old Multnomah County Courthouse was an eight-story, gray concrete building that occupied a block in the middle of downtown Portland. It had been constructed between 1909 and 1914, and had been abandoned in 2020 after the opening of a new, modern, seismically safer building that had been erected near the west end of the Hawthorne Bridge. The new location gave visitors and the courthouse staff a view of boats cruising the Willamette River and the magnificent snow-covered slopes of Mount Hood.

The courtrooms in the old courthouse featured high ceilings, ornate molding, marble Corinthian columns, and daises of polished wood. The courtrooms in the new building had none of the grandeur or historic character of the old courtrooms. They had flat, dull brown wooden desks with clean lines that could have been bought at IKEA and were built for function, not form. Attorneys could charge laptops or phones in outlets in their counsel tables. Videos and evidence were presented to jurors on wall-mounted screens.

The bail hearing in Otis Truax's case was set for three thirty. Margaret was at the defense counsel table when the guards led Truax to her. Neither Margaret Finch nor Otis Truax had the slightest interest in the décor of the courtroom or the people who were watching the hearing. That's why they didn't notice Alan Chen sitting among the spectators in the rear of the courtroom.

Stephen Reese, the judge who was presiding over the bail hearing, took the bench and the bailiff called the case. The State had the burden of convincing the judge that he should deny bail or set a high amount. The deputy district attorney who had been assigned to Otis's case called Portland detective Chet Marx to the stand. Marx told the judge the details of the insurance scam, Otis's part in it, and the horrific consequences of the staged crash.

Margaret pretended to pay attention, but she knew how the hearing would end. The Honorable Stephen Reese was not very honorable. Lloyd Standish had the erotic photos to prove it, and copies had been shown to Judge Reese the evening before the bail hearing. Bail was going to be granted, a reasonable amount would be set, and Otis would be out in the world in the next twenty-four hours.

The deputy district attorney sat down, and Margaret forcefully argued the defense case for bail, even though she knew that she would prevail even if she said nothing. Appearances were important if an investigation into the judge's decision was to be avoided.

When Margaret sat down, Judge Reese pretended to consider the arguments of counsel. Then he said that the State's case had a lot of merit, but he saw problems with it. He concluded by setting bail in the amount that Lloyd had told him to set.

The court took up a few housekeeping matters, then declared a recess. As soon as the judge was off the bench, Margaret turned to her client.

"That went well," she said with a smile.

Otis looked worried.

"What's wrong?" Margaret asked.

"I ain't got that kind of money," said Otis, who had already forgotten what Margaret had told him in the jail.

"I know that," Margaret said patiently, "and so do your friends. Bail will be posted for you within the hour, and you'll be on the street today. Now, do you feel better?"

Otis took a deep breath and nodded. "I sure do."

Margaret laid a reassuring hand on Truax's shoulder. "Everything is going to be okay, Otis, as long as you follow my simple rule. Do you remember it?"

"I don't say nothing unless you're with me."

"You got it. Now go back to your cell and wait for the guards to set you free. Then go home, take a shower, eat a nice meal, and get a good night's sleep."

"What about that deal the cop talked about?"

"I'm going to get all the details, and I'll have them for you when we meet at my office."

"Okay."

The guards led Otis away, and Margaret gathered her things.

She tried not to think about Otis Truax as she walked out of the courthouse and headed for her car, but she knew he was a loose end and she knew Lloyd Standish's approach to problem-solving.

The bail hearing had recessed shortly before five, so Margaret planned on going home instead of returning to her office. Her car was parked on the fifth floor of a lot a block from her office. She rang for the elevator and waited for the car to arrive. Alan Chen walked up to the elevator and stood behind the attorney. When the doors opened, he followed her in.

Margaret registered the fact that Alan was Asian, well dressed, well built, and pleasant looking, but she was still thinking about Otis Truax, so she didn't pay any more attention to him.

The door opened on five, and Margaret got out. Her car was in a back row, and she headed toward it, unaware that the man from the elevator was headed in the same direction. Margaret's car was in a narrow space between two other cars. She took out her key and pressed the button that would unlock the driver's door. Before she could open it, Alan stepped into the space between the cars, penning her in.

"Tell me who ordered your client to kill my wife," he commanded in a low voice that was more threatening than if he had yelled at her.

"Who are you?" Margaret demanded.

"I'm someone with nothing to lose, so tell me who's behind the insurance scam."

Margaret backed into the wall. "I'm just a lawyer. All I know about a scam is what I heard in court."

The man stepped so close to Margaret that she could smell the alcohol on his breath. "That's bullshit. You talked to Truax. He would have told you what he did."

"That's . . . that's a protected conversation. I can't tell you what a client said to me. It's against the law."

"You're not in a courtroom, Finch. You're face-to-face with the husband of the wonderful woman your client murdered."

At that moment, a woman with a young child walked up to the car that was next to Margaret's and smiled.

"Do you want me to pull out first?" she asked.

Alan turned to look at the woman, and Margaret squeezed by him.

"No. I'll pull out," Margaret said as she got in the driver's seat and locked her door. Alan leaned against the window.

"You'd better not be lying to me," he said. Then he walked away.

Margaret looked in her rearview mirror as she pulled out of her space. Alan Chen was watching her. Margaret had trouble breathing. She drove out of the garage and took a circuitous route toward her house until she was certain that Chen wasn't following her. Then she pulled into a supermarket parking lot and parked in between two cars that shielded her from anyone passing by.

Margaret got out her phone.

"Detective Marx?" she asked when the call went through.

"Yes. Who is this?"

"It's Margaret Finch, the lawyer representing Otis Truax."

"Oh, sure. What can I do for you?"

"I just had a very unsettling experience. I walked to my parking garage from the courthouse, and Alan Chen followed me. He backed me against the wall between my car and another car. Then he demanded to know what Mr. Truax had told me about the accident. When I refused to reveal a client confidence, he threatened me. The woman in the car next to mine came up with a child, and I was able to get in my car and drive away, but Chen really upset me."

"What do you want me to do?"

"I want you to tell him to stay away from me and my client. Investigating crimes is your job. He's acting like a private detective."

"Okay. I'll talk to Mr. Chen. He's just upset, and with good cause."

"I understand that, but he frightened me. I don't feel safe."

"No, what he did isn't right. Thanks for telling me."

Harry Claypool had been having the best twenty-four hours of his post-prison life until his meeting with his bitch sister spoiled his mood. Harry had gone four years without getting laid until he hooked up with Terri Lund at a bar down the street from his apartment. After many drinks too many, they had staggered back to Terri's place, and Harry learned that he had not lost a step when it came to pleasing the ladies.

Terri was a receptionist in a dentist's office, and she'd agreed to let him use her car if he'd drive her to work and pick her up. After dropping off Terri, Harry had driven to Margaret's office with high hopes that he could charm her into helping him get a job with one of her gangster clients, but she'd been the same old Margaret.

Harry didn't give up easily. He'd followed Margaret to the courthouse and learned what her car looked like. Then he'd waited for her to leave the parking lot after her hearing. He'd seen his sister pull into a supermarket parking lot and make a call. Then he'd followed her home and watched her house.

Harry had staked out the places he'd robbed, so staking out Margaret's house wasn't anything new. He settled in and took out his phone to look up the score of a game he'd bet on when he saw the text from Terri asking where he was.

Harry swore. Terri had said he could use the car if he picked her up from work at five. It was almost six, and he knew she would be pissed. He replied to her text with a bullshit story about a job interview that ran over and was starting to leave when he saw a young girl walk up the block to the Finches' front door.

Harry knew Margaret had two kids because he'd visited her a few times before he was arrested. The last time he'd seen Annie, she was in elementary school. It took Harry a few seconds to figure out that the hot chick who was entering the Finch home was his niece.

Annie had long black hair and a lot of curves she emphasized by wearing tight clothes. Harry knew she was jailbait, but he wondered if she might provide a way to get back at his sister for the way she'd treated him.

CHAPTER EIGHT

Robin Lockwood walked into the crowded ballroom where the Oregon State Bar Association was honoring Harold Wright and looked for her assigned table. When the award ceremony had been announced, Robin had been of two minds about attending. Wright was her favorite judge. She had tried many cases in his court and always looked forward to a trial where he was on the bench, because he was fair, brilliant, and had a wonderful courtroom temperament. But Robin could not hear Wright's name without reliving the worst moment in her life.

Judge Wright called on Robin occasionally to take court appointments in cases that no other attorney would handle. Three years ago, he had asked Robin to represent Lloyd Arness, a degenerate rapist who had left his victim with brain damage. The evidence against Arness had been overwhelming, and the jury had convicted in record time. At the sentencing hearing, the victim's distraught husband had shot Arness and turned his weapon on Robin. Jeff Hodges,

Robin's fiancé, had saved Robin's life by wrestling the husband to the ground, but he had been killed when the husband's gun went off. Robin's pain had softened during the intervening years, but the pain was always there, and Judge Wright's name was a trigger that shot it to the surface.

Robin knew that Judge Wright felt terrible about his part in Jeff's death, and she had concluded long ago that it was irrational to blame the judge for her tragedy, so she had decided to attend the award ceremony as one more step in dealing with her grief.

Robin's table was near the front of the ballroom, and she found the place with her name. She had just gotten seated when a man pulled out the chair next to her. Robin turned and found herself face-to-face with Tom McKee. McKee was in his early thirties, slightly taller than Robin, and slender. He had wavy brown hair, blue eyes, and a wonderful smile, which he used to his advantage in court.

Robin had battled the deputy district attorney several times, winning two of the three cases they had tried together. But the last time they had faced each other, McKee had pulled out a brilliant victory. Robin liked McKee because he tried a clean case and treated her with respect. When McKee was on the other side, Robin never had to worry about dirty tactics, the way she had to worry with some of the less scrupulous deputies. He was also one of the few deputy DAs who didn't bring up Robin's past as a nationally known professional fighter when he was questioning potential jurors.

"Hi, Robin," McKee said.

"Hi, yourself. What brings you to this shindig?"

"The judge teaches a class in civil procedure every other year, and I took it. He remembered me when I tried my first felony case in his court. I got my butt kicked, and he was kind enough to meet with me and tell me where I screwed up. So, I'm a big fan, even though he's never given me a break in any case I've tried in front of him."

"Did you ace civil pro?" Robin asked.

McKee smiled. "If I had, I'd be making the big bucks at one of the corporate firms instead of having to put up with sleazy criminal defense attorneys."

Robin laughed. "Hey, I don't ask my witnesses to perjure themselves until I see how much evidence your cops have planted on my innocent clients."

McKee's smile widened. "That's what I like about you. So many of your fellow defense attorneys lack a sense of humor."

Robin shrugged. "If you can't laugh at the absurd and insane, you have no business practicing criminal law."

"Amen. So, are you handling any interesting cases now?"

"No. And I don't regret it. The weird goings-on at Black Oaks were enough to last me a lifetime."

"Yeah, I heard. You don't get a case with werewolves and a murder in a locked room every day."

"Hopefully I never will again."

A couple Robin knew took the seats on her right, and she talked to them while McKee struck up a conversation with a law school classmate who took the seat next to him. Then dinner was served and the program started. The dinner broke up after the awards ceremony, and Robin got up to leave. McKee stood up at the same time.

"The word on the grapevine is that you work out every morning," McKee said.

"I try to keep in shape."

"I run before going to the office, and I try to get in some distance on the weekends. Care to join me sometime? I'm training for a marathon, and it's lonely running by myself."

Robin didn't show it, but the idea of doing anything even vaguely romantic scared her. She had gone out a few times since Jeff died, but there hadn't been any repeats, either because she'd been too sad when the evening ended or she hadn't liked her date enough to go out again.

"Wouldn't that create a conflict of interest?" Robin joked to stall for time.

"Only if you were faster than I am and bragged about it to a jury. So, what do you say? It's supposed to be nice on Saturday."

Robin heard herself say, "Okay," and wondered if she'd regret it.

"They've got some beautiful trails in Forest Park," McKee said. Let's meet at eight at the parking lot."

Robin heard herself say "Okay" again, and felt like someone else were answering for her. McKee walked to the street with her and said goodbye. Robin's condo was fifteen minutes from the hotel, but she didn't remember a second of the walk because she was too distracted wondering why Tom had asked her to run with him.

CHAPTER NINE

Lloyd Standish had entrusted the task of getting rid of Otis Truax to Martin Lebedev and Grigor Nikolaev, two thugs who were good at beating up people and, on occasion, making people disappear. Making Otis disappear had not seemed like much of a problem, but Otis was living in a fleabag motel on a brightly lit thoroughfare, and he had stayed in his room after being released from jail, subsisting on pizza and beer he ordered in from a pizza joint two blocks away.

"This is fucked up," Grigor had declared more than once during the second day of their stakeout. "What if he never comes out of his room?"

Martin wanted to drag Otis out, but Grigor, the brighter of the two—but not by much—had pointed out that there were always people going in and out of the parking lot or the motel rooms who would be able to ID them.

Then, just when Grigor was on the verge of agreeing to an assault on Otis's room, Otis went a little stir-crazy and decided to mosey down to a neighborhood bar.

"It's him!" Martin yelled as he started the car. When he was next to Otis, Martin rolled down his window and smiled.

"Hey, it's Otis, right?"

Otis stooped over to get a good look at the driver. "Do I know you?"

"I don't think we've had the pleasure, but we're friends of Lloyd Standish. He sent us to bring you to him. He's real proud of the way you've been handling yourself and he wants to thank you personally." Martin winked. "He also said something about a bonus."

Otis was confused because he understood that a bonus was something extra and he'd never been paid any of the money Lloyd had promised him if he crashed the car.

"Hop in," Martin said as Grigor got out of the passenger seat and opened the door for Otis.

Otis was torn. Mrs. Finch had told Otis not to talk to anyone, but she couldn't have meant Mr. Standish.

"I don't know," he stalled as he tried to decide the right thing to do.

"Hey, Otis, you don't want us to tell Mr. Standish that you re-fused to see him, do you? He hates to be disappointed, and you'd miss out on all that bonus money."

Otis did need the money, so he got in the passenger seat, and Grigor got behind him in the back seat. Grigor and Martin acted very friendly, and Otis relaxed, but he started getting nervous when they drove into the countryside. He had just started to ask where they were meeting Mr. Standish when Grigor knocked him uncon-scious.

*   *   *

Lloyd had instructed Martin and Grigor to find out everything Otis had told law enforcement about the accident scam. Otis was weak, and he had caved under torture very quickly. When his captors were certain that Otis had nothing more to tell them, Grigor garroted Otis with a strand of piano wire.

"I'm glad that's over," Martin said after Otis had been deposited in a shallow grave.

"Let's go tell Lloyd that Truax is in a better place."

As proof that Martin and Grigor were not very competent, the shallow grave was immediately discovered by various animals and, a few days later, by a hiker, who freaked out when he tripped over Otis's femur.

CHAPTER TEN

On Saturday morning, Robin ran with Tom McKee. He was in great shape, but so was she, and she was able to stay with him during a grueling fifteen-mile run. After the run, they ate lunch at a small café where the food was good and the small talk was enjoyable.

Robin headed home after agreeing to run with Tom the next weekend. As soon as she entered her condo, she stripped off her clothes and took a shower. While the hot water washed over her, she processed the emotions that had confused her during the ride home. She had to admit that she had enjoyed the run and lunch. Tom was funny and kind, and she hadn't hesitated when he had suggested getting together again. It was only when she was driving home that she started to feel guilty because she had enjoyed her time with someone who wasn't Jeff.

Many people had told her that Jeff would not want her to spend the rest of her life in mourning, that he would want her to be happy. But Robin had felt badly after every date she'd had since Jeff died, and she couldn't help feeling that she was betraying him whenever she was with a man. Did that still make sense?

Wouldn't you have wanted Jeff to meet someone new and fall in love again, if you were the one who had died? she asked herself. There was no question that the answer was yes, so why couldn't she break the cycle of grieving that kept her sad and lonely? She knew that it was logical for her to cast off the feelings of sadness and guilt that haunted her when she went out on a date, but logic and emotion were two different things.

Robin forced herself to stop soul-searching and got dressed. She had not had time to read the newspaper before her run, so she sat on the couch and opened the paper to the sports section. She was surprised to see an article about mixed martial arts because the paper rarely covered the sport. There was going to be a big, televised UFC event in Portland. The main event was a world championship fight, but it was a bout on the undercard that caught her eye. Mandy Kerrigan was fighting Kerrie Clark, a young, undefeated woman whom Robin had seen on television in a recent UFC event.

Robin had kept track of Kerrigan's career after their bout. The year after her fight with Robin, Kerrigan had won a world championship and had held on to it for two years. Then injuries had contributed to a string of losses that had downgraded her from a headliner to an opponent future contenders were paired with to beef up their résumés.

An idea occurred to her. If there was one thing Robin Lockwood had in abundance, it was self-confidence. That confidence had enabled her to wrestle boys in high school, excel in college, law school, and the courtroom, and best more than one murderer in life-and-death situations. But what she was thinking of doing made her heart race and her mouth go dry. Robin hesitated. Her hand shook. Then she steeled herself and called Tom McKee.

"Long time no see," he joked when he answered her call.

Robin laughed and hoped he couldn't tell how nervous she felt. "You know I used to fight professionally."

"Everyone in the DA's office knows that. It's the reason we're all terrified of you."

"There was a reason I quit. In my first year in law school, I got the chance to fight Mandy Kerrigan, the number two contender, on a big pay-per-view card in Las Vegas. If I'd won, I would have gotten a title shot. Only I didn't. She was way out of my league, and I got knocked cold. I had a concussion and short-term memory loss, and I decided to retire while I still had a few IQ points left.

"Anyway," Robin said, "the reason I'm calling is I just found out that Kerrigan is on a UFC card that's being televised from the Moda Center this Saturday, and I wondered if you'd like to go—that is, if you don't have other plans."

"That sounds great," Tom answered enthusiastically. "I've only watched a few MMA fights on TV, but I enjoyed them. You can explain what's going on."

"Okay. I'll get the tickets and let you know the time."

As soon as Robin disconnected, she closed her eyes and took a deep breath. She'd faced down armed killers and hadn't been this scared. Then she opened her eyes and laughed. She couldn't believe how silly she was being. She wasn't getting married to Tom. She was going to a fight with a nice guy.

CHAPTER ELEVEN

Margaret Finch was working on a matter that had nothing to do with the Russian mob when her receptionist told her that a Mr. Chen was in the waiting room and wanted to see her. Margaret's stomach clenched, and she started to perspire. What would Chen do if she said she was too busy to talk to him? Would he cause a scene?

Margaret made a decision. She took a few calming breaths the way she'd been taught in her yoga class. Then she stood up, smoothed down her skirt, and walked into the waiting room. Chen got to his feet when he saw her.

"Mr. Chen, I'm very sorry for your loss, and it's perfectly reasonable under these terrible circumstances for you to be upset. But you told me what you want in the parking garage, and I simply can't help you, because I don't have the information you require."

Chen stared at her. "I think you do, and I'm going to make you give it to me, one way or another."

"Threatening me won't make the information magically appear.

I do not know anything about any insurance scam. I can't tell you what I don't know. Now I'm going to ask you to leave, because I'm in the middle of an urgent matter and I have to get back to work."

"You're lying. I've done some digging, and I know your clients are Russian Mafia."

"Look, Mr. Chen, just because I represent people who are alleged to be criminals doesn't mean that I am a criminal or have inside information on the plans a criminal makes. Now, please leave and don't come here again. I'm being considerate because you've just suffered a terrible tragedy, but I will call security if you come here again."

Chen glared at Finch and said, "This isn't over." Then he left the office. Margaret exhaled.

"Is everything all right?" Stacey asked.

"No, it's not. If that man returns, call security and have him shown out."

One hour later, Margaret's receptionist interrupted her again, this time to tell her that two detectives wanted to talk to her. Margaret's normal contact with law enforcement was a prosecutor. Her curiosity was aroused, and she told her receptionist to bring the detectives to her office. When the door opened, she stood up to greet her visitors. She recognized Chet Marx. She did not recognize the detective who followed Marx into her office. He was young, slender, and sported a buzz cut, a goatee, and a wisp of a mustache that arched over his upper lip.

"Hello, Detective. What brings you to my office?"

"This is my partner, Darrell Price. I'm afraid we have some bad news about Mr. Truax."

Lawyers are trained to hide their emotions, and Margaret's facial features didn't twitch, even though she suspected that she knew what Marx was going to tell her.

"Yes?" she said.

"He's dead, Mrs. Finch. He was murdered, and he may have been tortured. We'll know more after the autopsy."

Margaret pretended to be shocked, and she collapsed on her chair. "What happened? Where was he killed?"

"A hiker found him on a trail out by the Columbia River Gorge."

"That's terrible." She shook her head. "Otis was so inoffensive. He was actually very slow. I can't imagine why someone would . . . You said he may have been tortured?"

"Yes, ma'am. And I'm guessing—given the type of client you represent—that you're not as surprised that Mr. Truax has been killed as you appear to be."

Margaret's head snapped up. "That's a terrible thing to say."

"Jack Kovalev and Lloyd Standish are killers without con-sciences. We both know that. Truax was a loose end, and they might see you that way. If you cooperate with us, we can protect you."

"I was only Otis's attorney. I don't know anything that would make me a threat to the men you just named."

"You keep telling yourself that and you might end up dead." Marx placed a business card on Finch's desk.

"If I were you," Margaret said, "I'd find out where Alan Chen was when Mr. Truax was murdered."

"I talked to Mr. Chen after you called. He assured me that he would stop investigating his wife's death."

"Then he lied. He was in my reception area this morning, and he threatened me. If anyone had a motive to harm Mr. Truax, it's Chen. You said Otis was tortured. Chen keeps asking me who is behind the insurance scam you say Otis was involved in. Chen would have tortured Otis to get the information he wants."

"I doubt very much that Alan Chen is a sadistic killer. And I know for a fact that Jack Kovalev and Lloyd Standish are. If you have a change of heart, call me, day or night. Thanks for taking the time to see us."

The detectives left. Margaret closed her eyes and did some more yoga breathing. When she was calmer, she got a burner phone from the bottom drawer of her desk and dialed Kovalev.

"I just had a visit from two detectives. They told me that Otis Truax is dead."

"That's terrible," Kovalev answered.

"I'm calling about a serious problem. You know who Alan Chen is?"

"The husband of the woman who died in the crash."

"After the bail hearing, he accosted me in my parking garage and threatened to hurt me if I didn't tell him who hired Otis."

"What did you say?"

"What do you think I said? I told him I couldn't reveal an attorney confidence. Then I got away from him."

"Why are you calling me now?"

"He came to my office today and threatened me again. Then Otis turns up dead and tortured."

"You think Chen might be responsible?"

"I don't know, but he's got me scared. Can't you do something about him?"

"Chen's a CPA, for Christ's sake. He might report you to the IRS, but I don't see him doing anything physical."

"You weren't here when he threatened me. I think he's dangerous."

"I can tell you're upset. Let me think about what to do with Chen. Meanwhile, try to relax. I can't believe you're in any danger."

Margaret disconnected. She didn't feel any better after talking to Kovalev. She probably shouldn't have done it. But Chen's and the detectives' visits had her rattled.

CHAPTER TWELVE

The Moda Center, a multimillion-dollar, multipurpose arena on the east side of the Willamette River, was the home court of the NBA's Portland Trail Blazers, but it hosted other events, including rounds of the NCAA's March Madness, rock concerts, and, on Saturday evening, a televised UFC card featuring a world championship.

Robin had been so nervous about going out with Tom that she'd spent too much time on her wardrobe and had been twenty minutes late picking him up at his condo. By the time she parked her car in the Moda Center lot and they'd worked their way through the crowds, the fights were only minutes away from starting.

An Octagon had been erected in the center of the basketball court, and the highest-priced seats surrounded it. Spectators who didn't want to pay premium prices sat in the stands. Robin's seats were in the front row on the floor where they had a clear view into the cage.

"These are great seats!" Tom said.

Robin smiled. "These are the best seats."

"They must have cost a fortune. Can I chip in?"

"No need. A year ago, I helped out a Trail Blazers exec who was in an embarrassing situation. I smoothed things over and kept it out of the papers. As a result, I get comped if I want to go to an event at the Moda Center."

"Ah, to work in the private sector. If I got a perk like that from a defendant, I would be disbarred and go to jail."

"No, you wouldn't. I'd represent you, and you would come out smelling like a rose."

Tom laughed. "Do you know a lot of the fighters on the card personally?"

"No. I follow MMA, but it's been ten years since I competed. There are still a few competitors I know who were fighting when I called it a day, but Kerrigan is the only person on this card who was fighting when I was around."

Tom was about to ask another question when the lights went down and the first bout started. Kerrigan's fight was third on the card, and Robin turned around when the announcer called out Kerrigan's name. Robin's seat was at the end of the aisle down which Kerrigan walked to the Octagon. Robin studied the woman who had ended her career and did not see the warrior she had faced.

There was no bounce to her step when Kerrigan walked to the cage. She had moved up a weight, and a layer of fat covered the six-pack abs and sculpted biceps that had impressed Robin, and the pent-up rage that had unnerved Robin was not on display.

When Kerrigan's fight with Kerrie Clark started, Kerrigan didn't charge across the ring and attack. She waited for Clark to make the first move and shuffled back while throwing jabs that had no power behind them. Kerrigan was still skilled enough to block a lot of Clark's kicks and punches and she landed a few of her own, but Clark was primarily a grappler, and Kerrigan was a step too slow to keep from being taken to the ground, where she struggled to fend off choke holds, arm bars, and punches.

By the third round, Kerrigan was bleeding from a cut over her left eye, her right eye was closing, and she was well behind on the scorecards. Her trainer wiped away the blood and checked her eye while the judges totaled up the score. Then the announcer called Kerrigan and Clark to the center of the ring to announce the winner. Clark was bouncing in place and had a big smile on her face. Kerrigan looked down at the ground and barely moved. It did not come as a surprise when the announcer raised Clark's hand in victory and the judge's scores revealed that she had won every round.

Kerrigan's head was still down, and she looked like all the fight had gone out of her when she passed by Robin on the way to the locker room. Robin made a quick decision.

"Stay and watch the next fight," she told Tom as she got to her feet. "I'll be right back. I'm going to say hello to Mandy. She looks like she can use some cheering up."

Robin followed Kerrigan down the aisle and through a tunnel into a concrete corridor that led to the women's locker room. When she walked in, Kerrigan was sitting on a bench with her head in her hands. She looked up when she heard the door open.

"If you're a reporter, fuck off," Kerrigan said.

"I'm not a reporter. I'm Robin Lockwood. I used to be a ranked fighter. We fought many years ago. I live in Portland now, and I just wanted to say hello."

Kerrigan stared at Robin for a minute. She looked confused, like a student who has no idea about how to answer a simple question on an exam.

"Who are you?"

"Robin Lockwood. I used to be called Rockin' Robin when I was fighting."

"I don't know you."

Robin smiled. "I'm not surprised I didn't make an impression. You knocked me out with a kick to the head in the first round of our fight and convinced me to retire. It was on a big card in Las Vegas, ten years ago."

Kerrigan's brow furrowed for a second. Then it smoothed out.

"Okay, yeah. Now I remember. You stepped in when Angelina Mendes broke her ankle."

"That's right. I was in law school when we fought. You convinced me that I wasn't going to be a champion in the UFC and should devote myself to my studies. I'm a lawyer now."

"Well, good for you," she said dismissively. "You did the right thing by getting out of this racket. You weren't much competition." She stood up. "I need to shower and get out of here, so, if you'll excuse me . . ."

Kerrigan turned her back on Robin and headed for the showers. Robin was shocked at how rude Kerrigan was, but she had just suffered a bad loss and she was pretty beat up, so Robin decided that she would cut Kerrigan some slack and not take the brush-off personally.

"Did you get to talk to Kerrigan?" Tom asked when Robin returned to her seat.

"Yeah, but she wasn't in the mood for chitchat, so I left when she went to take a shower."

"I'm not surprised. Her fight was pretty one-sided."

"That it was. But this next bout should be a barn burner."

The sun woke Robin on Monday morning. She kept her eyes closed and enjoyed the warmth. Saturday night had been so nice. After the fights, she and Tom had gone for a beer and talked for another hour. Just before Robin dropped him off, Tom had suggested dinner and a movie on Sunday. Robin had accepted and hadn't felt even a twinge of regret during the ride home.

She opened her eyes and looked at the clock on her end table. She had slept an hour later than normal, but work was slow and she didn't have any meetings or court appearances scheduled, so she got into her sweats and took off for McGill's gym, where she trained every weekday, with a spring in her step.

McGill's was in the Pearl District, which developers had transformed from a warehouse district populated by the homeless into a posh section of town filled with upscale condos, fancy restaurants, art galleries, and boutiques. McGill's was housed in a brick building that had escaped gentrification, and its owner, Barry McGill, was an irascible ex-boxer in his sixties who was one of Robin's favorite people.

"It's about time," McGill barked when Robin walked in. "It must be nice to be able to lie in bed all morning eating bonbons."

"Get stuffed, Barry," Robin sang out.

"Hey, I ain't rich enough to afford to stuff myself with bonbons."

Robin couldn't stop herself from smiling. "I had a late night."

McGill knew that Robin was still grieving and he was surprised, and pleased, by what he took as a hint that Robin had gone out on a nice date. He was curious, because he wanted Robin to be happy, but he was smart enough to keep his curiosity in check.

"Didn't you get your clock cleaned ten years ago by Mandy Kerrigan?" McGill asked to change the subject.

Robin smiled. "Ms. Kerrigan was instrumental in making me see the wisdom of devoting myself full-time to my studies."

"She fought at the Moda Center on Saturday."

"I know. I was at the fight."

"Hold up for a minute," McGill said. He walked into his office and returned with the morning paper. "Have you seen this?" He handed Robin the sports section. The article McGill had pointed to said that Mandy Kerrigan's purse had been suspended because she had flunked a test for performance-enhancing drugs.

CHAPTER THIRTEEN

Mandy Kerrigan's life had rarely been easy and hardly ever good. Her mother was an addict, and she had no idea who had fathered her, although her mother told her to call the string of men—many of whom had sexually or physically abused her—*Daddy* as long as they were paying the rent and stocking the refrigerator with food.

As a child, Kerrigan had been in and out of foster care. She'd dropped out of school as soon as it was legal and supported herself any way she could. While she was in school, Mandy had been suspended many times for fighting, and fighting provided a lifeline once she learned that she could be paid to beat people to a pulp.

One of the few bright spots in Kerrigan's life was the world championship she'd won a year after her brutal demolition of Robin Lockwood. But that moment in the sun was brief. Two years after winning the title, she suffered a shoulder injury that took a long time to heal. Then there was the ACL tear and the broken hand. By the time she was ready to defend her title, she was a shadow of the beast

Robin had faced, and she lost by a knockout that caused one of her many concussions.

Kerrigan still had a name and a reputation for ferocity that many remembered, so she continued to show up on the undercard of UFC events, never as a headliner anymore, but often as cannon fodder for up-and-coming prospects, who could build up their résumés with a win over a former titleholder.

One of the lowest points in a life filled with them came the day after her fight at the Moda Center when she was informed that a drug test had revealed the presence of a banned substance. Kerrigan needed her purse, which was being held up, and she depended on the money she would earn in the future bouts that might never come if she was suspended.

Kerrigan returned to the motel room she'd been living in while she trained for her fight in Portland as soon as she learned about the failed drug test. Her head hurt from the beating she'd taken. She tried to rest and come to terms with what she saw as a bleak future, but anger was the dominant emotion that kept her from resting. That anger was focused on Ryan Finch, who had sold her the PEDs he'd sworn could not be detected by any drug test. Finch had lied to her, and that lie might lead to the end of her career. The sun was setting, and that meant that Ryan Finch would be dealing at the bar where Mandy had found him. She put on gloves to protect her hands and headed toward a showdown with the man who had ruined her life.

The Gaslight was separated from the Willamette River by Naito Parkway and a strip of green space. The dimly lit bar, which was constructed of dark wood and illuminated by sconces held in place by brass fittings, was modeled after the bars that lurked across the Willamette in the 1800s, when the clientele were whores, card sharks, sailors fresh off the ships that anchored on the river, and the men who shanghaied those sailors. The present-day clientele were mainly techies, college students, the young associates of law and accounting firms, and the sons and daughters of Portland's upper classes.

Ryan Finch fit right in. He was six foot two, in his midtwenties, handsome and charming, and had a gym-toned physique. His casual clothes sported designer labels, and he hailed from a family with a residence in Portland's pricey West Hills. However, Ryan was not in school, because he had flunked out of Portland State, and he was unemployed, having been fired from his last job due to frequent unexcused absences and a suspicion that he was high when he did deign to show up for work.

When Mandy Kerrigan entered the Gaslight, Ryan was in a good mood. He'd made several drug sales that evening and was close to convincing a tipsy coed to go to a nearby hotel for some hanky-panky. Kerrigan wedged herself between Ryan and his prey.

"We have to talk," she said.

"Hey," said the coed.

Mandy turned to her. "Fuck off or lose some teeth."

"You'd better leave, Cassie," Ryan said. "I'll call you."

"I'm not letting some—" Cassie started, but she wasn't able to finish her sentence because Kerrigan had driven the air out of the young woman's lungs with a sharp elbow. While Cassie doubled over and gulped in air, Kerrigan glared at Finch.

"Outside, motherfucker."

Ryan looked at Cassie and decided that antagonizing Kerrigan was not in his best interest. There was a back entrance that led to an alley, and Ryan followed Kerrigan through it. As soon as the door closed, Kerrigan slammed Ryan into the brick wall and grabbed his shirt at the collar. She squeezed the collar tight enough to cut down

Ryan's air supply and pulled him up so that he was balancing on his toes.

"Hey, hey," was all Ryan managed to say.

"Your untraceable PEDs were traced, fucker. They're keeping my purse, and I'm going to be suspended."

Ryan held up his hands. "I never said my stuff couldn't be detected. I said it would pass most tests."

Kerrigan glared at Ryan. Then she broke his nose. Ryan was in shock for a moment. Seconds later, blood poured out of his nostrils, staining his expensive shirt, and the pain hit him.

"You lied to me when you sold me that shit, and you're lying now."

Kerrigan released the grip on Ryan's shirt and smashed her fist into his eye. He screamed, slid down the wall, and collapsed on the alley floor. Kerrigan kicked him in the ribs, oblivious to the people who were running to Ryan's rescue and the woman who was dialing 911.

Three football player–sized men had been drinking beer with their girlfriends in the alley when the attack started. They tackled Kerrigan and pinned her to the ground while their girlfriends saw to Ryan. A pair of police officers on patrol a block from the Gaslight ran into the alley moments after the 911 call.

Ryan was propped against the alley wall, groggy from his beating, blood dripping through the handkerchief someone had supplied. Kerrigan was screaming and cursing and struggling against her captors.

"Will somebody please explain what's going on here?" one of the police officers asked. Her nameplate identified her as Vivian Gold.

The woman who'd made the 911 call pointed at Kerrigan. "This . . . person attacked that man."

"Let me up, you motherfuckers!" Kerrigan screamed.

"That's a good idea," the other officer, whose name tag read James Rourke, said to the men who were looking to the officers for guidance. They released Kerrigan, and she leaped to her feet and squared off against the man closest to her.

"Hey, lady, back off," Officer Gold said as she inserted herself between Kerrigan and the man. Kerrigan glared at the officer for a second. Then she dropped her hands to her sides and stepped back.

"Okay. That's better. Now what happened?" Gold asked Kerrigan.

"There was a misunderstanding," Kerrigan said.

The officer pointed at Ryan's swelling eye and blood-soaked shirt. "That doesn't look like the normal outcome of a 'misunderstanding.'"

Rourke stared at Ryan's assailant. "Are you Mandy Kerrigan?"

Kerrigan looked at the officer. "So what?"

He smiled. "I'm a big MMA fan. I've seen you on TV."

"Who is she?" Gold asked.

"Don't you watch UFC? She's Mandy Kerrigan. She was a world champion."

Officer Gold looked directly at Mandy. "That makes what you did here a lot worse. You're a professional fighter. Your fists could be considered deadly weapons."

Ryan began to panic. If Kerrigan was arrested, she'd give him up.

"Hey, hold on, Officer," Ryan said as he struggled to his feet. "I wasn't in any danger. We just had a spat, and it got out of hand. But we're good, right, Mandy?"

"Yeah, we're good," she said, but Ryan deduced from her tone that they were anything but.

"So, you can see that everything is okay," Ryan said. "We just had a little disagreement. There's no reason to take up your valuable time any longer."

"You're lucky your boyfriend is so understanding," Officer Gold said. Then she studied Ryan's face. "How are you feeling? You might have a concussion."

Ryan managed a laugh. "Hey, thanks for your concern, but I'm fine. Everything is okay. Right, honey?"

"Yeah, *honey.*"

"Are you two lovebirds going to have another misunderstanding tonight?" Gold asked.

"We're cool," Ryan said, forcing a grin.

"And you?" the woman asked Kerrigan.

"Yeah. I'm cool," she said in a voice filled with menace.

"Great meeting you, Miss Kerrigan," Rourke said. "Are you in training for another fight?"

Kerrigan nodded, relieved that the cop didn't know about the suspension and the PEDs.

"Then you should go home and rest up."

Kerrigan stared at Ryan until he looked away. Then she walked out of the alley.

By the time Ryan was alone in the alley, his nose had stopped bleeding. He went inside and called his father.

"We have to talk," Ryan said when Nathan Finch answered his phone.

"Now? It's after eleven."

"One of our deals went south, and I got beat up."

"Are you okay?" Nathan asked with genuine concern.

"No, Dad. That's why we have to talk. Can you come down and get me?"

"Of course. I should be there in twenty minutes or less."

While he waited, Ryan swallowed two stiff drinks to help him calm down. He'd only met Kerrigan once before, when she bought the PEDs from him. But she'd made him nervous then because she seemed like she could explode at any second. Now he knew what happened when she did explode, and it scared the shit out of him. What really worried him was what would happen if he saw Mandy Kerrigan at her worst.

Ryan was waiting outside when his father pulled up. He jumped in the car, and Nathan leaned over to examine him.

"Jesus! Who did this?"

"That professional fighter I sold the PEDs to. You said no drug test would identify them."

"They won't."

"But they did, and now she's gonna be suspended and they won't pay her and she blames me."

"Geez, Ryan, I'm so sorry. I was sure they were undetectable."

"Well, they aren't. You screwed up."

"Yeah, I get that."

"I don't want to do this anymore. Two cops showed up when I was getting beaten. What if she'd told them I was dealing? I could have gone to jail."

"But she didn't. You're safe."

"This time. I'm sorry, but I want out."

"Please hang in there a little longer. I need the money. I may have a gambling problem. I've made some bets I was sure I'd win. Then there were upsets that should never have happened and . . . Well, the bottom line is that I'm in debt to some very dangerous people. If I don't pay up, I could be tortured or killed. Once I pay these people, I swear I'm done gambling. But I only have a week. Then they're coming after me, and that might not be the worst of it. These people have no boundaries. They could come for you or Annie or your mother. They have no conscience. It's what they do."

"You're scaring me, Dad."

"I'm just telling you the truth. But look. I almost have the money I need to get them off my back. I'm almost clear. A few more deals and we'll ride off into the sunset. What do you say? Just help me out a little longer and I'll never ask you to do any of this ever again."

Ryan was torn. He was scared of Kerrigan and scared of going to jail, but he couldn't let anything happen to his dad. And what if the men he owed did come for him or Annie or Mom to make an example? Ryan took a deep breath.

"Okay. I'll help you get out of your scrape. Then I'm through."

CHAPTER FOURTEEN

Alan Chen was depressed when he drove home from Margaret Finch's office. He knew that he hadn't accomplished a thing and that he was no closer to finding the proof he needed to bring to justice the person who had ordered Otis Truax to crash into Susan's car.

Chet Marx had come to his house and told him to stop bothering Margaret Finch, but he wasn't sleeping and he was drinking too much and he hoped that he would get some kind of closure if he could find the bastard responsible for Susan's murder. So, he'd confronted Finch again, and he was still no closer to finding Susan's killer than he'd been before he threatened her.

What if she was telling the truth? What if he'd terrified an innocent woman? Maybe she was just doing her job as an attorney and had no idea who had hired Truax. God, he was making a mess of everything because losing Susan had made him crazy. He wasn't a detective. Marx was right. He had to stop obsessing about finding Susan's killer. He had to let the police do their job.

Chen was exhausted from lack of sleep. He stood up and started for the bedroom when someone rang his doorbell. He looked at his watch. It was a little before eleven. Was Marx at the front door because he'd visited Finch after being told not to? But it wasn't Chet Marx who was standing on Chen's welcome mat. It was two very large, muscular men who had not shaved that day and who collected tattoos that displayed skulls, bloody knives, and other scary objects.

One of the men shoved Chen in the chest. Chen stumbled backward into his entryway. The other man closed and locked the door.

"Are you working for the person who's behind the insurance scam that killed my wife?" Chen asked.

The first man shook his head. "That's the kind of question that can lead to you ending up like your wife."

"You have to stop poking your nose in places it don't belong, and stop scaring people," the second man said.

"You mean Margaret Finch? Are you here because I went to her office?"

The first man turned to his companion. "This guy doesn't get it."

The other man looked at Chen and cracked his knuckles.

"I thought a guy with a CPA degree would be smarter than this," he said. "But I guess you didn't pay attention in the class that taught accountants that it isn't good to keep asking questions when someone tells you to stop poking your nose where it doesn't belong. So, we're going to have to help you learn that lesson."

Both men closed in on Alan.

Lloyd Standish was sitting in one of Jack Kovalev's upscale clubs, dining on a piece of Wagyu beef that had melted on his tongue and was so delicate he believed he could cut it with his fingernail. Seated next to him in a dimly lit booth upholstered in dark red leather was a very expensive call girl who was so beautiful and talented that she commanded an astronomical price to spend one night with a customer. The girl would never think of charging Lloyd for her services, but she knew that Lloyd treated his women very well and that there would be a wad of cash on her end table when he left in the morning.

Lloyd was cutting into the last piece of steak when he heard the ringtone of the burner phone that was only called in emergencies.

"Sorry, Jane," Lloyd said, calling his date by her real name and not the name she used with customers.

Lloyd fished out the phone and held it to his ear.

"Mr. Standish?" an unfamiliar voice asked.

"Who is this?"

"This is Alan Chen, and I'm calling to tell you that you made a big mistake when you sent your men to my house to intimidate me, and a huge mistake when you killed my wife."

"I don't know anything about these men and your wife."

"There's no one listening to this call, so we can speak freely. You can find your men in the trunk of their car on a logging road."

Chen gave Standish the coordinates.

"They should be alive. I think they have enough oxygen. I subjected both men to what is euphemistically called *enhanced interrogation*, and they are alive because they convinced me that they didn't know what I needed to know. But they did tell me that you sent them to teach me a lesson. I've concluded that means you do know who ordered the crash that killed my Susan. Give me his name and I won't kill you."

"You're a dead man," Standish said. Then he ended the call. "I'm sorry, Jane, but I have to leave. The bill is taken care of, so stay and finish your meal."

Standish left the table and signaled the bodyguards who were watching his back from two tables that were positioned nearby.

It was a little past two in the morning when Standish found the car parked on a remote logging road that led to a highway that passed over the Coast Mountains. Chen had left the key for the trunk on the ground.

"Get those assholes out of the trunk," Standish told one of his men.

Inside the trunk were the two men he'd sent to work over Alan Chen. They were only wearing underpants; their mouths were taped shut, and they were hog-tied. Standish's bodyguards dragged the men out of the trunk, ripped off the tape that sealed their mouths, and cut them loose. The men flopped around on the ground, gasping for air. Standish could see marks of torture on their faces and torsos.

One of the men started to struggle to his feet, but Standish used the toe of one of his beautifully polished shoes to push him back onto the ground.

"Stay where you are until I tell you that you can get up. Understand?"

"Yes, boss," one man answered, while the other man nodded. They looked terrified.

"It's Grigor and Martin, am I right?"

"Yes, sir," Grigor answered.

"Which one of you pathetic losers wants to tell me how you ended up in the trunk of your car?" Standish asked.

"You told us he was an accountant," Martin said. "We didn't see it coming."

"He was so fast, boss," Gregor said. "We let down our guard because of what you said."

"So, I'm to blame?" Standish asked.

"No, no. I didn't mean that. It's just . . . An accountant. We didn't think—"

"Exactly," Standish said. "You dumb fucks didn't think. I have a few questions that I hope aren't too difficult for you morons. Mr. Chen called me to tell me where to find you. Wasn't that nice of him?"

The men looked at each other.

Standish looked at one of his bodyguards. "Kick these losers until they answer me."

Martin raised his hand in defense. "Yeah, yeah. That was nice," he said to ward off the kick.

Standish stopped the bodyguard, who had just raised his leg.

"That was easy, wasn't it? So far, you're acing your exam. So, next question. How did Mr. Chen know my number and name?"

The two men looked away. Standish nodded, and the bodyguard delivered a blow to Grigor's ribs.

"We had to tell him!" Martin shouted. "He said he'd kill us if we didn't."

"We tried to hold out," Grigor said, "but you can see what he did to us."

"So, you gave me up to avoid a little pain?"

The men looked down.

"Did Mr. Chen ask you questions about an auto accident insurance scam?"

"Yeah, yeah, he did," both men answered quickly.

"What did you tell him?"

"We didn't know anything about that," Martin said. "No one ever clued us in about any scam. Honest, Mr. Standish."

"I believe you," Standish said. Then he turned to his bodyguards. "Put them back in the trunk."

"No, please," Grigor begged as Standish's men grabbed them.

Martin threw a punch, and Standish shot him in the head. Martin's eyes rolled back, and he dropped.

"Fuck," Standish said as his men beat Grigor unconscious. "I wanted all the blood in the trunk. Oh, well. The best laid plans, et cetera."

Standish's men dumped Martin and Grigor in the trunk, and Standish shot Grigor.

"Shut the trunk," Standish said.

Jack Kovalev lived in a mansion in the middle of several acres that backed on the Willamette River. A high metal gate blocked the only access to the house from the road that ran through forest to the estate, and a high stone wall topped with broken glass and surveilled by security cameras twenty-four hours a day ringed the property. Near the river, a locked gate separated the dock where Kovalev's speedboat was secured from the grounds. Dogs and guards roamed the property at all hours to keep out the riffraff and Kovalev's rivals.

Jack Kovalev was not happy about being awakened from a deep and peaceful sleep at three in the morning. But he knew that Lloyd Standish wouldn't have called unless it was very important.

"Go back to sleep," the Russian mobster told his wife as he went into the master bathroom to speak to his lieutenant.

"It's the middle of the night, Lloyd, so this had better be good."

"It's not, and it isn't something I'm comfortable discussing over the phone. I'll be at your place in twenty minutes."

Kovalev's physique had been developed during the years of his youth when he had been a heavyweight wrestler good enough to win championships in Russia. His bald head was oversized, as was the rest of his body. He had massive shoulders, a neck so thick it almost touched them, large biceps and forearms, and a barrel chest covered in curly black hair. The mobster dressed and was waiting in his study when his houseman showed Standish in.

"What's so important, Lloyd, that you couldn't tell me over the phone or in the morning?"

"We may have a big problem. You know Otis Truax fucked up and killed a woman named Susan Chen?"

"Yeah. Margaret told me Chen's husband has been harassing her."

Lloyd nodded. "He's been trying to find out who hired Truax, so I sent Grigor and Martin to knock some sense into him."

Kovalev looked alarmed. "Why did you do that? Truax isn't a problem anymore."

"In hindsight, I probably made a mistake."

"Why? What happened?"

"Chen beat up Grigor and Martin. Then he put them in the trunk of their car and called me."

"How did he know who to call?"

"Chen tortured the idiots until they talked."

"You're kidding me! Didn't you tell me that Chen is an accountant?"

"He is now, but I had him checked out as soon as he called. Before he became a CPA, Chen was Special Forces. He's been in combat in Afghanistan, Iraq, and on missions that are classified. And worse still, he's a sniper. So, we could be targets."

Kovalev was quiet for a while, and Standish let him think. After a while, Kovalev looked up. "Find him and kill him."

"I already have our people on it. But what about Margaret Finch? If he could make Grigor and Martin talk, he'd have no problem getting Margaret to tell him everything she knows about the insurance scam and a lot of other information she has about our business. And she could also run to the cops."

"You make a good point, Lloyd. Margaret has been useful, but lawyers are a dime a dozen. Take care of both problems."

CHAPTER FIFTEEN

"It was the blood and the smell," the runner told Chet Marx.

"Yeah, you get a pretty pungent odor when a corpse has been marinating for a couple of days," Darrell Price said.

Marx cast a withering look at his partner. They were standing next to the detective's car, which was parked on the logging road far enough away from the crime scene so they wouldn't be in the way of the medical examiner who was looking at the decaying corpses of Grigor and Martin and the forensic team that was working the area.

"I run distance races, and these forest trails are great for endurance. I vary my routes, but the trail that passed the car is one of my favorites. Anyway, I've been past this spot dozens of times, and I've never seen a car here. Then I saw the blood on the ground and I stopped. That's when I got hit by the smell and called you guys."

"I'm glad you did. We might not have found the bodies for days," Marx said.

"Do you need me anymore? I'm supposed to be at work. I did call my boss, and he told me it would be okay to be late, but . . ."

"We have your statement, so you can go. Thanks for being a good citizen."

The runner took off.

"There's no ID on either victim, but we'll get fingerprints and we'll know who they are pretty soon," Price said.

"I know who they are already," Marx told him. "You're looking at Martin Lebedev and Grigor Nikolaev. They're muscle Jack Kovalev uses to collect debts."

"So, a mob hit?"

"Looks like it." Marx sighed.

"Which means the odds are slim to none that we'll ever make an arrest."

The next day, Chet Marx was finishing a report so he could go home when his phone rang.

"Hi, Chet. This is Eleonore Park from the crime lab."

"Hey, Elle. How are you?"

"Great."

"You had a kid graduating, didn't you?"

"Last year. She's at the U of O."

"Majoring in biology like her mom?"

Park laughed. "Theater. She wants to be a movie star."

"So, what's up?"

"We got a hit on prints we found on the trunk of that car with the two dead men."

"Lebedev and Nikolaev, right?"

"Yeah, but there was another one."

"Oh?"

"It's a man named Alan Chen."

"Chen? Are you sure?"

"He's in the database."

"For a criminal conviction?"

"No. Military. He's got a pretty impressive record. Medals, some classified stuff."

"And you're certain the prints belong to Alan Chen?"

"One hundred percent sure."

"Thanks."

"Price," Marx said as soon as he hung up. "Let's go for a ride."

Half an hour later, the detectives were standing at Alan Chen's front door. There were no lights on in the house, but Marx rang the doorbell anyway.

"I don't think he's in," Price said after Marx had rung the bell again, knocked, and called Chen's name.

There was a mail slot in the front door, and Marx peered through it.

"The mail is piled up, so I'm guessing that he hasn't been home for a few days."

"What do you want to do?"

"There are only two possibilities. He's dead or he had something to do with those two in the trunk. Either way, we need to find him."

PART THREE

All Dead

CHAPTER SIXTEEN

Roger Dillon got out of his unmarked car and hunched his shoulders in an ineffective attempt to avoid the icy drizzle that was chilling his bones. On days like this, Dillon wondered why he had moved from the Midwest and its subzero winters to Portland, where the sun only shone a few months each year, instead of San Diego or Arizona.

Dillon's partner, homicide detective Carrie Anders, didn't even bother to put up the hood on her rain jacket when she got out of the car, apparently unconcerned about the rain and cold.

Anders and Dillon, the Portland Police Bureau's smartest and most effective homicide team, were a study in contrasts. Dillon was a lanky African American man who wore his salt-and-pepper hair short and was nearing retirement. Anders, who was many years younger than her partner, was a large woman who topped six feet and was as strong as some men. She had sad brown eyes, a large, lumpish nose, and short, shaggy black hair. Her lumbering appearance and slow drawl often led people to conclude that Anders was slow-witted, which gave the college math major an edge.

That evening, Anders had phoned Dillon at his house a little after nine o'clock.

"Sorry to call so late," Anders had said, "but 911 got a call from a schoolteacher. He said he went over to the home of one of his students and found the whole family dead. The first responders say there are four victims. They've all been shot. One of them is Margaret Finch."

"She's the lawyer who represents Jack Kovalev, isn't she?"

"And other members of the Russian mob."

"Do you think this is a mob hit?" Dillon asked.

"I'd just be guessing."

"Chet Marx has been bitching about a case involving Russians."

"That auto accident where the woman was killed," Anders confirmed.

"Yeah. He thought the accident was planned as part of an insurance scam Kovalev's mob has been running. Wasn't Finch representing the guy who drove the car?"

"Otis Truax was the driver, and Finch represented him," Carrie said. "From what I heard, Marx offered Truax a deal if he'd tell them who was running the scam and testify. Then, Truax was murdered."

"With Finch and Truax dead, there's no one who can tie Kovalev to the fraud scheme. Makes you wonder," Dillon said.

"Tut, tut, Mr. Dillon. You know better than to start a case with preconceived notions about whodunit."

"You're no fun, Carrie."

Anders laughed. "One of us has to behave like a professional. I'm almost at your house. Pick you up in fifteen."

Twenty minutes after Anders picked up her partner, the detectives parked in an upper-class Portland neighborhood in front of a large, cheery red-and-brown Craftsman-style house that backed on part of Portland's urban forest.

"Doesn't seem like a place where you'd find a mass murder, does it?" Carrie said.

"Life is full of surprises," Dillon said. "Shall we?"

A uniformed officer was standing under the cover of the front porch huddled in a poncho, holding the log in which he recorded everyone who entered the crime scene. The detectives gave him their names and put on protective gear that would keep them from contaminating the scene.

Anders and Dillon wound their way through techs from the crime lab who were gathering evidence and stopped in front of the living room, where the medical examiner was hard at work. A television was on, but someone had muted it, and a man and a woman were slumped on a couch across from the wall-mounted set. Their heads lay against the back of the sofa, and their mouths were open as if they were caught by surprise when the end came. Both victims' chests were covered in blood that had poured from bullet wounds.

The detectives turned toward a staircase that led from the second floor to the entryway. A teenage girl was sprawled at the bottom. The autopsy reports listed the heights of the Finches. They were all above average, and the girl was just shy of five foot eleven and heavyset, her weight more muscle than fat. She had been shot in the face and torso. Roger had a daughter in college. The sight of the dead girl hit him hard.

"That sucks," Carrie said, her voice only slightly above a whisper.

Dillon just shook his head. He'd been to more crime scenes than he could count, and he'd grown used to the smell of blood, the stench of emptied waste products, and the desecrated bodies of adults, but he had never gotten used to seeing the children whose lives had been cut short before they could grow up, marry, start families, and experience what a good life could offer.

"What do you think?" Carrie asked. "Thirteen, fourteen?"

Dillon didn't answer. He turned away and walked over to Sally Grace, the medical examiner, a slender woman with sharp blue eyes, whose frizzy black hair was concealed by a plastic cap.

"Have anything for us yet?" he asked.

"Just the obvious. Death caused by gunshots. We have a witness who found the victims. He got here around eight thirty, so we should be able to get a close estimate of the time of death if you can find out when any of the victims were last seen alive."

"I recognize Margaret Finch. Any ID on the male?" Carrie asked.

"Her husband, Nathan. The lab guys took his wallet, and there are pictures of the two of them all over the house."

Dr. Grace pointed toward the dead girl. "That's Annie, their daughter. She's fourteen and in middle school."

"We were told that there were four victims."

"Ryan, the son, is in his bedroom. Gunshots to the head and body. He had a headset on and was listening to loud music. There's a possibility that entry was made from the rear of the house, which is near his bedroom. So, either the killer got him first, or he didn't hear the shots in the living room and the killer found him after he shot the rest of the family."

"We'll let you get back to work," Dillon said. "Let us know if you find anything you think we should know."

"Will do," Dr. Grace said as she turned back to Nathan Finch's corpse.

A hall led from the staircase to the rear of the house. A door at the end of the hall was open, and lab techs were dusting for fingerprints, sweeping for trace evidence, and performing the other tasks they were trained to do.

Ryan Finch was in bed with earphones covering his ears. He had a surprised look on his face and a bullet hole in the middle of his forehead. But that was not the extent of his injuries. Carrie leaned in close and examined Ryan's face.

"His nose has been broken, his lip's split. It looks like someone worked him over."

"I don't think it was the person who killed him. Those bruises look like they're healing."

A uniformed officer walked into the bedroom. "Are you the detectives in charge of the case?" he asked.

"Roger Dillon and Carrie Anders," Anders answered.

"Good. I know something that might help."

"And you are?" Roger asked.

"Oh, sorry. Harry Nguyen."

"Let's step into the hall and let these guys do their job," Anders said.

The officer and the two detectives went to the end of the hall where they had some privacy.

"So, Officer Nguyen, how can you help us?" Roger asked.

"I'm a big MMA fan, and so is Jim Rourke, another officer. We went to the academy together. Anyway, Jim was called to the Gaslight, that bar on Naito Parkway. Someone reported a fight. When he got there, he found this victim. He recognized him as Margaret Finch's son."

"Why did he know he was Finch's son?" Carrie asked.

"Ryan was a drug dealer. We've never arrested him, because he's small-time, so we never put much effort in. But everyone knows who he is because everyone knows Margaret Finch."

"Okay. Go on. Sorry I interrupted you."

"This is what might help you. Ryan was really busted up, and Jim recognized the person who delivered the beating right away. It was Mandy Kerrigan."

"Who?" Roger asked.

"Do you follow MMA?" Nguyen asked.

"No," the detectives answered.

"Okay, well, Kerrigan was a world champion for a few years. That was some time ago. But she's still fighting and she was on the undercard of a big televised event that was held at the Moda Center. She lost. Then she failed a drug test and had her purse held up. She could face a suspension. One of the witnesses thought she heard Kerrigan accuse Finch of selling her bad drugs."

"Was Kerrigan arrested?" Dillon asked.

"No. Jim told me that Finch refused to press charges and said it was a misunderstanding."

"Okay. When you see Rourke, tell him we want to talk to him."

"I will."

"Didn't a schoolteacher call in the 911?" Roger asked.

"Arthur Proctor. He's in the den if you want to talk to him."

"In a minute," Dillon said. "And thanks, Officer Nguyen."

Nguyen walked to the front of the house, and Carrie turned to her partner.

"Now we have two suspects," she said.

"Not bad for twenty minutes' work."

Carrie followed the hall to the kitchen in the back of the house. Outside, on the other side of the kitchen wall, was a patio. The sole piece of furniture left on it was a heavy glass-topped table. Dillon guessed that the rest of the patio furniture was probably stored in the garage until the spring. There was a door that separated the kitchen from the patio. It was half-open, and a pane had been punched out. Glass was strewn across the kitchen floor.

"The killer comes through the woods at the back of the house, enters through the back door, and leaves the same way," Carrie said.

"Seems right," Dillon agreed.

"Good luck tracing his escape route," Carrie said. "This tract is part of the largest urban forest in the world. If I remember correctly, we have more than five thousand acres with miles of hiking trails, fire lanes, and roads inside Portland."

"I'll get one of the lab techs to look for evidence of an escape route. Maybe we'll get lucky."

"Let's talk to Proctor," Carrie said.

The detectives asked directions to the den and found Arthur Proctor seated on a sofa in a small, book-lined room. He was leaning forward, his forearms resting on his legs, but he sat up when the detectives walked in and stared at them with clear, brown eyes that sat on either side of a Roman nose. A well-tended, sandy-brown beard and mustache framed a firm mouth and covered a strong chin.

For some reason, the word *dapper* popped into Roger's head. It was an old-fashioned word that was not in vogue nowadays, but Roger thought that it described Proctor. The teacher was wearing dark slacks with a knife-edge crease, a blue blazer, a dark sweater vest, and a school tie that was evidence that he was an alumnus of an Ivy League university.

Roger guessed that Annie's teacher was in his late thirties or early forties, but his face hadn't started to show his age. It was obvious that Proctor had been running his fingers through his full head of hair, but nothing else about the man seemed out of place. The detectives could see that he was very upset. They pulled up chairs and sat across from him.

"I'm Roger Dillon, and this is my partner, Carrie Anders, Mr. Proctor. I know this is difficult, but it would really help us if you can tell us why you came to the Finch home and what happened when you got here."

"Of course. Anything to help."

Someone had brought Proctor a glass of water. He lifted it off the coffee table that separated him from the detectives and took a sip.

"I teach honors English and run the theater club at Marie Curie Middle School. Annie is in my eighth-grade English class."

Proctor paused and took another sip of water.

"Annie was . . . *Complicated* is an apt description. She was a loner without many friends and she was quiet in class. I could tell that she has . . . had a high IQ, but her grades weren't reflecting her intellect. She was doing A work for me, but her other grades were Cs and Ds, and she was skipping class. In other words, she was underperforming and it was obvious that there was a problem, but I had no idea what it was. I did feel that she needed a change of scenery, and I told her parents that she would benefit by going to a private school with smaller classes."

Proctor held up a file that had been lying on the sofa. "Mr. Finch was worried about the cost. This file contains information about scholarships. That's why I came here. I told Annie to tell her parents I'd drop in around eight thirty with information I'd found about financial assistance."

Proctor took a deep breath, then blew it out.

"I . . . I parked out front and rang the doorbell."

"Do you remember what time you parked?" Carrie asked.

"Somewhere around eight thirty. I had the radio on, and the news had just started when I parked out front. They start the news on the half hour."

"Did you see anyone outside the Finches' house or on the street?"

"No."

"Okay. Go on."

"I could hear the television. It was very loud. But no one came to the door to let me in. I rang the bell twice more. Then I tried the door. It was open."

Proctor shut his eyes for a second. "I'm going to have nightmares about this for the rest of my life," he said when he opened them.

"Take all the time you need," Roger said.

Proctor took another sip of water. Then he shook his head as if he was trying to rid himself of the images that were seared into his brain.

"I saw Annie first. She was lying there, and there was so much blood. I wanted to run out, but I had to see if anyone was alive and needed help. One look told me that Mr. and Mrs. Finch were gone. That's when I got out of the house and called 911."

"Did you see anyone or hear any sounds that might indicate that there was someone in the house?" Carrie asked.

"No."

"Did you go into any other part of the house?" she asked.

"No. I just wanted to get out of there."

"Can you clear up something for me?" Carrie asked. "In the 911 call, you said that they were all dead. When you made the call, did you know that Ryan Finch had also been murdered?"

"No. When I said 'all,' I meant everyone I saw."

"Thank you, Mr. Proctor. Have you given a statement to one of the officers?" Roger asked.

"Yes. Soon after the police arrived."

"I imagine you'd like to go home. Unless Carrie has another

question for you, you can leave. Do we have your contact information?"

Proctor nodded. Roger looked at Anders. She shook her head.

"Okay. Thanks again. I'm sorry you had to see this," Roger said.

A raincoat had been thrown haphazardly over one end of the sofa's cushions and one of the sofa's arms. Proctor put it on, grabbed his file, and left.

"Poor bastard," Carrie said.

Officer Nguyen walked into the den. "There's a witness, Megan Radcliffe, a neighbor. You need to talk to her."

Nguyen walked out of the den, and the detectives followed him across the street to a yellow-and-white Dutch Colonial house. A woman was talking to a female officer in the entryway. She was in her late thirties, with short red hair and green eyes, and was dressed in jeans and a blue, man-tailored shirt. A tall man in casual dress was standing behind her, and two teenage boys were standing in the entrance to the living room.

"Mr. and Mrs. Radcliffe," Nguyen said, "this is homicide detective Roger Dillon and his partner, Carrie Anders. Mrs. Radcliffe, can you tell them what you just told me?"

"Of course. This was a little before eight o'clock. I'm going to say seven fifty or seven fifty-five because my show started at eight and I wanted to get a snack in the kitchen. I was here in the foyer when I looked out the window and saw a woman outside the Finch home."

"What was she doing?"

"Just standing there and pounding on the door. I could hear her yelling, but I couldn't hear what she was saying."

"Go on."

"I fixed my snack and walked back toward the living room. I'd recorded the show, so I wasn't in a hurry. When I passed the window again, I saw the woman leave the porch and walk down the block."

"Did you see where she went?" Carrie asked.

"No."

"What time was this?"

"Eight oh five to eight ten. I can't be certain."

"Did you get a good look at the woman?" Carrie asked.

"Yes. There's a streetlight outside the Finches' house, and she stopped under it for a moment before walking away." Radcliffe nodded toward Officer Nguyen. "He showed me a picture of her on his phone."

Nguyen held up his phone. On the screen was the picture of two women at a weigh-in. The letters *UFC* were emblazoned in red behind them. Mrs. Radcliffe pointed at one of the women.

"That's her," she said.

Carrie turned to Officer Nguyen. "I take it that's Mandy Kerrigan?"

"Yes, ma'am."

"Did you see or hear anything else after the woman left?"

Radcliffe nodded. "At some point during my show, I looked out the living room window at the Finch house and there was no one there."

"Do you know what time that was?" Carrie asked.

"Maybe eight fifteen. I can't be certain."

"Okay. Go on."

"At eight thirty, I heard a car across the street. I looked out the window, and I saw a man get out of his car. My kids went to Marie Curie Middle School, and I recognized Arthur Proctor. He taught my boys English.

"Mr. Proctor went to the Finches' door. I believe he rang the bell. Then he went inside, and I went back to my show. About ten minutes later, I looked out of the window and I saw Mr. Proctor run out of the house. He'd left the Finches' door open, and he looked very upset. I walked across the street. He was standing on the porch talking into his phone to 911. I asked him what was wrong, and he said I should go back to my house. That something awful had happened and the police would be there soon. Shortly after, several police cars drove up."

Carrie turned to the policewoman. "Have you been taking Mrs. Radcliffe's statement?"

"I'm almost done."

"Okay. Finish up. We're going back to the crime scene. Thanks, Mrs. Radcliffe. You've been a big help."

The detectives ran through the rain to the Finches' front porch.

"Kerrigan?" Roger said.

Carrie nodded. "As soon as we can find out where she's staying."

CHAPTER SEVENTEEN

Tom McKee was floating as he made his way to the restaurant where he was going to meet Carrie Anders and Roger Dillon. It seemed like everything was going his way. First and foremost, there was Robin. She was terrific and every date had been great. He knew about the death of her fiancé, so he had kept the romance one hundred percent platonic. Tom had never felt about someone the way he felt about Robin, and he was willing to wait for her to let him know when she felt comfortable moving the relationship along.

Then there was his job. Two weeks ago, Vanessa Cole, the Multnomah County district attorney, had asked him to come to her office and had praised his work. Then she'd told him that one of the attorneys who was trying murder cases was leaving the DA's office to work at a large civil firm, and she was going to promote him to the section that handled homicides.

Mike Greene, the head of the capital crimes unit, had asked Tom to be his second chair in an aggravated murder case that would be going to trial in two weeks, so he could learn how to try a death penalty case, but Tom had a suspicion that he might have a case of his own soon. Carrie Anders and Roger Dillon had invited him to have lunch at a restaurant near the courthouse and had been very mysterious when he'd asked them why.

McKee spotted the detectives sitting at a table near the sushi bar. Roger saw him come in and waved a hand.

"I hope you like Japanese," Roger said.

"Japanese is a favorite of mine," McKee said as he took a seat.

A waitress came over and took their order.

"So, why aren't we meeting in my office?" Tom asked.

"We've never worked with you, and we like to get to know the deputies who are working on our cases."

McKee smiled. "As far as I know, I'm not working one of your cases."

"You will be. But first, we need a search warrant."

"Are you guys springing for sushi instead of a Big Mac because probable cause is questionable?"

Roger turned to Carrie. "I told you that Mr. McKee was nobody's fool and we couldn't tempt him with a cheap bribe."

"I get to eat my chirashi bowl even if I turn you down, right?"

"Yup."

"Okay, then. Hit me with your facts."

"Four people were murdered in the West Hills yesterday evening. One of them was Ryan Finch, Margaret Finch's son."

"She's a criminal defense attorney, isn't she?" Tom asked.

"Yes. And he's a drug dealer, but he doesn't sell weed or coke. We talked with Nick Borelli in Vice and Narcotics this morning. Ryan's father was a chemist, and Ryan was selling designer drugs. One product his father concocted is a performance-enhancing drug that

Ryan had been touting as untraceable. He sold it to a Trail Blazer and two members of the Portland Timbers. Last weekend, he sold it to Mandy Kerrigan, an MMA fighter who was in a bout at the Moda Center recently."

"I was at that fight. Kerrigan lost and she didn't look that good, so the PED must not be that effective."

"Worse," Roger said, "it was detected during a post-fight drug test. Kerrigan's purse is being held up, and she's facing a possible suspension."

"She didn't take it well," Carrie said. "Shortly before Ryan was murdered, Kerrigan found him at the Gaslight tavern and beat the crap out of him. Then she was seen at Ryan's home just before the bodies of Margaret, her husband, their fourteen-year-old daughter, and Ryan were found. The lab says that they were all shot with the same gun. We haven't found the murder weapon yet."

"Kerrigan is staying in a motel," Roger said. "We want to search her room for the weapon, clothes that may have blood on them, and anything else that will prove Kerrigan was inside the Finch home and murdered the family. So, what do you think?"

McKee didn't answer right away, and the detectives left him alone. The waitress brought miso soup for the table. McKee raised his bowl to his lips and sipped the soup. When he set down the bowl, he looked across the table.

"I won't be able to give you an opinion until I read the reports. When I get back to the office, I'll start researching. Get me everything you have."

Carrie handed Tom a thick file. "We're way ahead of you, Mr. McKee. This is everything we've got so far."

McKee smiled. "It looks like you were pretty confident I'd help you."

"We were confident that you are young and ambitious," Carrie answered.

"How soon will you know if we've got the goods?" Roger asked. "Kerrigan could skip town or get rid of evidence anytime."

"I'll get back to you this afternoon."

As soon as he was back at the district attorney's office, Tom booted up his computer, logged on to LexisNexis, and started bringing up cases he thought would help him decide if he could convince a judge to issue a warrant.

He was reading an Oregon Supreme Court case that looked promising when a thought occurred to him. He had poured himself a cup of coffee before starting his research. He looked away from the case and took a sip.

Robin had talked to Kerrigan after the fight. Had Robin told her that she was an attorney? If she had, would Kerrigan hire Robin if she was arrested, and, if she did, how would that impact their relationship?

He and Robin had tried cases against each other, and she was still willing to go out with him. He'd even won a case she thought she would win, and she hadn't held the loss against him.

Kerrigan wasn't under arrest and might never be. A judge might not issue a search warrant. If the detectives did get one, they might not find enough evidence to take Kerrigan into custody. And if Kerrigan was charged with murder, she might not have the money to afford Robin or she might hire someone else. Tom decided that there were too many ifs. He shook his head to rid himself of negative thoughts and plunged back into the world of search and seizure law.

CHAPTER EIGHTEEN

It had been a nail-biter, but McKee delivered. The detectives and the deputy DA had rushed to the chambers of a judge just before five in the afternoon on the day of their lunch date. After a brief discussion of the law that McKee had handled beautifully, the judge had signed the warrant.

With the warrant in hand, Dillon and Anders sped across town to serve it at the motel where Mandy Kerrigan was living while she waited to find out how much of her purse she would receive and whether she was going to be suspended.

The detectives were followed by a car with uniformed officers, who had been alerted to the fact that they would be confronting a trained fighter. Kerrigan's room was on the second floor of the Paris Motel. The detectives and the uniforms stood on the landing under an overhang that provided some shelter from the light rain that was falling. Carrie knocked on Kerrigan's door and announced that there were police officers outside it.

When Kerrigan opened the door, the detectives identified them-selves and held out their IDs. Anders thought that Kerrigan didn't look good. There were shadows under her eyes and an air of despair about her.

"What took you so long?" the fighter asked.

"You've been expecting us?" Anders asked.

Kerrigan held up the front page of the newspaper. In bold let-ters, the headline told readers about THE WEST HILLS MASSACRE.

"As soon as I read that Ryan Finch was one of the victims, I knew someone would come calling."

"Can we come in?"

Kerrigan stepped aside, and the detectives entered a squalid room that smelled of sweat and take-out food.

"I guess you'll want to search for evidence, so go ahead," Kerri-gan said, negating the need for the search warrant. "You won't find anything."

"Is that because you've gotten rid of the gun and anything else that might incriminate you?"

"No, Detective. That's because I didn't kill anyone."

"Do you have a car?" Carrie asked.

"It's the brown Kia," she said. "Here are the keys."

"So, we can search it?" Carrie asked.

"Be my guest."

Anders signaled the officers who were waiting outside. She gave the keys to the car to one of them and ushered the others inside. They came in and began a methodical search of the room after An-ders and Dillon led Kerrigan outside.

"We have a witness who saw you outside the Finch home just before their bodies were found, pounding on the door and scream-ing," Carrie said. "Why were you there?"

Kerrigan looked down, embarrassed. "I wanted to kill that motherfucker Ryan. All I've got going for me is fighting, and I was going to be suspended because his supposedly untraceable drugs showed up in my post-fight test. I know I should have stayed away, but I get headaches and I wasn't thinking straight, and the next thing I knew, I was pounding on that bastard's door."

"Did they let you in?"

"No. When I was there, the TV was really loud, so I thought they didn't hear me. Or they saw who was at the door and Ryan told them that I'd beaten him up. Now I know that they were probably dead."

"You didn't see the bodies when you went inside?"

"I never went inside the house."

"Why didn't you?"

"The door was locked."

It was raining, cold, and windy. Kerrigan was shivering even though she had put on a jacket.

"You look uncomfortable," Roger said. "Why don't we continue our talk at the station where it's warm and I can get you some coffee."

"Is this a nice way of telling me that I'm under arrest?"

"Absolutely not," Roger fibbed.

Kerrigan aimed a weary smile at the detective. "Let's go," she said. "I'm tired of sitting in this room."

CHAPTER NINETEEN

Robin slept well and had a terrific workout at McGill's before going to her office. She was in a great mood when she stopped at her favorite coffee shop to purchase a latte and a scone. As she walked across town, it dawned on her that she'd been a lot happier since she started going out with Tom and, recently, she hadn't felt guilty about being happy. She wondered if she was at a turning point in dealing with her grief.

She took bites of her scone and sipped her latte while she checked the emails on her computer. She had positioned pictures of Jeff on her desk, her bookshelves, and other places in the office so she could see him anywhere she looked. When she turned away from the monitor, Robin found herself staring at a framed selfie of her and Jeff on the beach at the Oregon coast in front of Haystack Rock. They had taken the picture a month before he died. For a moment, Robin imagined Jeff seated across from her desk in one of the client chairs.

"I'm seeing someone I really like, Jeff."

In her mind, she saw him smile and say that he was happy for her.

Robin's chest heaved, and a tear trickled down her cheek. She missed Jeff so much and she would never stop loving him, but maybe it was time for her to take a chance.

Her intercom buzzed. She took a breath and wiped her eyes.

"There's a collect call from the jail on line two," the receptionist said. "Should I accept it?"

"Is it one of my clients?"

"It's a Mandy Kerrigan. I don't recognize the name."

"Hi, Mandy," Robin said when the receptionist put the call through. "Why are you in jail?"

"I've been arrested for a quadruple homicide. I looked you up after you visited me in my locker room. That's right up your alley, if I'm not mistaken."

"It's definitely the type of case I'm comfortable handling. Hang tight. I'm coming to the jail right now."

A guard let Robin into one of the contact visiting rooms. Ten minutes later, the locks on the door that led to the cells snapped open and another guard ushered Mandy Kerrigan into the room. Robin thought that Mandy looked sad and defeated. Her shoulders slumped, and the ferocity that had unnerved Robin when they'd fought was nowhere to be found.

"Thanks for coming," Kerrigan said.

"It's the least I can do for the person who convinced me to quit fighting and concentrate on my studies," Robin said in an attempt to lighten the situation. It didn't work.

"Look, Robin. I really appreciate your coming over here, but I want to be honest. I'm not sure I can afford to hire you. My career has been going downhill and so have my paychecks. When I looked you up, one of the articles said that you've gotten a national reputation. I'm guessing that translates into big retainers, which I can't handle. But I do have enough to pay you for an hour's worth of advice."

"Isn't there anyone you can rely on who can help you financially? Family, friends?"

"My mother died five years ago, and I hadn't spoken to her for a long time before she passed. My father is some guy among many who she spent a night with, and I have no idea who he is. There aren't any brothers or sisters. And, before you ask, I've run through trainers and I've fired my last two managers."

"Okay. Let's worry about the money after we talk. And you should know that anything you tell me is confidential, so you can be completely open and honest without worrying that I'll tell anyone what you told me. That's true even if you tell me that you murdered someone."

"But I didn't."

"Then why are you in jail?"

"You know I might be suspended for failing a drug test?"

"I read about it in the paper."

Kerrigan sighed. "I've been fighting since I was a teenager, and I'm not a kid anymore. I don't move as fast, and I've had a lot of injuries. In the last few years, I've lost more fights than I've won. My career is winding down. Soon I'll have to stop, but I can't stop because I don't have anything else. My career is my life. All I've got is fighting. If I hang up my gloves, it will be like dying. So, I have to do anything I can to win or, at least, put on a good show. That's why I took the PEDs."

"What does that have to do with the Finches?"

"Ryan Finch sold them to me. They were supposed to be top

of the line and untraceable. That's what the guy who told me about Ryan said."

"Who was that?"

"Sorry, I can't tell you. I promised. But he's another fighter who used them. And he told me where I could find Ryan. Ryan swore they wouldn't show up in a drug test, but they did, and I realized that could be the end of everything. I was so angry that I wasn't thinking."

Kerrigan stopped talking and looked down at the top of the metal table that separated her from Robin.

"I've had a few concussions. I black out. It scares the hell out of me."

"I had that problem when we fought," Robin said. "You hit me so hard that I had short-term memory loss." She shook her head. "I couldn't remember anything about our fight. It scared me too. So I know what you're talking about."

"My head was killing me after the fight with Clark. I may have blacked out when I got back to my motel room. The point is, after an episode, there are times when I don't think straight, and I definitely didn't have my shit together after I found out that I'd flunked the drug test."

"What did you do?"

"I went back to the bar where I bought the drugs and beat up Ryan Finch in front of witnesses, giving myself one hell of a motive for murder. Someone called the cops, so there was a record of me beating up one of the victims shortly before he was murdered.

"Then, to make matters worse, I went to Ryan's house just before the cops came. The door was locked, and I made a fool of myself by pounding on it and screaming." Kerrigan shook her head back and forth slowly. "They must have been dead while I was screaming at them. That's why no one answered the door."

"Did you see anyone in the house or hear anything?" Robin asked.

"I couldn't see in the house because the shades were down, but I thought I heard a scream or a shot when I was pounding on the door. But the TV was blaring, and I thought it was from a show."

"How did you know where Ryan lived?"

Kerrigan looked embarrassed. "I was still furious after the cops broke up the fight, so I followed Ryan home from the bar. A man picked him up. Probably his father. By the time I saw where they lived, I'd cooled down."

"Were you arrested at the Finch house?"

"No. I left before the cops arrived. I've been staying at a motel. The detectives went there. They asked me to go down to the police station while they searched my room and my car. They questioned me. Then they arrested me."

"Did they have a warrant to search your motel room?"

"I don't know. I just let them look. I wasn't worried. There was nothing to find."

Robin was worried. In her experience, there had been occasions when evidence magically appeared that should not have been in a place the police searched.

"Do you remember the names of the detectives who arrested you?"

"One of them was a big woman, and the other was Black. I think the woman was Carrie something and the man was Roger."

Robin had mixed feelings when she learned who had arrested Kerrigan. Carrie Anders and Roger Dillon would never set up a defendant, but they wouldn't have arrested Mandy if they weren't convinced that she was guilty.

"I think I have enough to work with. I know the detectives who arrested you. I'll call them and find out why they think you killed the Finches. We'll meet again when I have more information."

"What about your fee?"

An idea popped into Robin's head. "Let's talk about that when I know more. Don't worry about it for now."

CHAPTER TWENTY

Robin felt terrible when she left the jail. Mandy Kerrigan's tale was similar to the story so many fighters told. A sad early life, a momentary climb out of poverty and into the bright lights that shone on a winner who sacrificed his or her body for some measure of success. Then the downward spiral brought on by age or injury that is the fate of all athletes, no matter how good they are at their sport. Fighters like Mandy Kerrigan did not get a retirement plan or health insurance, and purses in mixed martial arts bouts were not like the multimillion-dollar payouts top boxers earned.

And there was something else that had touched Robin. She knew that she could be fooled as easily as anyone else, but her gut told her that Mandy might be innocent.

Robin stepped out of the Justice Center and into a biting wind. The cold brought clarity to an idea that had started to form in the contact visiting room and became fully formed in the elevator that brought her down to the reception area.

It cost a fortune to finance a death penalty case, and Mandy had made it crystal clear that she didn't have that kind of money and didn't know anyone who could help her. That meant that she was going to have a lawyer appointed by the court if the DA charged her with aggravated murder, a category of crime that carried a potential death sentence. And there was no doubt that would happen if the district attorney believed that Kerrigan was responsible for a quadruple homicide.

Robin headed to the Multnomah County Courthouse.

The first time Robin appeared before Harold Wright, she wondered if someone had dropped his double helix when he was born and forgot how to put the judge's DNA back together in the proper order. The judge had the barrel chest of a weight lifter, but his torso was supported by legs so thin you expected him to topple over at any moment. His wavy white hair could have adorned a model in a magazine on aging, but his nose reminded Robin of a bird's beak, and his bushy eyebrows and wild mustache made Robin think about Groucho Marx in the black-and-white comedies Jeff liked to watch on Turner Classic Movies.

When his secretary showed Robin into his chambers, the judge broke into a big grin.

"Good to see you," he said. And he meant it, because Robin had avoided him since Jeff was killed. "Sit, sit."

"That was a nice tribute," Robin said when they were seated across from each other.

"Were you there?"

Robin nodded. "I almost didn't come, but I knew I had to try to put what happened behind me. And I know it wasn't your fault."

Judge Wright's smile disappeared. "I did ask you to represent Arness."

"There was no way anyone could have foreseen what happened."

"That's true, but it hasn't stopped me from feeling awful."

Robin smiled. "I absolve you of all guilt, Judge. If you were Catholic, you'd have a clear path to heaven again."

Wright smiled. "You're forgetting all of my other sins."

"There's nothing I can do about those."

The judge sobered. "Thank you. That means a lot to me. So, I don't think any of your cases are on my docket. What brings you here?"

"You read about the four people who were murdered at the home of Margaret Finch?"

"She was in my court two weeks ago."

"My last fight in the UFC was against Mandy Kerrigan. I was in my first semester in law school, and she beat me up so badly that I stopped fighting professionally. Kerrigan was a world champion for a few years. Then her career started to go downhill. She's close to rock bottom now because they found PEDs when they tested her after her last fight.

"She just called me from the jail. She's been arrested for the Finch murders, and she's probably going to be indicted for a capital offense, but there's no way she's going to be able to afford private counsel. I feel a real connection to her because we both went through the wringer in the UFC."

"And you want the appointment."

Robin nodded.

"I can make a call. You'll know by this afternoon."

"Thank you."

CHAPTER TWENTY-ONE

Robin was appointed to handle Mandy Kerrigan's case an hour after she left Judge Wright's chambers. An attorney who was appointed to represent a defendant in a death penalty case was required to have a cocounsel assisting her. It was important to have a sounding board in a death case because of the horrific consequences that could ensue if lead counsel made a mistake. Amanda Jaffe and her father, Frank, were two of the best criminal defense attorneys in Oregon, and Amanda had been second chair in a capital case that Robin had tried a few years ago. As soon as the call appointing her ended, Robin was on the phone to Amanda.

"Why are you calling?" Amanda asked.

"Is that any way to greet an old friend who wants to give you an amazing opportunity to become famous?"

"Oh, shit. This can't be good."

Robin became serious. "You know that Margaret Finch and her family were murdered?"

"The infamous West Hills Massacre. Don't tell me you have the case."

"I was just appointed to represent Mandy Kerrigan. If the DA goes for the death penalty—which he's bound to do with four dead—I'll need a second chair. Are you available?"

"Maybe. I'll have to ask Mike if he's involved."

Amanda was engaged to Mike Greene, who headed up the unit in the Multnomah County District Attorney's Office that prosecuted death cases.

"Fair enough. Get back to me when you know."

Robin and Amanda made small talk for a few minutes more. When Robin hung up, she made her next call to Carrie Anders.

"I figured Kerrigan might try to hire you when I learned that she was an MMA fighter," the detective said.

"Can you tell me why you arrested her?"

"Not yet."

"Why? Didn't you find anything incriminating when you searched her motel room?"

"You know you don't get discovery until there's an indictment."

"If you're playing this so close to the vest, you must be worried about your case."

"Sorry I can't be more open with you, Robin, but you'll have to talk to the DA who's handling the case. I can't tell you anything right now."

"Okay. I respect that. Who has Kerrigan?"

"The new guy in Homicide, Tom McKee."

Robin hung up and took a deep breath. What should she do? One thing she couldn't do was drop Mandy Kerrigan as a client because she was dating the person who was prosecuting her. Could she ask Tom to ask his boss to take him off the case? The answer to that question was easy. The last time she had gone out with Tom, he had told her how excited he was to be promoted to the unit that prosecuted capital crimes. If she asked him to drop Mandy's case and he agreed, it would torpedo his career.

There was only one solution, and it broke her heart when she realized what she had to do.

"Tom," she said when he took her call. "Can you meet me for coffee?"

"Now? I'm in the middle of something."

"Does what you're doing concern Mandy Kerrigan?"

There was silence on Tom's end for a moment. "Are you representing her?"

"Let's get a cup of coffee, okay?"

Robin got to the coffee shop first and was sitting with two lattes when Tom walked in.

"This could be considered a bribe," he joked when she pushed his drink across the table. Robin didn't smile, but she did look directly at McKee.

"I knew this might happen after we started going out, and I've given this situation a lot of thought. My fiancé died three years ago. Dating anyone has been very difficult for me since Jeff died. I haven't done much of it in the past three years, and you are the only person I've gone out with more than once. That's because I really like you."

"I know what happened to Jeff," Tom said. "Friends have told me how hard this has been for you, and I've been honored by the fact that you've been willing to see me."

A tear formed in Robin's eye. She reached across the table and covered Tom's hand with her own. "Thank you."

She sat back and took a breath to calm herself. Tom waited until she was ready to speak again.

"Before we started seeing each other, being on opposite sides of a case wasn't a problem. Now, it is."

"I can ask to be taken off the case," Tom said.

"No, you can't. You have as much right to represent the State in Mandy's case as I do to represent her."

"I'd do it if prosecuting Kerrigan meant I'd be losing you."

"Think about the impact that would have on your career and how you'd be viewed in the office."

"You're more important to me than any case or any job."

"Wow!" Robin said. Then she laughed. "This is getting way too serious, and it doesn't have to be. I want to keep seeing you, and I have a solution. It will be painful, but I think it can work."

"What's your plan?"

"I'll tell Mandy that we've dated. If she has any reservations, I can get off the case. If she doesn't, I'll tell you and you can tell Mike we've been dating, but we're going to stop meeting out of court until the case is over.

"Here's where it gets interesting. Mike Greene's fiancée is the defense attorney, Amanda Jaffe. A few years ago, she was second chair on one of my capital cases, and I asked her to second chair Kerrigan before I knew that you were going to be lead counsel for the State."

"Jesus! This sounds like one of those incest cases they get in hillbilly country."

Robin smiled. "It does, doesn't it? So, what do you think?"

Tom thought for a minute. Then he smiled. "I think it could work. And they say absence makes the heart grow fonder."

"We won't really be apart. We'll see each other in court."

"Where we'll bicker like an old married couple."

Robin laughed. "Thank you for being so understanding."

"I am now, but don't expect me to cut you any slack in court."

"I won't if you'll promise that you won't cry when I win all the motions."

"You wish."

Robin stopped smiling and touched Tom's hand again. "What I wish is for a just and speedy end to the *Kerrigan* case, so things can go back the way they were before the Finch family was murdered."

Robin went to the jail as soon as she left the coffee shop and was escorted to a contact visiting room. Soon after, a guard brought Kerrigan to the room.

"There are a few things we have to discuss," Robin said as soon as the guard left Robin and her client alone. "First, I've been appointed to represent you. That means that you won't have to worry about paying me. The court will do that."

Kerrigan closed her eyes for a moment and took a deep breath. Then she opened her eyes and stared at Robin. "Thank you. I know you won't get paid anywhere near what you're worth, and I promise you that if I'm ever in a position to pay you, I'll make up the difference."

Robin smiled. "I hope I can get you out of this mess and that you get your career back on track, but you'll never owe me a dime. So, forget the money." Robin stopped smiling. "There is something else you need to know before I continue as your attorney."

"Oh?"

"The DA who will be prosecuting your case is Tom McKee, and we've been dating."

"What?"

"We haven't been going out very long, and the relationship has been one hundred percent platonic. We haven't even kissed. I didn't know that Tom would be prosecuting you the first time I spoke to you, and he didn't know I was going to represent you when his boss assigned the case to him. We met just before I came to see you. We agreed that while the case is active, we wouldn't see each other out of court, unless, of course, it was to discuss the case.

"If you don't want me to represent you because of my relationship to Tom, I'll get off and you can have another lawyer appointed. If you want me to continue as your lawyer, Tom will talk to his boss to see if his office wants him to continue as your prosecutor.

"You should know that Tom and I have tried three cases against each other. Tom will work hard to convict you, but he's very ethical, so you won't have to worry about him trying to pull anything."

Kerrigan took a minute to digest what Robin had just told her. When she spoke, she sounded concerned.

"Is he a good lawyer?"

"Yes. He's very smart and creative."

"How did you do in the three cases?"

"I won two of them and lost one."

"I need an honest answer, Robin. Are you going to be able to give me the same representation you'd give me if McKee wasn't your boyfriend?"

"I wouldn't be here if I didn't think I could. Tom and I got along in court before we started seeing each other, and it didn't affect the job I did."

Kerrigan smiled. "Okay, then. Let's do it."

"Great. The next thing I want to do is to brief you about the way a case with a death penalty is tried, because it differs procedurally from every other type of criminal case."

"Go ahead."

"The big difference has to do with the way your sentence will be determined if you're found guilty of a charge of aggravated murder. In every other criminal case, the judge decides the appropriate sentence, and there are several weeks between the conviction and the sentencing hearing. In a death penalty case, the jury decides whether the defendant should be sentenced to death, to life in prison without the possibility of parole, or life in prison with the possibility of parole. To protect the jurors from outside influences, the jury is brought back immediately after the guilt phase to hear evidence by both sides about what the sentence should be. There are times when the sentencing hearing is longer than the trial. This difference in the way your sentence will be determined has a major impact on how I prepare for your trial.

"When I get a death case, I have to assume the worst and start preparing for the sentencing phase at the same time I prepare for the part of the case where your guilt or innocence is decided, because I won't have time to prepare for the sentencing phase if I wait to see if you are convicted. And I'm going to need your help in preparing for the sentencing phase."

"What do you want me to do?"

"If you're convicted, all the jurors will know is that you killed a whole family. To save your life, I have to convince the jurors that you aren't a monster. To do that, I need to tell the jurors the story of your life so they can see that you're a decent human being even though you committed a terrible act.

"I'll need you to write your autobiography starting with your earliest memories up to the date of your arrest. I'll have investigators interviewing everyone who ever knew you so we can present positive evidence to the jurors.

"When you write your bio, I don't want you to sugarcoat it. If there's something awful like sexual or physical abuse, I need to know about it. What you write is protected by the attorney-client privilege, so no one but me will learn about it unless you give me permission to tell someone else—like an investigator—about it. I also want a list of witnesses who you think will have good things to say about you with as much contact information as you can give me. So, do you have any questions?"

"No, I'll start on the bio today."

"Great. Is there anything else we need to discuss?"

"Not that I can think of. And thanks. I appreciate everything you're doing for me."

PART FOUR

Suspects

CHAPTER TWENTY-TWO

Tom McKee, Carrie Anders, and Roger Dillon sat across a conference table from Mike Greene, the deputy district attorney in charge of the unit that prosecuted death penalty cases. Greene had curly black hair, blue eyes, and a shaggy mustache. His head was larger than normal but didn't seem out of proportion because he was six feet, five inches tall and had the massive body that people associated with NFL linemen. People who met Mike for the first time assumed that he'd played football. Mike had to explain that he'd never played and didn't even watch sports on TV. He did play chess and was a rated expert. He also played tenor sax in some local jazz clubs.

"If we decide to indict Kerrigan, will you be able to prosecute her the way you would if Robin weren't on the other side?" Mike asked after Tom told Greene and the detectives about his potential conflict.

"I don't see it as a problem," Tom replied. "I've liked Robin since the first time I met her, and I was toying with the idea of asking her out by the time we tried the *Costello* case. Robin put on one hell of a defense, but I won anyway. Robin congratulated me and didn't seem to resent the fact that I'd outlawyered her. I felt the same way when she won our first two trials. We both fought really hard and were very professional."

Mike turned to the detectives. "What do you think?"

Roger shrugged. "I've been involved in several cases where Robin has represented clients. She's very ethical, and I can't see her taking advantage of their relationship."

"If Tom thinks it won't be a problem, I have no objection," Carrie said.

Mike sighed. "I've been through this before when Amanda second chaired the *Lattimore* case with Robin, so I can hardly object. Just be open with me if a conflict does pop up."

"I will," Tom said.

"Our next order of business is deciding if we have the evidence to indict. Tell me what you've got."

"Kerrigan attacked Ryan Finch shortly before he was murdered, and we know why," Roger said. "Kerrigan was on a fight card at the Moda Center. She's on the downside of her career, so she was probably desperate to win. Ryan sold Kerrigan PEDs that were discovered during a drug test. That led to her purse being held up and a suspension that could lead to the end of her career."

"So, we have a motive for one of the murders," Greene said.

"We also have opportunity. A witness can place Kerrigan at the Finch home, standing on the front porch during the time period Sally Grace fixed for the time of death."

"I did an Internet search," Tom said. "Kerrigan has an arrest for assault in 2019."

"Was there a conviction?" Greene asked.

"It was a domestic thing, and the boyfriend dropped the case. That's not why the incident is important. The Finches were killed with 9 mm ammunition. A Glock 19 shoots 9 mm ammunition, and Kerrigan threatened her boyfriend with a Glock 19."

"Did you find her gun when you searched her room and car?"

"No."

"Did the search turn up any incriminating evidence?" Greene asked the detectives.

"We found gloves with Ryan's blood on them in Kerrigan's gym bag, but the blood probably got on them when she beat him up."

"Anything else?" Greene asked.

"No, but Kerrigan made a fatal slip when we questioned her," Roger said before explaining what Kerrigan had said and why it was important.

"Are there any suspects who also had it in for Ryan or any of the other victims?" Greene asked.

Carrie told Greene about the auto accident insurance scam and the murder of Otis Truax.

"Margaret also represented other members of the Russian mob," Carrie said. "She might have been able to blow the whistle on Jack Kovalev, but no one saw anyone but Kerrigan in the vicinity of the house."

"The killer may have come in through a back door," Roger said, "so someone could have entered and left that way without being seen."

Greene turned to Tom. "You're the one who has to prosecute, Tom. What's your opinion?"

"I think it's going to be close, but I think she's guilty."

Greene closed his eyes and analyzed the information he'd been given as if it were a chess problem with a conviction being the equivalent of a checkmate.

"Give me everything you've got," he said when he opened his eyes. "I'll make my decision tomorrow."

CHAPTER TWENTY-THREE

The morning after Mandy Kerrigan was indicted, a messenger from the district attorney's office delivered a thick package containing the discovery in the case. Robin had her secretary send a copy to Amanda Jaffe and make copies for her investigator, Ken Breland, and Loretta Washington, one of her associates. Then she buzzed them and told them to read through the discovery and meet her in the conference room after lunch.

When Robin got the originals back, she went through the police reports, autopsy reports, and reports from the crime lab and took notes to prepare for her meeting. As soon as she finished going through the discovery, Robin called Tom.

"Thanks for sending the discovery so soon," she said when the deputy DA was on the line.

"I wanted you to see what we've got so you'd see how hopeless your case is, and be ready to discuss a plea."

Robin laughed. "Cute. Now that I've read what you've got, I'm thinking that you might have a hard time getting past a motion for judgment of acquittal."

Now it was Tom's turn to laugh. "One of the things I love about you is your keen sense of humor. So, tough guy, besides trying to psych me out, why are you really calling?"

"I want to look at the Finch house. Is that a problem?"

"It's still a crime scene, but I'll make sure you can get in. When are you thinking of going?"

"Sometime this afternoon. I'm not sure of the exact time. I'm bringing Ken Breland, my investigator."

"I'll clear both of you."

"Thanks."

"No problem, and I'll entertain a plea offer anytime."

"I like your sense of humor too," Robin said before she disconnected.

Robin's associate and her investigator were leafing through the copies of the discovery in the *Kerrigan* case when Robin walked into the conference room shortly before one. Loretta Washington was a five-foot-one-inch African American dynamo who had grown up in New York City. Like Robin, Loretta was the first person in her family to graduate from college, where she had excelled. A full ride to Lewis & Clark Law School in Portland had lured Loretta to Oregon, and Robin had hired her after she completed a clerkship at the Oregon Supreme Court. Loretta was a brilliant researcher and wrote excellent briefs and memos. Robin had been developing Loretta's trial skills by giving her misdemeanor cases to try, and she was turning into a very good trial lawyer.

Ken Breland was a prime example of why—to borrow a cliché—one should not judge a book by its cover. He was slender, five foot ten, and with his full head of prematurely white hair he could easily be mistaken for a bookkeeper or a librarian, but before becoming Robin's investigator, Breland had been a police officer, a Navy SEAL, and an agent of the CIA.

"We have a new client, Mandy Kerrigan," Robin said. "Mandy is a former world champion mixed martial artist and the last person I fought when I was competing. The weekend before the murders, she was on a fight card at the Moda Center. Miss Kerrigan has just been indicted for the murders of Margaret, Nathan, Ryan, and Annie Finch. Amanda Jaffe is going to be my second chair."

"The West Hills Massacre!" Loretta said.

"Let's not use that term in this office or anywhere else, please," Robin said.

"Margaret was a criminal defense attorney, wasn't she?" Loretta asked.

Robin nodded.

"I've been through the discovery, and I'm a little surprised they indicted," Ken said.

"Playing devil's advocate," Robin answered, "Mandy has a motive to murder two members of the Finch family. Ryan Finch sold her PEDs his dad, Nathan, manufactured in a basement lab in their house. After her fight, a drug test revealed the presence of the PEDs; Mandy's purse was held up, and she faces a suspension. Mandy beat up Ryan Finch shortly before he was murdered, and the police found gloves with Ryan's blood on them in her gym bag.

"Next, Mandy had the opportunity to commit the crimes. She was seen outside the Finch home around the time of the murders.

"Finally, the Finches were murdered with 9 mm bullets, which are fired from a Glock 19. Kerrigan owned one."

"That sounds like a good case to me," Loretta said.

"On the surface, but the Finches were shot inside their home," Ken said. "The murder weapon hasn't been found, and Miss Kerrigan's fingerprints were found on the handle of the front door, but no fingerprints, DNA, footprints, or other trace evidence belonging to her were found in the house. And when the police searched her motel room and her car, they didn't find any evidence that connects her to the murders."

"What about the gloves?" Loretta asked.

"Witnesses say that Kerrigan was wearing gloves when she beat up Ryan, so that explains the blood on the gloves."

"What do you want us to do?" Loretta asked.

"I need you to do a deep dive into each victim, Loretta. You'll also be in charge of preparing the jury instructions, our juror questionnaire, and drafting legal motions. The police searched Mandy's motel room and car, and she made statements. If you see anything we don't want in evidence, work up a motion to suppress. But also review the discovery for ideas about our defense.

"Which brings me to your assignment, Ken," Robin went on. "In the discovery, there are police reports about an auto accident insurance scam that was run by the Russian mob. Susan Chen, the wife of Alan Chen, was killed when Otis Truax drove his car into hers. Truax was arrested for vehicular homicide, and Margaret was representing him. Both of them could have testified about the scam, and both of them have been murdered.

"You'll also find reports about two confrontations Alan Chen had with Margaret Finch."

"You want me to see if Chen or the Russians could have murdered the family?" Ken asked.

Robin nodded. "I also want you to see if you can find anyone else who had a motive to kill any of the victims. Nathan was manufacturing designer drugs and Ryan was selling them, so the killer could have been a disgruntled client."

"Has anyone thought that the killings might be the work of a serial killer?" Loretta asked. "If you're thinking that one of the victims was the real target, wouldn't it have been simpler to just kill that individual? But killing a whole family, that's weird."

"Good thinking, Loretta. Why don't you search the Internet to see if there's someone out there who's murdering entire families?"

"I'm on it," Loretta said.

"Right now, I want to have a look at the crime scene. Want to tag along, Ken?"

"Nice house and nice neighborhood," Robin remarked as she parked at the curb in front of the Finches' Craftsman home.

"Not the type of surroundings where I'm used to finding mass murders," said Ken, who had seen violence in war zones.

A policeman had been sitting on the porch, and he walked over to them when Robin and her investigator got out of their car. Robin checked his name tag and smiled.

"Hi, Officer Bradley. I'm Robin Lockwood. I'm representing Mandy Kerrigan, and this is Ken Breland, my investigator. I think Tom McKee called you."

The policeman nodded. "The door is open and you have the run of the place, but I'm supposed to tag along."

Robin grinned. "That will make it harder for us to plant evidence that will clear our client."

"I think that's the general idea," Bradley said, returning the grin.

Robin studied the porch and the front door where Mrs. Radcliffe said she'd seen Mandy screaming. Then she turned and looked across the street at the Radcliffes' house. After a minute, she climbed the stairs to the porch and walked inside.

Robin had brought a folder with the photographs from the crime scene. She walked into the foyer and looked at the bloodstains on the floor at the bottom of the stairs. Then she looked at the photo that showed where Annie Finch had lain. Ken looked over her shoulder as Robin examined the photograph.

Robin was used to seeing dead bodies, but she still found it hard to look at the picture of this young girl who had been brutally murdered. She switched her attention to the living room sofa and the photos of the bodies of Margaret and Nathan Finch. The bodies had been removed, but the bloodstains remained.

The group headed upstairs and walked into a bedroom at the top of the stairs. A large window gave Robin a view of the forest behind the house. Under the window was a makeup table on which sat a multilevel jewelry box. The window cast pale light on a king-sized bed that dominated the room. A quilt and throw pillows decorated it, and an antique wooden chest stood at the foot of the bed.

Robin wandered over to a walk-in closet that was filled with women's clothing, accessories, and shoes. Then she looked in the bathroom, where she saw makeup, but no shaving items.

"This looks like it was Margaret's bedroom. I don't see any sign that a man stayed here."

"Agreed," Ken said.

Robin and Ken walked down the hall and into a small bedroom with an unmade queen-sized bed. Men's clothing was thrown over a chair, and men's toiletries were strewn across the sink in a small bathroom.

"I'm guessing that the Finches were not experiencing connubial bliss," Ken said.

Robin and Ken walked to the other end of the hall and opened another door. There was no question who had lived in this room. A poster from a Harry Styles concert hung on the wall next to a bed covered with too many pillows and a blanket decorated with purple and blue forget-me-nots. Next to one of the pillows was a well-worn teddy bear. Robin guessed that the stuffed animal had been Annie's companion since she was a toddler.

A fake marble bedside table was covered with hair ties and makeup brushes. There was also a small organizer for Annie's jewelry that held an abundance of random earrings and a few simple silver and gold necklaces. Next to the table was a bag overflowing with makeup.

T-shirts and a dress lay on the floor in front of a closet. A full-length mirror hung to the left. Robin opened the closet. It contained more jeans and dresses, shoes and sneakers, and a chest of drawers. The top drawer was halfway open. Robin opened it all the way. It was filled with T-shirts, tops, and gym clothes. The next drawer was filled with bras and cotton underpants. Robin opened the bottom drawer, which was stuffed with swimsuits, basketball shorts, and tops.

Robin started to close the closet when she saw a gym bag behind a bunch of shoes and sneakers. She fished it out and opened it. The bag was stuffed with gym gear. Robin was about to close the bag when she saw the edge of a ziplock bag that was concealed under a sweatshirt. She picked up the bag and frowned. Inside was a very sexy black thong.

"Ken, come here, will you?"

When Ken walked up to the closet, Robin held up the ziplock bag.

"I found this buried under workout gear in Annie's gym bag. What do you think?"

Ken looked at the thong for a few moments. Then he looked at Robin. "Boyfriend?"

"Why don't you see what you can find out."

Robin put the ziplock bag back where she'd found it and walked to the other side of the room, where the light from a window that faced the front of the house shone on a white desk with a matching white chair. A few schoolbooks were stacked on one side of the desk. Robin knew from the inventory in the police reports that Annie's laptop was at police headquarters.

A paperback was lying on the other side of the desk. Robin picked it up. It was the first book in the Hunger Games series.

"This is too sad," Robin said.

Ken nodded.

"Let's take a look at Ryan's room," Robin said.

Officer Bradley followed Robin and Ken downstairs and down the hall that led off the living room to Ryan Finch's room. After a brief scan, Robin went to the kitchen, the area she really wanted to see.

The forensic team had taken the glass to the crime lab, but the photos showed the debris on the kitchen floor. Glass shards that had been dusted for prints remained in the damaged pane. Robin walked into the backyard. A fence with a latched gate separated the lawn from a wall of trees. She unlatched the gate and led Ken into the forest on a path while Officer Bradley waited on the Finches' property.

The sun was out and it was in the high fifties, but Robin zipped up her jacket when the shade in the forest brought the temperature down. Portland's urban forest was well maintained in the West Hills, and the trail was clearly marked. After a short walk, Robin noticed trails leading off in other directions that ended in other parts of the West Hills' neighborhoods.

"Our killer could have parked anywhere, gone through the woods to the house, then returned to his car," she said.

"I'll take a video of these trails to show a jury," Ken told her.

"Good idea."

Ken frowned. "Something's been troubling me ever since I read the discovery. Loretta touched on it."

"Oh?"

"Why did the killer murder the whole family?"

"You're not seriously suggesting that Hannibal Lecter is running loose in Portland?"

"Not really, but killing a whole family . . ." Ken shook his head. "It just bothers me. Let's take Margaret Finch. If she was killed because Jack Kovalev was worried that she'd rat him out to the DA, wouldn't they get her alone and make her disappear? Same thing with Ryan. He's selling drugs at night in bars. He goes to his car and you walk up and pop him. Why go to his neighborhood where there are a lot of witnesses and kill everyone in the house?"

"I see your point," Robin said. "Can you think of an answer?"

"One has occurred to me."

"Spill it."

"Do we know who inherits, now that all the Finches are dead?"

CHAPTER TWENTY-FOUR

The next morning, Loretta walked into Robin's office shortly after Robin arrived.

"Got a minute?" Loretta asked.

"Sure. What do you have for me?" Robin said.

Loretta took a chair across from Robin and opened a folder on her side of Robin's desk.

"I've been working up bios of the victims, and I've found some interesting stuff."

"Go on."

"It looks like Nathan Finch was a genius. According to his obit and online profile, he had Harvard and MIT degrees in chemistry. What stands out is that he was fired from his job at King Pharmaceuticals recently."

"Do you know why?"

"No. I called the company, and they sent me to HR. The woman

I spoke to told me he'd been terminated a few weeks before he was killed, but she wouldn't tell me why."

"That is interesting. Give the info to Ken. What about Margaret?"

"U of O undergrad, summa cum laude. She stayed in state for law school at Willamette, also graduating with honors. Then she went with the Reed, Briggs firm for a few years. Margaret met Nathan when the firm defended a lawsuit filed against King. Nathan testified for the company as an expert witness."

Robin frowned. "Reed, Briggs only hires the cream of the crop. If they hire someone who isn't a graduate of a top-ten national law school, the associate has to be exceptional. Do you know why Margaret left the firm?"

"They didn't keep her on a partner track."

"Do you know why?"

"Not a clue. After she was let go, Margaret started her own practice. Soon after she started, she was appointed to handle a drug case for a street dealer with ties to the Russian mob. She won, and she started getting hired by other people with ties to Jack Kovalev. She scored some impressive victories and became the mob's go-to attorney."

"Was she only handling cases for the Russians?"

"No. She established a reputation and built a successful practice. She doesn't have a partner, but she does have two associates."

"Any dissatisfied customers who might want to do her in?" Robin asked.

"I have no idea, but I'm talking to a friend in the DA's office and checking into court documents. I'm also looking at auto accident cases that might have been part of the insurance scam and trying to get information about Alan Chen."

"Tell me about Ryan Finch."

"A classic loser. He started at a private school and was kicked out. Same thing at the next private school, so it was off to a public high school, where he made it through by the skin of his teeth. Then he dropped out of PSU.

"Ryan had been involved in drugs forever, and he was selling marijuana in high school and college. Now that it's legal in Oregon, he got a job at a cannabis store that was run by one of his dealers who went legit. He was canned from that job. Recently, he's been peddling his dad's designer drugs."

"Have you gotten any background on Alan Chen yet?"

"He's next on my list."

"Okay. That's pretty good for such a short time. You've given me a lot to work on. Now I have one more task for you. Can you find out who inherits now that all of the Finches are dead?"

Loretta left, and Robin leaned back in her chair. What Loretta had found out was definitely interesting. One thing was certain. If Mandy's defense was centered on someone else killing the Finches, they had more than enough ammunition.

Loretta had opened several areas of inquiry, but Robin thought she knew how to answer one question that Loretta's information had raised. A year ago, she had been hired by Lucy Timmons, a Reed, Briggs partner, to represent her son, who had been arrested for driving under the influence. Robin decided to call her to see if she could tell her the reason Margaret Finch hadn't made partner.

"Hi, Robin. What's up?" Lucy asked when she and Robin were connected.

"I've got a new case, and I was hoping you could help me answer a question that came up about someone who worked at your firm."

"Is this about Margaret Finch?"

Robin laughed. "Are you auditioning for a part in the next Sherlock Holmes movie?"

"No, but it's been the talk of the office."

"My associate's been working up background on the victims, and she told me that Margaret had a stellar academic background but hadn't been placed on the partnership track. I was wondering if you can tell me what happened?"

Lucy didn't answer right away.

"I don't want to put you in a tough spot. If this is confidential . . . ?"

"No. I wasn't directly involved, and all I know is what was rumored."

"This is just background."

"Okay, but don't tell anyone I told you."

"Of course not."

"I heard it was drugs. She met her husband, Nathan, when he testified for her as an expert witness. They started dating after the trial. As far as I knew, until then, she'd been doing great. Then the partners she was working for started complaining about mistakes and missed deadlines. The word was that Nathan was using and he'd gotten Margaret hooked. But I can't swear that was the problem. Like I said, this is all hearsay and rumors."

"Thanks, Lucy. It fits what I know. According to the police reports, Nathan was using his son to deal drugs he was concocting."

"How sad."

"Yeah. The whole case is sad. On another topic, how is Kevin doing?"

"Getting arrested was a real wake-up call, and I can't thank you enough for getting him out of his scrape in one piece. His grades are way up, and he's talking about law school, but not what I do. He wants to be a criminal defense attorney."

"Oh, boy. It sounds like I really messed him up."

Lucy laughed. "It was good talking to you. We should get to-gether for lunch sometime."

Robin agreed and hung up. Then she swiveled her chair so she could look out at Mount Hood. The more she learned about the Finch family, the more fucked up they sounded.

CHAPTER TWENTY-FIVE

King Pharmaceuticals was the sole tenant of a seven-story steel-and-glass building that stood in the middle of a manicured lawn on a plot of land in Washington County that had once been the pasture of a dairy farm. Ken Breland parked in the visitors' lot and checked in with the security guard sitting behind a polished wood desk in the lobby. Ten minutes later, the elevator opened and a muscular man impeccably dressed in a black pin-striped Armani suit, white silk shirt, and navy blue tie walked across the atrium to the couch where Ken was waiting.

"Mr. Breland?" the man asked.

Ken nodded and stood up.

The man held out his hand. "Wayne Driscoll," he said as they shook. "I'm head of security for King. Why don't we go up to the second-floor conference room and I'll try to answer your questions."

Ken followed Driscoll up an escalator to a glassed-in conference room that looked out on the Columbia River and a stretch of the

Cascade Range. Driscoll had been carrying a folder, and he opened it on the conference table.

"Thanks for seeing me," Ken said.

"We've all been shocked by what happened to Nathan. I heard about the murders on the evening news and couldn't believe it."

"It is horrible," Ken agreed.

"I'll be honest. When you said you worked for the lawyer representing the person accused of killing Nathan, I wasn't certain I should meet with you. But the boys upstairs told me to cooperate."

"There's a chance Miss Kerrigan is innocent, so we appreciate the position you've taken."

"What do you want to know?" Driscoll asked.

"Can you fill me in on Mr. Finch's background?"

"It's quite impressive. Summa cum laude in chem at Harvard, then MIT for graduate school. We hired him as a research chemist, and he was very good at his job. His job evaluations were always top-notch. That's why it was a difficult decision to let him go. But we really had no choice."

"Why was he fired?"

"We discovered that Nathan was embezzling money from a grant his department had received. When we confronted him, he said he had a gambling addiction and he begged us to let him get help. But it was decided that we couldn't trust him."

"Did you refer the case for prosecution?"

"No. We thought about it, but he'd been a good employee until the theft, so we agreed not to prosecute if he paid back what he'd stolen."

"Was Nathan gambling online or at a casino?"

"He said he owed money to a bookmaker named Mario Messina. He said that the man was a criminal and he regretted getting involved with him, but he swore he was going to settle what he owed and get involved with a program."

"Do you know anything about Messina?"

"Actually, I do. I have contacts with law enforcement, and I asked one of them about him. He's small-time, but he has a reputation for violence. He's never been arrested, but some of the men who collect debts for him have been picked up after people who owed him money were roughed up. None of the arrests went to trial, because the victims wouldn't testify. The police are pretty certain they or their families were threatened."

"Interesting."

"Anything else?"

"Not that I can think of. Can I get back to you if I have some more questions?"

"Of course."

After he retired from the CIA, Ken had volunteered to work with a group of detectives at the Portland Police Bureau who looked into cold cases. One member of the group was Mary Simpson, a detective in Vice and Narcotics. When Ken was in the parking lot of King Pharmaceuticals, he called Simpson.

"Hey, Mary, do you have a minute?"

"Sure, Ken. What's up?"

"You know I'm Robin Lockwood's investigator?"

"Yeah?"

"We're representing Mandy Kerrigan. She's charged with murdering the four members of the Finch family, and I'd like to get some background information about Mario Messina. I understand he's a bookmaker and that Nathan Finch, one of the murder victims, owed him money."

"What do you want to know?"

"Anything you can tell me about Messina and his connection to Nathan Finch."

"Mario Messina is not a nice man. We know he runs an illegal gambling operation, but he's smart and we've never been able to shut him down. We also know that he uses strong-arm tactics to collect bets, and he doesn't have any qualms about going after a man's family if the threat will make a person pay up."

"I learned that Nathan Finch owed Messina money. Do you know anything about that?"

"A little. Messina owns an auto body shop on Sandy Boulevard in Northeast Portland. We suspect that he's laundering money from gambling through the business. Messina runs a poker game in the back of the shop, and Finch played in the games. From what I hear, he usually won."

"That makes sense. He has a genius IQ, and I bet he was a whiz at math. But I've learned that he has a gambling addiction, so he probably lost his winnings and more on other bets."

"Messina takes bets on NFL games, horse racing, you name it."

"Anything else I should know?"

"Yeah, Ken. You should know that Messina is a very bad dude who would have no problem going after you if he sees you as a threat."

CHAPTER TWENTY-SIX

The next morning, Robin worked out, then grabbed a latte as she headed to Barrister, Berman, and Lockwood. Loretta was waiting for her boss in Robin's office, and she looked excited.

Robin grinned. "You'd make a lousy poker player, Loretta. What's got you pumped?"

"I found some really good stuff," Loretta said as Robin shed her jacket and walked behind her desk.

"Spill it."

Loretta leaned toward Robin. "I reviewed the cases that the DA thinks are part of the auto accident scam."

Loretta paused dramatically, and Robin rolled her eyes.

"Am I going to have to guess the big reveal?" Robin asked.

"There are commonalities," Loretta answered. "Dr. Truman Alcott, for one."

"And he is . . . ?"

"The physician in almost every case."

"He swore that the plaintiffs were injured?" Robin asked.

Loretta nodded.

"Did the insurance company have their doctors examine the plaintiffs?"

"No, they settled, and the agent who signed off on most of the settlements was Dale Gibbs."

"Oh, my. It's Tinker to Evers to Chance," Robin said.

"Huh?"

"That's a famous double-play trio from way before your time. Mine too."

"I get it," Loretta said. "Margaret represents the plaintiffs, who are examined by Alcott, whose diagnosis is accepted by Gibbs, who signs the check that ends up in Jack Kovalev's bank account."

"Exactly. Terrific work, Loretta. Fill in Ken. He should be in by now."

"Don't you want to hear about Annie?" Loretta asked.

"Annie? What have you got on her?"

"A family named Faber was suing the Finches. They had a daughter, Donna, who was a classmate of Annie's. She died by suicide, and the suit alleges that she killed herself because Annie cyberbullied her."

Loretta handed Robin a copy of the lawsuit, a newspaper article about the case, and articles she'd found on the Internet.

Robin looked sad when she finished reading. She remembered the worn teddy bear on Annie's bed and sighed. "Annie looked like the only decent human being in the Finch family. Now, it seems that she was no angel."

"Apparently not, if she did what's alleged in the lawsuit. The only good news is that the Fabers would have a motive to kill all the Finches."

Robin barked out a humorless laugh. "I guess that proves that every cloud has a silver lining."

"Reporters talked to several of Donna's and Annie's classmates and teachers after the suit was filed. I made you a list of the students and teachers mentioned in the articles. You might want to see what they have to say."

"Anything else?"

"You asked me who inherits now that all the Finches are dead. I'm assuming that Annie and Ryan didn't have wills, and they didn't have children, so they wouldn't have heirs.

"I don't know the contents of Nathan's and Margaret's wills. The DA might know. If they had a normal arrangement, the wife's money would go to the husband if she predeceased him and vice versa. Then, if they both die, the money goes to their kids. But everyone is dead, so the kids wouldn't get anything.

"According to the Oregon probate statutes, in a case like this, the next of kin would inherit. I read Nathan's and Margaret's obits. Nathan's parents are deceased, and he was an only child. Margaret's parents are deceased, but she has a brother named Harry Claypool. I think he'd be in line to inherit Margaret's estate.

"Here's the interesting part. I looked Claypool up online. He just got out of prison, where he was serving a term for a really vicious armed robbery."

"So, we have another possible killer with a reason to murder all the Finches?"

"Yup."

"You're doing great work, Loretta. Get Ken up to date and tell him I want him to find out what Claypool has been up to since he got out of prison."

"Will do."

When Loretta left, she took Robin's good mood with her. Robin should have been excited by all the ammunition her associate had given her, but the information about Annie Finch left her depressed. Despite having a job that put her in contact with the worst people in society, Robin liked to think that people were basically good. She hated having her illusions shattered.

CHAPTER TWENTY-SEVEN

Robin asked Ken to come to her office as soon as Loretta left, and filled him in on the Fabers' lawsuit against the Finches, Harry Claypool, and the new information that Loretta had given her about the insurance scam.

"I'll need a list with the addresses of the drivers who claimed they were injured in the car crashes, and Dr. Alcott's and Dale Gibbs's office and home addresses," Ken said. "If we can convince a jury that Margaret was killed to keep her from going to the police after she learned Truax was murdered, we'll have a good shot of raising a reasonable doubt."

"Agreed," Robin said. "Have you spoken to Alan Chen?"

"I can't find him. His house is dark, and I can see that mail has been piling up. His neighbors haven't seen him for a while, and he's MIA at work."

"Sounds like he's hiding," Robin said. "But why?"

"He'd have a reason if he murdered Margaret. I read his military record in the discovery. He certainly has the training. The problem is that I can't see him killing everyone in the Finch family."

"Keep looking," Robin said, "but Chen is a low priority. Concentrate on the insurance scam and the Russians. From what I've learned about Kovalev, he'd have no problem wiping out a family."

"What are you going to do?"

"I'm going to talk to Annie's teacher and see what I can find out about this lawsuit."

The West Hills was home to professionals with high incomes and high aspirations for their offspring. Marie Curie Middle School was a public school, but the students' parents held auctions and hosted garden tours to raise additional funding for things like tennis courts and state-of-the-art computer labs. As a result, the school had a reputation as good as Portland's exclusive private schools.

The original school had been renovated, and the redbrick exterior was overlain with ivy, making it reminiscent of the colleges that many of the parents had attended. Robin parked in the visitors' lot shortly after school let out. On her way to the main entrance, she waded through a tsunami of chattering, laughing students, many of whom were approaching, or had crossed the border of, puberty. She noticed how well dressed they were, even when their clothes were manufactured to look distressed.

Robin checked in at the school office and asked where she could find Arthur Proctor. The secretary told her how to find the auditorium, and Robin walked in just as Proctor was talking to a group of students who were gathered on the stage. The teacher had made no concessions to the trend of dressing down to fit in with his charges, and he was wearing a blazer over a crisp white shirt that was tucked into neatly pressed khaki pants. A sweater vest partially concealed a tie with the colors of Proctor's college.

Robin took a seat in the back and watched Proctor direct a scene from the school play. She was impressed by how well the students related to him. After the scene was finished, he complimented the cast and told them they were dismissed for the day. Robin walked up front as the students filed out.

"Arthur Proctor?" Robin asked.

"Yes?"

"Are you directing a modern version of *A Midsummer Night's Dream*?"

Proctor smiled. "I am."

"The kids seem pretty professional."

"They're delightful. Just when you think there's no hope for today's youth, a group like this comes along and restores your faith in humanity."

Robin smiled. "Do you think I just watched some future Oscar winners?"

Proctor laughed. "You aren't by chance a Hollywood talent scout?"

"I'm afraid not," Robin said as she handed the teacher her business card. "I'm an attorney, and I wondered if I could talk to you about the Finches?"

Proctor's smile disappeared. "You're the lawyer who's representing the woman who was arrested for the murders."

"I am, and Mandy Kerrigan insists that she did not murder anyone."

"The police must not be convinced."

"It's been my experience that the police often jump to conclusions about who perpetrated a crime and stop looking for other possible suspects."

"And you think that's the case here?"

"I think it's a real possibility. That's why I'm trying to get as much information about everyone who was killed as I can."

Proctor sat down, and Robin took a seat next to him.

"I don't know how I can help you, but ask your questions," the teacher said.

"I just learned that Donna Faber's parents sued the Finches. They claim that Donna died by suicide because Annie Finch cyberbullied her. You were Annie's teacher. What was she like?"

"I already answered that question for the police."

"I know, but I'd appreciate your insight."

"I had Annie as a student when she was in seventh-grade honors English. She was happy, bright, a normal thirteen-year-old. She changed by the time I had her for eighth-grade English. I have no idea what happened, but she was obviously troubled. She was a good student in my class, but her other grades plummeted. I could see that she was unhappy, but I didn't know why. Then there was this horrible incident with Donna. I have no idea why she would do something like that."

"Did you initiate the conversation about private school with her parents?"

Proctor nodded. "At our parent-teacher conference."

"Were they receptive?"

"They were both concerned about the finances, and Mr. Finch seemed very opposed to sending Annie away."

"Did you know Donna too?"

"I did. Donna was in the drama club. She had a role in last year's production."

"Were you surprised when she killed herself?"

Proctor took a moment before he answered. "Surprised, of course, like everyone who knew her. She was a sensitive young woman. That's why she was such a good actress. But suicide . . . No, I can't say I saw that coming."

"Do you think Annie caused Donna to kill herself?"

"I can't possibly answer that. I didn't know that she'd bullied Donna until Donna killed herself and it became the talk of the school."

"Why did you think Annie should leave Marie Curie?"

"Before Donna's suicide, I became concerned because of the change in Annie's personality. And then there was the fact that her grades had dropped so precipitously. That led me to believe that Annie would benefit from a change of scenery. Then the cyber-bullying went public after Donna killed herself, and Annie's life at school . . ."

Proctor shook his head. "Children can be very cruel. Annie was ostracized, she was reviled on social media. I lobbied her parents to send her out of state."

"I didn't see any mention of Donna's suicide or the lawsuit in the police reports. Is there a reason you didn't tell the police about them?"

"I suppose, in your line of work, you see blood and dead bodies all the time." Proctor shook his head. "I still have nightmares about what I saw. Especially Annie. I didn't even think about the lawsuit when I was at the murder scene. Later, when I did remember it, I didn't feel right about defaming Annie. And I assumed that the police would learn about it anyway."

"Can you think of anyone who might want to hurt Annie?"

"You mean, kill her?"

"Yes. You said her life at school was difficult after the cyberbullying lawsuit became public. Did she get death threats?"

"I have no idea. I assume that the police have examined her computer for threats. They probably have a record of that sort of thing."

"So, no students you can think of?"

"Absolutely not." Proctor hesitated. "If you're asking me to guess, the only people I can think of who might want to do her harm would be Donna's parents. But I've met them, and I can't imagine either of them intentionally murdering anyone, let alone an entire family."

"Thanks for taking the time to talk to me," Robin said as she stood to leave. "You've been very helpful. If you think of something that's relevant, please call. You have my card."

Robin walked to her car with only a minimal awareness of her surroundings. Proctor had said that Annie had gone through a major personality change between seventh and eighth grade. What had caused it? An answer occurred to her, and she felt sick.

Robin could not imagine a more dysfunctional family than the Finches. They were all bent. Margaret was a lawyer for the Russian mob and involved in their criminal enterprises, Ryan was a drug dealer, and Nathan was addicted to gambling and manufacturing the drugs he had his son selling.

Robin turned her thoughts to Nathan. He and his wife had separate bedrooms, which probably meant that they weren't having sex. Nathan had no trouble using his son to sell drugs, even though dealing could land him in prison. Would he have any moral qualms about using his daughter for sex? Arthur Proctor had told Robin that Nathan was very opposed to sending Annie away to school. Was he afraid that she would tell someone about their relationship if he wasn't there to control her, or did he want to keep her in the house where he could use her?

Priority number one was getting the contents of Annie's computer to see if there was any mention of a lover.

CHAPTER TWENTY-EIGHT

When Ken walked into the garage at Rose City Auto Body Repairs, a mechanic in grease-covered overalls was working on a BMW that was floating in the air on a lift.

"Do you know where I can find Mr. Messina?" Ken asked him.

"Try the office," the mechanic said, gesturing toward an enclosure at the back of the garage.

A large pane of glass let the occupants of the office see what was going on in the garage, but it also let Ken see that there were two men in the office. One of them was huge and was wearing a short-sleeved shirt that let him display bulging biceps and thick tattoo-covered forearms. He was sitting in a chair in a corner, thumbing through a magazine with a naked woman on the cover.

The other man was seated behind a metal desk and talking on a phone he had pressed to his ear. He was short and stocky with a swarthy complexion and slicked-back jet-black hair that looked dyed.

When Ken walked into the office, the man in the corner looked at Ken for a moment before going back to his magazine. The other man held up a finger to indicate that Ken should wait until he finished his call. Ken took a chair and listened to the man discuss the purchase of some auto parts.

"Mr. Messina?" Ken asked the man behind the desk when he ended the call.

"Yeah?"

Ken handed Messina his card. Messina studied it, then looked at Ken.

"What can I do for you, Mr. Breland?"

"I work as an investigator for Robin Lockwood, an attorney. She's representing Mandy Kerrigan, who is charged with murdering Nathan Finch."

"I'm confused. I don't know anything about Mandy Kerrigan."

"But you do know Nathan Finch."

"I do?"

The man in the corner looked up from his magazine and studied Ken. He did not look friendly.

"I've talked with a number of people in law enforcement. They told me that Nathan Finch placed bets with you and owed you a lot of money."

"They're misinformed."

"Misinformed about you knowing Mr. Finch or misinformed that he owed you money?"

"Are you suggesting that I had something to do with killing this person? Are you looking for someone to blame so you can get your client off the hook?"

"We're looking at all possibilities."

"Let me be clear, Breland. I don't appreciate anyone sticking their nose in my business, and I especially don't appreciate a person suggesting that I'm a murderer. You do that and bad things can happen."

"Did you murder Nathan Finch?" Ken asked the bookmaker, watching for Messina's reaction.

Messina's features clouded over. He leaned toward Ken and looked directly into the investigator's eyes. Ken met the stare and didn't blink. The man in the corner put down his magazine.

"A question like that can get you seriously injured," Messina said, "but I'm going to answer it. As soon as I do, you will stop bothering me. If you don't . . ." He shrugged. "That will be on your head. So, here is my answer.

"Let's assume, for the sake of argument, that this guy Finch did owe me money. Do you know why I'd have to be an idiot to kill him? Dead men can't pay off their debts."

"A spectacular murder might work as a warning to other deadbeats."

"That's true," Messina agreed. "But why would I kill the whole family? With so many victims, how would anyone know that Nathan Finch was the target? And with his heirs dead, who would pay me what he owes?"

"You make a good point."

"I also have a good alibi. I read all about the murders in the paper. *The Oregonian* said that the family was killed around eight o'clock. At eight o'clock on the night the Finches were murdered, I was here, and I could parade a bunch of witnesses in front of a jury if I had to."

Ken nodded toward the man in the corner, who had been following the exchange.

"You wouldn't have to kill Nathan yourself. You could have sent someone to do it."

"I could have, but I didn't. And we're done here. Defending a person in a death penalty case who looks so guilty can't be easy. But you're wasting your time if you're thinking of pinning Nathan's murder on me."

Ken stood up. "Thanks for taking the time to talk to me."

"We won't be talking again. Remember what I said about things that can happen to people who annoy me."

Ken left the auto body shop and was almost at his car when his phone rang. It was Robin.

"Where are you?"

"I just had a talk with Mario Messina, Nathan Finch's bookie."

"And?"

"I think we can move Messina to the bottom of the list of suspects. I'll tell you why when I get back to the office. Did you just miss me, or did you have a reason to call?"

"When you get back to the office, look at the list of the items the police seized from the Finch home and see if a diary was found in Annie's room. Then see if we have a readout of the stuff on Annie's computer. I don't remember seeing one. Finally, give me as much background as you can on Donna Faber's parents. We're going to visit them tonight."

CHAPTER TWENTY-NINE

A little before six, Robin poked her nose into Ken's office at Barrister, Berman, and Lockwood.

"Did Annie Finch have a diary?" Robin asked.

"It's not in the discovery. I called Tom McKee. He says they didn't find a diary when they searched Annie's room."

"What about her laptop?"

"The discovery doesn't contain the contents of her computer because the techs at the crime lab are still compiling the information."

"Okay. What did you find out about the Fabers?"

"Harry Faber owns a local grocery chain, with four stores in various parts of Portland and one in the suburbs. Millie Faber owns a boutique real estate agency that concentrates on homes in the wealthier sections of Portland and its suburbs. Both parents were born and raised in Portland. They met at the U of O. Donna was their only child."

"Let's go talk to them."

* * *

Fifteen minutes later, Robin steered her car up Vista, a winding road that led up a steep incline toward the top of one of the two hills that loomed over Portland on the west side of the Willamette and Columbia Rivers.

"This isn't going to be easy," she said.

"Agreed. I listened to an interview they gave on TV after the lawsuit was filed. They're really bitter."

"For a good reason, if Annie did what they say she did."

A few minutes later, Robin parked in front of a Tudor house surrounded by a wide lawn. A light rain was falling as she and Ken got out of the car. Robin looked at the beautiful homes on either side of the Fabers' home and across from it. Those lawns were well tended, edged by boxwoods or bordered by flower gardens. The contrast with the Fabers' grounds was stark. The lawn looked like it hadn't been mowed in months, weeds had sprung up in spots, and the house looked like it had been abandoned.

Robin rang the doorbell. When no one came to the door, she tried again. This time someone yelled, "I'm coming!"

The woman who answered the door looked used up. She was almost as tall as Robin, but she slouched. Her skin was pale, and there were dark circles under her eyes that poorly applied makeup didn't quite hide.

"Mrs. Faber?" Robin asked.

"Yes?" she answered as she looked back and forth at Ken and Robin.

"I'm Robin Lockwood. I'm an attorney. This is Ken Breland, my investigator."

"What do you want?" Millie Faber asked warily.

"I represent Mandy Kerrigan. She's been charged with the homicides at the Finch home."

"If she killed those . . . people, she deserves a medal."

"Because Annie Finch was responsible for your daughter's death?"

"Why are you here?" Millie asked.

"Can we discuss this inside? It's starting to rain pretty hard."

Millie looked like she was torn between being a good hostess and getting rid of unwanted guests. Her middle-class upbringing won out, and she stepped back.

Ken followed Robin into a dark entryway. It opened into a living room that looked as unkempt as the lawn. Robin imagined that Donna's death had ripped the Fabers' life apart and drained them of the energy it took to do anything but mourn.

"Will you please tell me why you're here?" Millie asked.

"We're trying to get some background on Annie Finch. We can't figure out why she was so horribly mean to your daughter."

"Who is it?" a man shouted from another room.

"Lawyers about Donna!" Millie Faber shouted back.

A thickset man with thinning black hair and a ruddy complexion stormed into the entryway. He was wearing gray suit pants and a white shirt open at the neck, but no jacket or tie.

"Who the hell are you?" he demanded.

Robin smiled, hoping to defuse the situation. "I'm representing the woman who's accused of killing Annie Finch."

"Tell her that we appreciate what she did, but we have nothing to tell you."

"Do you know why Annie terrorized your daughter?" Robin asked.

"She did it because she was a pervert like everyone in that family."

Robin nodded. "The Finches were criminals, but was there some special reason that Annie tormented Donna?"

"If there was, the reason died with her," Millie said. She choked up, and her husband put an arm around her shoulder and hugged her to him. "Our daughter was an angel, and that monster . . ."

Millie started to cry.

Harry glared at Robin. "We're done here," he said.

Robin decided that it was time to leave. She followed Ken outside, and Harry Faber slammed the door shut.

"Is there anything in the reports about the Fabers having an alibi for the time of the murders?" Robin asked as they walked to their car.

"I don't remember a report about them, but I'll follow up."

Robin shook her head. "I should be mad at the way they treated us, but their situation is so damn sad."

"Amen," Ken said as he got in the car.

CHAPTER THIRTY

A little after nine the next morning, Ken parked in front of an apartment in a low-rent section of Portland.

"Serafina Gutierrez?" Ken asked the young woman who answered the door of a second-floor walk-up. Ken could hear a television with the volume turned low.

"Yes?" the woman said.

"I'm an investigator working for Robin Lockwood," Ken said as he handed Gutierrez his card. "We're representing the defendant in a murder case, and we can use your help."

"I don't know anything about a murder," Gutierrez said, looking both nervous and puzzled.

Ken smiled. "We know that, but one of the victims is Margaret Finch, the lawyer who helped you when you sued because of injuries you received in an auto accident. She was your lawyer, wasn't she?"

"Yes," answered Gutierrez, now noticeably more nervous.

"Mrs. Finch represented several other people who were in auto accidents and claimed they'd been injured. I don't want to alarm you, but evidence has come to light that suggests that many of the accidents were staged, that they were part of a scheme to defraud the insurance company. Miss Lockwood and I think that there is a good reason to believe that your lawyer was murdered by the people who devised this scheme."

"Why are you telling me this?" Gutierrez asked.

"We're worried about your safety. If you are willing to tell us how you became part of this scheme, we can talk to the authorities about protecting you."

Gutierrez looked sick. She stepped back into her apartment. "I don't want to be rude, but I don't know anything about a scheme. You have to go."

Ken started to say something, but the door slammed in his face.

Ken didn't even get in the door with the next two plaintiffs. He wondered if Serafina had called someone after he'd left, who had started a telephone tree to warn the other plaintiffs that they might get a visitor.

It was almost one by the time Ken left the home of plaintiff number three. He checked the address for Dr. Truman Alcott and programmed it into his GPS. Twenty minutes later, Ken walked into a doctor's office in a strip mall. The only people in the waiting room were a poorly dressed man and woman sitting next to each other on a green Naugahyde couch.

Ken walked over to a seated receptionist, who was looking at a computer screen behind a plastic shield with a slot at the bottom. Her long curly hair was dyed blond. She had thick lips covered in too much bright red lipstick, and she was starting to put pounds on a body that had probably been very attractive ten years ago.

Ken smiled. "I don't have an appointment, but I'd like to see Dr. Alcott, if he can fit me in."

"Name?" she asked, barely looking up from the computer screen.

"Ken Breland."

"Insurance?" she asked.

"I'd rather pay cash. How much does a consultation cost?"

The receptionist eyed Ken, evaluating his income bracket. "It's one hundred for the consult."

Ken pulled out his wallet and paid.

"Have a seat."

Ken sat down on a cheap plastic chair and picked up a six-month-old issue of *People* from a pile of magazines on the end table next to his chair.

Twenty minutes later, a teenage girl walked through a door next to the receptionist's desk. She looked upset. The couple came over to her. While they were leaving, the receptionist spoke into an intercom.

"Dr. Alcott can see you now," she said before opening the door next to her desk and leading Ken down a hall to an office with a plaque proclaiming it to be the domain of Dr. Truman Alcott.

The doctor was seated behind his desk. A diploma from a medical school in Grenada hung on the wall behind him. Ken thought that Alcott had the emaciated look of addicts Ken had known and, from his thinning hair and sallow complexion, Ken guessed that Alcott was pushing a hard fifty.

Alcott smiled, revealing nicotine-stained teeth. "Have a seat, Mr. Breland, and tell me how I can help you."

Ken handed Alcott his card. "I'm not here as a patient, Dr. Alcott. I work for the lawyer who is representing the woman charged with killing Margaret Finch and the other members of her family."

Alcott feigned surprise. "I read about the tragedy, but that's the extent of my knowledge about what happened."

"You knew Mrs. Finch."

"In a professional capacity. She sent some of her clients to me."

"Clients who were injured in auto accidents?"

"And other incidents."

"Your reports in the cases involving the auto accidents said that these patients were injured. Those reports were used to get settlements from their insurance company."

"I assume so, but I didn't know what happened after I submitted my report to Mrs. Finch."

"I've talked to people at the district attorney's office and the Portland police who think you are part of a scam that is being engineered by Jack Kovalev. Two people who could have testified against Mr. Kovalev were murdered recently. The driver of a car that was involved in a fatal crash was one of them, and Mrs. Finch was the other one. Doesn't that make you nervous?"

"Please leave, Mr. Breland. I have no interest in continuing this conversation."

"Fine. But you'll be continuing it in court when you are subpoenaed to testify for the defense so that we can establish that Jack Kovalev had a motive to kill Margaret Finch. If you can help us prove that Kovalev was responsible for the murder of Margaret Finch, I can get you protection."

"There's no way I can do that because I don't know anything about her murder. Now please leave."

"I apologize for springing this on you, but you could be in real danger. Take some time to think about the smart thing to do."

*   *   *

As soon as Ken left, Truman Alcott slumped in his chair and thought that he might throw up. When he was calm, he took a burner phone out of his desk and called Lloyd Standish.

"I just had a visit from an investigator who is looking into Margaret's murder."

"And?"

"I didn't say anything, Lloyd, but he threatened to subpoena me. He said Lockwood would question me about the auto accidents. What should I do?"

"First thing you have to do is calm down."

"How am I supposed to stay calm? He said he was talking to people at the DA's office and the cops. They're investigating us, and he knew about Margaret's part and that guy Truax I was supposed to write a report on. Did you kill them, Lloyd?"

"Of course not, Truman. Please pull yourself together. You have nothing to worry about unless you create problems for yourself. You're a doctor. You see patients who are injured all the time. That's what every doctor does. If the police or the DA ask you about any of the people who sued, just tell them the truth. Margaret referred one client to you and liked your work, so she continued to send injured clients to you. You were their doctor, you treated them, and you gave a truthful diagnosis. Who can prove you wrong? Stick to the truth and you'll be okay. Do you see that?"

Alcott assured Lloyd that he did, but he was still afraid, and he didn't know if he would be able to lie convincingly if he was questioned by the police or by Lockwood under oath in court. He was also afraid of Lloyd. Standish had assured him that he hadn't killed Truax and Finch, but Alcott couldn't help thinking that he might have been lying. If Margaret had been murdered to get rid of anyone who could connect Kovalev and Standish to the auto accident scam, he could be next.

"Marie, do I have any other appointments?" he asked his receptionist when he walked to the front of the office.

"There are three patients scheduled between two and four."

"Call them and cancel."

"When should I reschedule?"

"I'm not sure. I may be gone for a while."

The receptionist looked concerned. "Where are you going, Truman?"

"I'm taking a vacation."

"A vacation? Where?" she asked. But Dr. Alcott was already out the door.

As soon as he was in his car, he drove to his bank and emptied most of his accounts. Then he drove home as fast as he could. He planned to pack and drive until the sun set. Kovalev had hackers on his payroll who could trace a person's credit card purchases. Alcott planned to stay at a motel he'd select randomly and pay cash. Then he would figure out his next move.

Alcott's grades hadn't been good enough to get him into a medical school in the States, so he'd gotten his medical degree in Grenada. While he was there, he'd become fluent in Spanish, and he'd traveled around South America. There were any number of places he could hide once he was out of the country. He hoped Kovalev wouldn't see him as a threat if he wasn't stateside. He thought his chances of surviving would be pretty good if he lay low long enough for the events at the Finch home to blow over.

CHAPTER THIRTY-ONE

Robin called Loretta into her office after Loretta returned from lunch.

"Beth Wrigley was one of Annie Finch's friends. I spoke to Beth's parents yesterday and explained why I wanted to talk to Beth. Beth's mother just called. Beth is willing to talk about Annie. We're going to her house around four."

"You want me to come along?"

"Beth is African American. You'll be conducting the interview."

"Would you be asking me to go with you if Beth was white?"

"Maybe, but she isn't. And before you accuse me of being a racist, let me remind you that you win cases by gaining the confidence of witnesses who might be reluctant to help you. You're younger than me, so you might have a better chance of getting her to open up. Another thing you need to keep in mind, Loretta, is that this case isn't about the Fourteenth Amendment. We are trying to save Mandy Kerrigan's life. I will do what I have to in order to keep our client off death row, even if it means playing the race card. Do you get that?"

Loretta looked embarrassed. "Yeah. Sorry."

Robin smiled. "If it makes you feel better, look at this as a chance to hone your investigative skills. Are you in or out?"

Loretta laughed. "I'm in!"

"Good. Let's go over the ground I want to cover."

The Wrigleys lived in a modern, two-story home. Large picture windows gave the family a panoramic view of Portland's rivers and the snowcapped peaks of the Cascade Range.

Rose Wrigley, Beth's mother, opened the door for Robin and Loretta and led them to a large kitchen at one end of the house. Beth looked anxious when her mother escorted the attorneys to a carved wood table that stood in a kitchen nook where Beth was eating an after-school snack. The teenager was wearing jeans and a T-shirt under a light green sweater. She was tall for her age, and the newspaper article said that she'd played on the school basketball team with Annie and Donna in seventh grade.

Rose indicated two seats across from Beth that looked out on a flower garden.

"Hi, Beth," Loretta said. "I know this can't be pleasant for you, and Robin and I appreciate your seeing us."

Beth looked at Robin. "I read about you in an article about Annie's murder. Did you really fight on TV?"

Robin laughed. "You checked me out?"

Beth looked embarrassed and nodded.

"That's what I'd have done if our places were reversed. You have the makings of a good private investigator."

Beth flashed a shy smile.

"To answer your question," Robin said, "in another life, I was Rockin' Robin Lockwood, and I fought on TV in UFC events."

"Were you good?"

"Beth, don't be so nosy," Rose said.

"I'm not embarrassed by the question," Robin said with a smile. "Yeah, I was pretty good. I was ranked in the top ten in my weight class when I retired to concentrate on law school. Why? Are you thinking of training in mixed martial arts?"

"No. I don't want to get hit in the face and kicked."

"Smart girl. Basketball sounds like way more fun."

"Were Annie and Donna on the team with you last year?" Loretta asked as a way of easing into the questions she and Robin wanted answered.

"We'd been playing basketball together for years."

"How did you do?"

Beth blushed. "We usually won."

"Was Annie good?" Loretta asked.

"Yeah. She was our tallest player, and she was strong."

"How about Donna?"

Beth hesitated.

"It's okay to be honest," Loretta said. "We're just trying to get a picture of Donna and Annie."

"Donna was okay. She didn't start. She wasn't as tall or strong as the rest of the team, but she tried really hard."

"When did you three begin playing together?"

"Fourth grade."

"So, the three of you were pretty tight."

"Until this year. Annie was always nice until this year, or maybe the end of seventh grade. All of a sudden, she stopped hanging with me and her other friends. Once, she beat up Donna in the girls' bathroom."

"She hit her?" Loretta asked.

Beth nodded. "She was much bigger and stronger. Donna had a bloody nose."

"Did Donna report Annie?"

"No. She said she slipped and hit her nose on the sink. But we knew that wasn't true. And then Annie started saying all of this horrible stuff about Donna."

"What was she saying?"

Beth looked at her mother, who nodded.

Beth looked at the tabletop. "She called Donna a . . . Well, she said she was a whore and a slut and things like that. It was disgusting, and it really upset Donna."

"How do you know what Annie said to Donna?"

"She would text her and send screenshots to everyone in our class." Beth looked up at Loretta. There were tears in her eyes. "Donna was really sweet, and she was shy. What Annie did . . . Donna was really upset. She cut school. And then Annie was telling Donna that Donna didn't deserve to live and she should kill herself. And then she did."

Beth paused and looked back and forth between the attorneys. "I just want to know why Annie did it. Do you know?"

"It's what we're trying to find out," Robin said. "And I do have a question for you about Donna. Calling someone a whore and a slut implies that the person is having sex with someone. Did Donna or Annie have a boyfriend?"

"Donna definitely didn't date, but Annie went out with Steve Reynolds a few times. I don't know if they were still seeing each other."

"Is Steve in your class?"

Beth nodded.

"Beth, it sounds like you were good friends with Donna and

Annie," Robin said. "And it sounds like Annie and Donna were pretty happy and normal in seventh grade. Do you have any idea what happened to make them change?"

Beth shook her head. "I've thought about it and thought about it. It had to be something that happened near the end of seventh grade, because that's when Annie started acting strange and she and Donna stopped hanging with us. But I don't know why. We even asked Ryan, but he said he had no idea what was up with Annie."

"Are you talking about Annie's brother, Ryan Finch?"

"Yes."

"How did you know Ryan?"

"He was an assistant coach for our basketball team. He was a good player in high school, and he volunteered to help us when Annie started playing."

"Beth, did you know that Ryan was dealing drugs?"

Beth glanced at her mother. "We heard stuff last year, but he never did anything with us."

"You're certain Donna wasn't using?"

"You think Ryan was getting her high and that's why Annie was angry?"

"We haven't seen any evidence that Donna was using, but it could explain why Annie was mad at her."

"Yeah, I guess, but I never saw it, and none of my friends suggested it."

Robin and Loretta stayed a little longer. Then they got Steve Reynolds's address and phone number from Beth and left.

"What did you take away from the interview?" Robin asked Loretta when they were driving back to the office.

"There was an event late in the term in seventh grade that

started all the drama. I thought it had to do with sex, but with Ryan's name coming up, maybe it was drugs. What are you thinking?"

"We have four dead people, and history tells us that sex and drugs have provided powerful motives for a great many murders. See if you can get Donna Faber's autopsy report. I want to know if the medical examiner found any drugs in her system."

CHAPTER THIRTY-TWO

After Ken left Dr. Alcott's office, his next stop was the office where Dale Gibbs sold the insurance that all the alleged accident victims had purchased. The office, like Dr. Alcott's office, was in a low-rent strip mall in a part of town where decent citizens rarely went after the sun set.

"How can I help you?" asked the young woman who greeted Ken with a smile when he walked in.

"I'd like to talk to Dale Gibbs."

"Mr. Gibbs isn't in. Would you like to talk to Mrs. Clift?"

"No. I was referred to Mr. Gibbs. When do you expect him?"

"I really can't say. He's usually in first thing, but he must have had an appointment outside of the office."

"Did he say when he'll be back?"

"No."

Ken was worried, but he didn't show it. "Could you call Mr. Gibbs and find out when he'll be here? I can come back."

The receptionist hesitated. "I really shouldn't bother him. He could be in a meeting."

"It's important," Ken insisted.

"All right. What did you say your name is?"

"Ken Breland."

The receptionist checked a list of numbers and called Gibbs. She listened for a few seconds.

"Mr. Gibbs, this is Clarice. A Mr. Breland is in the office and wants to see you. Can you let me know when you're going to be in? He's here now."

Clarice disconnected. "Mr. Gibbs didn't answer. That was a voice mail message. If you leave your phone number, I'll call you when he gets back to me."

"Thanks," Ken said as he handed the receptionist his card.

"You're an investigator?"

"Yes. I'm hoping Mr. Gibbs can give me some insight into an insurance question that's come up. I've been told that he's quite the expert."

As soon as he was in his car, Ken programmed Dale Gibbs's home address into his GPS. With Truax and Margaret Finch dead, only Gibbs and Dr. Alcott could give evidence about the way the insurance scam worked.

Gibbs lived in an apartment complex that formed a horseshoe around a central courtyard. Ken parked in front and walked past a young woman who was carrying a bag of groceries. Ken knocked on Gibbs's door.

"He's not in," the woman said.

Ken turned.

"He left early this morning," the woman said.

Ken smiled, but he didn't feel happy. "Was he alone?"

The woman started to answer. Then she stopped. "Why do you want to know?"

"Are you a friend?"

"We're neighbors, so we see each other around."

"My name is Ken Breland, and I'm a private investigator. I'm working on a murder case. I hope I'm wrong, but your friend might be in danger."

"Oh my God. He wasn't alone. There were two men with him."

"Miss . . . I'm sorry. I didn't get your name?"

"It's Laurie Cohen."

"Laurie, did Mr. Gibbs appear to be going with the men willingly?"

Laurie started to answer. Then she hesitated. "I really can't say. I was headed out for a appointment when I saw Dale. I said hi and he said hello, but . . . Well, he did sound nervous."

"What did the men look like?"

"They were big, and they walked on either side of Dale. They were tall, and they looked like bodybuilders."

"When you can, please write down as detailed a description of the men as you can. It might be important."

"Do you think the men are going to hurt Dale?"

"Probably not. I might be overreacting," Ken said. He handed her his card. "If Dale comes home, can you ask him to call me?"

"Of course."

"Thanks. You've been a big help."

Ken called Robin as soon as he got in his car and told her about his visits to Dr. Alcott and Dale Gibbs.

"Do you think Kovalev is getting rid of anyone who can implicate him in the scam?" Robin asked.

"We'll have an answer if Gibbs turns up dead."

CHAPTER THIRTY-THREE

Vasyl Listnitsky and Lev Sokolov were parked across the street from Truman Alcott's house.

"Alcott just got home," Sokolov told Lloyd Standish on a burner phone when Truman pulled his car into his garage.

"Take care of him," Lloyd said.

"Let's go," Sokolov told his partner.

Listnitsky checked his gun before following Sokolov across the street.

"Go around back in case he tries to run," Sokolov said.

Listnitsky disappeared around the side of the house. Sokolov picked the lock on Alcott's front door and crept inside. The shades in the front room were drawn, and Alcott had kept the lights off so it would look like no one was home.

Sokolov held his gun by his side and walked down the carpeted hall toward Alcott's bedroom without making a sound. The door was open, and the doctor's back was to Sokolov, who paused in the doorway.

"Going somewhere, Truman?"

Alcott gasped and spun around. "Who are you?"

"A friend. Lloyd sent me. He wants to talk to you."

"I . . . I just talked to Lloyd."

"He enjoyed the conversation so much that he wants to keep it going."

Sokolov waved his gun in the direction of Alcott's suitcase. "Why don't you finish packing. Be sure to bring your passport. Lloyd said he wants to finance a trip to a very nice place where you can stay for a while. He mentioned somewhere in the Caribbean."

Alcott wasn't stupid. He knew if the police searched his house and found his passport, clothes, and toiletries missing, they would think he'd left the country. But Truman knew he wasn't going to be alive at the end of the day and that his possessions would be buried with his body.

"I have money," Truman said. "Take it and let me go. You can tell Lloyd I wasn't home."

Sokolov smiled. "I told Lloyd you were home before I came in. And I'm going to take your money anyway. Now stop stalling. We have things to do and places to be, and you'll enjoy them more if you're not in pain."

Alcott turned away and kept packing. He wasn't a fighter, but he tried to remember karate moves he'd seen on TV that he might try if he had the chance. Then he heard the back door open and knew that his captor wasn't alone, which meant that he was helpless.

Alcott started to cry. He didn't have much of a life. His wife had left him years ago, and he didn't have any children. Except for the occasional evening with his receptionist, his only sexual encounters involved Internet porn, and his only other escapes from reality were accomplished through the use of drugs to which his medical license gave him access. By any measure, his life was a pathetic failure. Even so, he didn't want to die.

Alcott fought to keep his sobs quiet. His shoulders shook, and he thought he might vomit. He was almost finished packing when he heard a thud behind him. When he turned, he saw that the man who was kidnapping him was sprawled on the floor and an Asian man was kneeling next to him, securing his hands and ankles with zip ties.

"Who are you?" Alcott blurted out.

"I'm your new best friend. Close up your suitcase, and let's get out of here."

Alan Chen led the doctor through the kitchen, where another unconscious man was lying near the back door with his hands and ankles bound. Alcott stepped around him and followed Chen, who walked through the backyard and onto the next street, where he used his electronic key to unlock the doors and trunk of a black Volvo.

"Put your bag in the trunk."

"Where are we going?"

"Someplace Jack Kovalev and Lloyd Standish won't be able to get to you," Chen said.

As soon as Alcott was in the car and they were on their way, Chen made a phone call and put it on speaker so Alcott could hear the conversation.

"Detective Marx?" Chen said.

"Yes."

"This is Alan Chen."

"Where are you, Mr. Chen? We've been trying to find you."

"Where I am is unimportant. The person who is riding with me is very important, because he can give you the evidence you need to put Jack Kovalev in prison."

"Who's in your car?"

"Dr. Truman Alcott. He played a major part in Kovalev's insurance fraud by issuing medical reports that stated that Kovalev's drivers suffered injuries when they did not. Kovalev just sent two men to murder Alcott. You'll find them at his house."

"Are they dead like the men we found in the trunk of a car on a logging road?"

"If those men were dead, someone else killed them. A man named Lloyd Standish, who works for Kovalev, sent them to my house to beat me up. When I left them, they were alive, but I did call Lloyd Standish and tell him where he could find them, so maybe you should talk to him."

"Why are you calling me?"

"You have to protect Dr. Alcott. In exchange for your protection, he'll tell you what he knows about the insurance scam. Can I tell him that you'll keep him safe?"

"Yes."

Chen pulled into the parking lot of a motel and parked in front of the office.

"I'm going to tell you where you can find Dr. Alcott sometime in the next half hour. Send several officers to protect him."

"Will you be with him, Alan?"

"No, Detective. I still have work to do."

CHAPTER THIRTY-FOUR

Steve Reynolds's parents agreed to let Robin talk to him in the principal's office after school, and Mrs. Lee, the principal, and Karen Reynolds, Steve's mother, were waiting with Steve when Robin arrived.

Steve had a buzz cut, a slender, athletic build, and the acned face of a boy who was new to puberty. He looked nervous when Robin walked in and introduced herself. She knew that Steve was on a club wrestling team, and Robin broke the ice by telling Reynolds that she wrestled in high school. They talked about cutting weight and what it was like to fight in mixed martial arts competitions until Robin felt that Reynolds felt comfortable enough to talk to her about Annie Finch.

"You know I'm the lawyer for the woman who's accused of killing Annie and her family?"

Reynolds nodded.

"Mandy Kerrigan swears that she never hurt anyone on the

night the family was killed. She was at the house, but she says that she never went in, and there's no evidence like fingerprints or DNA that says she's lying. If Mandy is innocent, then the real killer is out there. One problem I have is that no one knows who was the intended victim. It could have been any one of the Finch family. And that's why I want to talk to you about Annie.

"Now, I know this is uncomfortable for you. Annie's dead, and no one likes to say bad things about someone who has passed away, but Mandy could go to death row if we don't uncover the truth. Before I ask you any questions, I want you to know that I'm not writing a report about our conversation and, right now, I have no intentions or reason to call you as a witness. Unless you have vital information, this talk is just background for me. And I want you to know that you don't have to answer any of my questions if you don't want to. Do you get that?"

Steve nodded.

"Okay, then. Let's talk about Annie. I understand that you and Annie were dating."

Reynolds blushed. "Not really. I mean, we went to a movie and a dance in seventh grade, but we only went out those two times."

"Did you like her?"

"Yeah, for a while. Then she turned into a real . . ."

Reynolds caught himself.

"Uh, she got real mean."

"So, you stopped going out?" Robin asked.

Reynolds broke eye contact. "Yeah."

"I don't want to embarrass you, but I have a reason for asking. It's important that you give me a straight answer. Did you break up with Annie, or did she tell you she didn't want to go out with you anymore?"

"It was Annie. I'd go up to her in the hall and she'd brush me off. She'd started acting really strange. I texted to ask what was wrong, and she never texted back. Then, one time, she texted and said she didn't want to go out with me and I should stop bothering her. It hurt my feelings because I thought she liked me. But I'm not sorry now after what she did to Donna."

"Everyone I've talked to says that Annie was really nice until the end of seventh grade. Then she became a completely different person. Do you have any idea what made her change?"

"Honestly, I don't. Believe me, I've thought about it a lot, especially after she did that stuff to Donna, and I've talked to our friends. No one knows."

"You or her friends must have had ideas about what could cause her to become so mean and so different."

"Oh, sure, but we were just guessing."

"What were some of the guesses?"

Reynolds looked at the principal.

"It's okay, Steve," she said.

Steve shrugged. "I mean, everyone in her family was weird. I was over there once. Her brother was high, and her mom and dad didn't say a thing about it. Her mom was the most normal, but after saying hi, she left us alone. And her dad . . ." Steve shook his head. "He looked like he might have been high too. I wondered if Annie was using drugs, but she never seemed spacey. Just different. So, it might have just been living with those people that screwed her up."

"Any other theories?"

"Well, there was one more. I think she was seeing some guy, only not someone at school. That's what we all thought."

"Did you ever see her with someone?"

"No, but she started acting . . . I don't know. Older. She treated us like we were kids and she was so grown-up. So, I thought, maybe, she was dating someone at the high school and keeping it quiet."

"I was told that Annie was really savaged on the Internet after Donna killed herself. Do you know if there's anybody who hated her so much that they might kill her?"

"You mean someone at school?"

Robin nodded.

"You're way off base. No one liked Annie after she bullied Donna, but we just stayed away from her. I never heard anyone say they wanted to beat her up or, like, kill her."

CHAPTER THIRTY-FIVE

Robin talked to Steve Reynolds a little longer. Then she wished him luck in a match he had over the weekend. After thanking the principal and Steve's mother, Robin walked to her car with a dozen thoughts swirling through her head. That's why she didn't notice the handsome blond-haired, blue-eyed man dressed in a blazer, open-necked blue silk shirt, and tan slacks who was leaning on her car until she was only a few steps away.

Humans are wired to have a fight-or-flight response when confronted with danger. Robin's first choice was always to fight. Even though the stranger didn't seem to pose a threat, she kept some space between them so she would have room to strike if that became necessary.

"You're leaning against my car," she said.

Lloyd Standish saw what Robin was doing, and he smiled. "I know it's your car. That's why I've been waiting for you here. And you don't have to worry about your personal safety, Miss Lockwood.

I know all about your martial arts background, and I promise, you won't have any reason to kung fu me."

"Why are you waiting for me, Mr. . . . ?"

"Standish. Lloyd Standish. Jack Kovalev would like to speak to you about the Finches, and I'm here to invite you to meet with him."

"Just where are we supposed to have this meeting?"

"He would like you to accompany me to the Jazz Bar, one of his clubs. You'll be quite safe."

"Mr. Kovalev has a reputation as a violent gangster, so I'd prefer to talk to him at my office."

Lloyd shrugged. "Jack is a busy man. Going to your office would be very inconvenient."

"It would also be inconvenient for me to go to a club owned by a mobster with a stranger, so I'll pass."

"If you're worried about your safety, call your office and tell them what you're doing. Jack just wants to talk."

Now Robin was curious. She hesitated. Kovalev would be crazy to harm her if she told several people where she was going, and the chance to talk to one of the biggest suspects in the Finch murders was too good to pass up.

Robin took out her phone and called Ken Breland. "Hi, Ken. I'm standing in the parking lot at Marie Curie Middle School with a charming gentlemen named Lloyd Standish."

Robin held the phone toward Standish and snapped a picture. Standish stopped smiling.

"Jack Kovalev wants me to go with Mr. Standish to the Jazz Bar so we can talk."

"About what?"

"The Finches."

"Do you think that's wise?" Ken asked.

"I don't think I'll be in any danger. But you might want to tell Deputy District Attorney McKee where I'm going in case I disappear."

Robin disconnected and put the phone in her pocket. "Shall we?" she said.

"Why don't you leave your car here and drive with me?" Standish asked as he pointed to a Porsche that could have been part of a museum exhibit.

"Nice wheels, but I'll follow in my beater."

Standish laughed. "Afraid of being taken for a ride? I think you've been watching too many gangster movies."

"I'm just following one of my golden rules, 'Better safe than sorry.'"

Even though the Jazz Bar was only a few blocks away from McGill's, it might as well have been on a different planet from Robin's gym. McGill's stood on the edge of the Pearl District among the few remaining warehouses and within view of makeshift tents that housed the homeless. Jack Kovalev's flashy nightclub was in the gentrified part of the district surrounded by boutiques, upscale restaurants, and shiny steel-and-glass condos.

Lloyd Standish led the way to the club and parked in front of the valet station. Robin stopped her car behind his. The club wasn't open yet, but Standish must have called ahead, because a valet was on duty. The valet took Robin's keys and drove off just as Lloyd Standish led her into the darkened interior.

A team of waiters was covering tables with white tablecloths so the dining area would be ready for the guests who would arrive in a few hours, and a trio was rehearsing on a small stage. Three men with the build of bouncers were seated near a corner by the stage, sipping beers and talking sports. They paused to eye Robin as she followed Standish to the back of the club, then continued their analysis of a recent Seahawks trade.

Standish stopped in front of a door and knocked. Then he opened the door and stepped aside so Robin could enter Jack Kovalev's office. When Robin was inside, Standish followed her and shut the door. Then he drifted to one side of the office and sat down on a sofa.

Kovalev was wearing a navy blue Zegna suit. His pale pink shirt was open at his massive neck, displaying tufts of thick, curly black chest hair and a set of gold chains. When Robin entered, Kovalev walked over to her.

"It's a pleasure to meet you in person after seeing your fights on television."

"I haven't fought on television for ten years."

"But I still have vivid memories of your battle with Valerie Machado."

"And you're being polite enough to avoid mentioning the fight I had with my client Mandy Kerrigan."

Kovalev laughed. "Just so. And it is about Miss Kerrigan that I wish to speak. I've been told that your investigator has been talking to people who have been involved in auto accidents. That surprised me, because I thought you practiced criminal law."

"You do understand that I have an obligation to represent Miss Kerrigan to the utmost of my ability. That would include presenting alternative suspects to the jury."

"You're not suggesting that I am a suspect in the death of any of the Finch family?"

"Margaret Finch represented a number of people in criminal cases who have connections to you."

"Alleged connections. I don't believe any of these people who were represented by Margaret were ever connected to me by evidence."

"Which could mean that you had no connection to them or that you skillfully hid one."

"I still don't understand why you are looking into these auto accidents."

"Margaret represented the plaintiffs who recovered money from an insurance company after participating in staged auto accidents. A lot of people think you are running the scam. If Margaret was going to go to the authorities and tell them about your involvement in the scheme, you would have a reason to silence her."

"If the police had proof that I murdered Mrs. Finch, they would have arrested me. But there is no proof because I had nothing to do with her death. Suggesting that I killed her is slander, and introducing such a theory at Miss Kerrigan's trial would be unethical."

"I believe I can put on enough evidence to get over the bar I have to hurdle to raise the possibility that someone other than my client murdered the Finches. Remember, the State has the burden of proving that Miss Kerrigan is guilty 'beyond a reasonable doubt.' Even if they don't completely buy another person's involvement, the jurors have to acquit if I present evidence that creates a reasonable doubt in Miss Kerrigan's case."

Kovalev stopped smiling. "Looking into the accident cases could be dangerous."

"You aren't threatening me, are you, Mr. Kovalev?"

"I'm just making you aware of a potential problem. I also want to assure you that whether or not I am involved in this insurance scheme, I definitely did not have anything to do with the death of Margaret Finch or any other member of her family."

"If you had nothing to do with the killings at the Finch home, you have nothing to worry about," Robin said.

"Are you still going to try to involve me in Miss Kerrigan's trial?"

"I'll do whatever is necessary within legal and ethical limits to clear my client."

"That's not a direct answer."

"I can't predict the future. That's the best answer I can give you. It was nice meeting you and Mr. Standish, but I'm afraid it's getting late and it's time for me to go home."

Robin turned toward the office door, and Lloyd Standish stood up. The door opened and Alan Chen walked in.

"Who—?" Kovalev started to ask, stopping in midsentence when he saw the gun Chen was pointing at him.

Chen shut the door behind him and locked it. "You killed my wife," he said. "Now you're going to pay."

"I had nothing to do with your wife's death," Kovalev said.

"And I suppose you didn't send men to kill Truman Alcott either. He's alive, by the way, and with the police, and he's telling them all about the staged auto accidents."

"I don't know what you're talking about," Kovalev said.

"Then your death will be a tragic mistake."

"Look . . . ," Kovalev started.

Chen shook his head. "No more talking."

"Alan, I'm Robin Lockwood. I'm a lawyer representing the woman charged with killing Margaret Finch, and I've been investigating Kovalev. He may have been behind Margaret's murder. If Dr. Alcott is talking, we can prove Kovalev was behind the staged crash that killed Susan. He'll go to prison where he belongs, but you don't belong behind bars. Think. If you kill Kovalev, you'll spend the rest of your life in a cage, but he'll be free. That's what death does. It ends suffering. Don't let him off the hook by killing him."

Chen hesitated for a moment, and the barrel of his gun dropped an inch. Robin hoped that she'd defused the situation. Then all doubt disappeared from Chen's features, and he aimed his gun at Kovalev's chest. Out of the corner of her eye, Robin saw Lloyd Standish pull out a handgun that had been concealed under his blazer. Robin pushed the gun to one side just as Standish pulled the trigger. The bullet went into the floor, and Robin smashed her elbow into Standish's nose. The pain blinded Lloyd, and he dropped the gun. Robin torqued her body, sending her other elbow into Lloyd's temple with enough velocity to poleax him.

Robin's actions distracted Chen and gave Kovalev time to pull out his gun. The movement brought Chen's attention back to the mobster. Kovalev fired and hit Chen in his left shoulder. Chen staggered, but he got off two shots that hit Kovalev in the chest. Kovalev stumbled backward against the edge of his desk and let go of his gun. Then he slid down the side of the desk and sat on the floor. As Robin stooped to retrieve Standish's gun, she saw Kovalev make a feeble attempt to grab his weapon. Robin kicked it away. Then she turned back to Chen, who had taken a step toward Kovalev to set up a kill shot. Robin stepped between him and the Russian.

"Enough! Kovalev and Standish are down. I'm going to call Detective Marx. Let the police take care of these bastards."

Chen stopped. His gun hand angled down. Someone tried the door, then pounded on it. "Is everything okay?" someone shouted. "We thought we heard shots!"

"Don't try to come in," Robin called back. "It's not safe. There are armed men in here. I'm calling 911 and the police. I'll open the door when they arrive."

Robin could hear an argument through the door but couldn't make out what the people were saying. She pulled out her phone.

"Can I call Marx?" she asked Chen.

Chen hesitated. He looked exhausted. Then he nodded and collapsed on the sofa. He pressed one hand to his wound and laid down his weapon next to him.

Robin dialed 911 and asked for an ambulance and Detective Chet Marx. While she waited to be connected to the detective, she held out her hand. "Will you let me have your gun?" she asked.

Chen's head was back, and his eyes were closed. "Take it," he said just as Robin was connected to Chet Marx.

"This is Robin Lockwood, Detective. I'm in Jack Kovalev's office at the Jazz Bar with the door locked. There's been a shooting. Kovalev is seriously injured. Alan Chen is wounded, and Lloyd Standish is unconscious. Please come as fast as you can."

"What happened?" Marx asked.

"I'll tell you when you get here, but I can't talk now. I've got to help Mr. Chen until the EMTs arrive."

Robin disconnected and walked over to Chen. "How badly are you hurt?" she asked as she picked up his gun.

"I think the bullet went through, but I need to stop the bleeding."

There was a bathroom attached to Kovalev's office. Robin went into it and returned with a first aid kit and towels. Chen gritted his teeth and pulled his shirt off his injured shoulder.

Robin started to work on the wound when Lloyd Standish opened his eyes. He took some deep breaths. Then he focused on Robin.

"You're dead, bitch," he said as he started to struggle to his feet.

Robin turned Chen's gun on the gangster. "Sit the fuck down, Lloyd. And don't think I won't use this."

Standish looked at the gun. Then he grinned and continued to get up. Robin took a step and kicked Standish in his knee. He screamed and fell down.

"Don't test me," Robin said.

Standish glared at Robin. "You won't always have that gun, and I'm very patient."

Chen had been following the exchange as he worked on stopping his wound from bleeding. He didn't say anything, but he was studying Standish the way he'd studied his targets on his missions in combat zones.

CHAPTER THIRTY-SIX

While she waited for the ambulance and Chet Marx, Robin called
Ken Breland and told him what had happened at the Jazz Bar. When
Ken arrived, EMTs were loading Alan Chen and Jack Kovalev into
separate ambulances, another EMT was examining Lloyd Standish
for a concussion and broken nose while a police officer looked on,
and a team from the crime lab was processing Kovalev's office.

Ken spotted Robin sitting at a table in a corner of the nightclub.
Chet Marx and Darrell Price were sitting across from her, and Price
was recording everything Robin said. Marx had never arrested a person whom Robin had defended, but he knew police officers and DAs
who had been involved in her cases. They all said that you had to
bring your A game when Robin was the defense attorney, and they
all said that she was a straight arrow.

"Mind if I sit in?" Ken asked when he walked up.

"Yeah, we do," Price answered.

"Well, I don't," Robin said, "and I'm not answering any questions unless you let my investigator join us."

Price started to answer, but Marx laid a hand on his partner's forearm.

"It's okay, Darrell. Miss Lockwood isn't under arrest. She's a witness, and we want her to feel comfortable. So, Miss Lockwood, can you tell us what happened in Kovalev's office?"

Robin had spent the time between tending to Chen's wound and being brought to this table by the detectives thinking about how she was going to answer their questions.

"It all happened very fast, and I couldn't see everything that was happening at times."

"Just try to be as accurate as you can, and don't be afraid to tell me if you're not certain about something," Marx said.

"Okay. I finished interviewing a witness at Marie Curie Middle School, and I walked to my car. Lloyd Standish was waiting for me. He said that Jack Kovalev wanted to talk to me at this club. I followed him here, and Kovalev and I talked."

"What did you talk about?"

"I knew that Margaret Finch was involved in Kovalev's insurance scam and that she represented Otis Truax, who killed Alan Chen's wife. I also knew that Truax had been murdered. That meant that there was a possibility that Kovalev had ordered a hit on Margaret to make sure she couldn't tell the police about the scheme. If that's what happened, someone like Kovalev would have no problem killing all the witnesses, and that would explain what happened at the Finch house and lead to an acquittal for my client."

"Did you ask Kovalev if he'd had someone kill Margaret?"

"He assured me that he had nothing to do with her murder, but he also told me that he'd heard that we were talking to people who were involved in his plan and he tried to warn me off."

"He threatened you?" Marx asked.

"Not directly. But he did tell me that investigating the scam could be dangerous. That's when I decided to leave."

"How did the shooting start?" Marx asked.

"I turned toward the door to go, and Lloyd Standish got up from the couch. The door opened, and Alan Chen came in. He accused Kovalev of killing his wife. Kovalev denied it, and Chen accused him of sending men to kill Truman Alcott. Kovalev denied that too. Chen was holding a gun, and I tried to calm the situation. I think I said something about letting the police arrest Kovalev and how Chen would spend the rest of his life in prison if he killed Kovalev. That's when everything got out of hand."

"What do you mean?" Marx asked.

"While Chen was thinking about what I'd said, Standish pulled out a gun. I pushed the gun aside and knocked him out. While I was doing that, Kovalev shot Chen. Chen returned fire and wounded Kovalev. I couldn't have stopped Chen from killing Kovalev, but he didn't try to do anything after Kovalev went down. That's when I called 911 and you, and I helped Chen stop his wound from bleeding."

"From what you're saying, Chen went into the office with a gun and threatened to shoot Kovalev," Marx said.

Robin could have told the detective that Chen had raised his gun and aimed at Kovalev just before Standish pulled out his weapon, but she'd decided that she would leave out that detail. Chen had suffered enough, and she wasn't going to be the one who was responsible for having him charged with attempted murder.

"Yes," Robin said, "but he didn't start the shooting. He was starting to calm down when Standish pulled his weapon and Kovalev shot him."

Darrell Price didn't look like he believed Robin. "If I've got this right," he said, "Chen had a gun and threatened Kovalev, but he didn't try to harm him. But Standish, who could reasonably believe that he was in danger, tried to defend himself, and you knocked him cold before he could fire a shot."

"Yes," Robin said.

"Then Kovalev, who could reasonably believe he was in danger, shot Chen, who returned fire, arguably in self-defense."

"Yes."

"So, according to you, no one committed a crime?"

"That's for the DA to decide. I'm just telling you what I remember."

"You're saying that Chen didn't commit a crime, even though he broke into Kovalev's office with a gun?"

"That he didn't use until he'd been shot," Robin reminded Price.

"There's something you're not telling us," Price persisted.

"If I remember something more, I'll let you know. And now, I'd appreciate it if you would let me leave. I've had a long, stressful day, and I'm exhausted."

Marx also looked skeptical, but he told Robin she could go.

"Did you hold something back?" Ken asked when they were standing next to Robin's car, out of earshot of anyone.

"I'm going to pretend you didn't ask me that," Robin answered.

"You told Marx that you accused Kovalev of ordering Margaret Finch's murder, and Kovalev denied it. Do you believe him?"

"He sounded like he was telling the truth, but Kovalev is a sociopath, and they're excellent liars."

CHAPTER THIRTY-SEVEN

It was dark by the time Robin left the Jazz Bar. Ken asked if she wanted to grab a bite, but she was exhausted and running on fumes, and she told him that she was just going to head to her condo.

She parked in the condo's garage and took the elevator to her floor. When she got out of the elevator, she saw Tom McKee sitting on the floor in front of her door reading a paperback book. When he saw Robin get out of the elevator, he jumped to his feet.

"What are you doing here?" she asked.

"I know we aren't supposed to see each other, but I heard what happened at the Jazz Bar, and I had to see you to make sure you were okay."

"How did you get past the security guard?" Robin asked, not really interested but stalling for time to think about what she should do. Part of her was thrilled that Tom had taken a risk because he was worried about her, and part of her was alarmed at the problems his visit might cause for the *Kerrigan* case.

Tom smiled. "That was easy. I flashed my credentials and told the guard that you're the mistress of a notorious drug lord who's in witness protection."

Robin couldn't help herself. She threw back her head and laughed, grateful for a light moment in an otherwise awful day. "You did not."

Tom smiled. "You got me. Actually, I told the truth. I did show him my credentials. Then I said we were on opposite sides of a death penalty case, and I had to discuss something important that had just come up." He stopped smiling and looked into Robin's eyes. "So, are you okay?"

"Yeah. I survived in one piece, and I was the only one. Let's get inside before anyone sees us, and I'll tell you what happened."

Tom followed Robin into her condo. She turned on the lights and started toward the kitchen.

"Nice digs," Tom said. "I bet you have a fabulous view. Can you see any mountains when the sun is out?"

"A few. I'm starving. Have you eaten?"

"No."

"I've got some pasta, a jar of marinara sauce, and two spicy Italian sausages in the fridge. There's also a bottle of Chianti somewhere. Are you game?"

"Is that a trick question?"

Robin smiled and realized how much it meant to have Tom with her.

"Can I do anything to help?" Tom asked.

Robin found the Chianti and handed the bottle and a corkscrew to Tom. "Can you uncork the wine?"

"I have some experience in that line of work."

"Good. That's your job while I put dinner together. Cooking

helps me relax, and, after my afternoon adventure, I need all the relaxation therapy I can get."

While she whipped up dinner, Robin told Tom about her meeting with Jack Kovalev and the shoot-out.

"Jesus, Robin. You could have been killed," Tom said as Robin dumped the spaghetti into a colander.

"That only dawned on me after everything calmed down. I was just lucky that I wasn't hit by a stray bullet."

Tom uncorked the wine. He didn't say anything while Robin put together the dinner and brought it to the table. She could see that something was troubling him.

"What's got you so deep in thought?"

"You beat up Lloyd Standish. He's the enforcer for the Russian mob, and I'm guessing he's not the type who turns the other cheek and forgives and forgets."

Robin had been so tired that she hadn't thought about possible aftermaths of her run-in with Kovalev. Now, she was worried. "He did threaten me. Do you think he'll come after me?" she asked.

"I don't have any idea, but, first thing in the morning, I'm going to ask some people who would know. In the meantime, watch your back."

"Thanks, Tom. I will."

"Do you own a gun?"

Robin nodded. "I've had a few bad situations where I needed one. So, I have a license to carry."

"Good. Don't leave home without it. I'll clear things with courthouse security."

Robin and Tom were both hungry, and they dug into the food without much more conversation. When they were finished, they carried their plates to the sink. Robin emptied her leftover pasta into the disposal. When she turned away from the sink, she was inches from Tom. They stood looking at each other, and emotions swept through Robin that she hadn't felt since the last time she'd made love to Jeff. She knew she should back away. Instead, she said, "To hell with it," and kissed Tom.

"Do you think . . . ?" Tom started.

Robin laid a finger across his lips and said, "I don't want to think." Then she leaned in and kissed him again. Tom wrapped his arms around Robin, and they stood together for a moment, their hearts beating wildly.

Robin stepped back and took Tom's hand. "Come with me."

Robin tried to stay calm when she led Tom into her bedroom, but she was very nervous. Robin wasn't inexperienced. There had been adolescent experimentation with two boys in college, a brief affair with another fighter in her gym when she was competing in the UFC, and a longer affair with a professor at Yale while she was in law school. But Robin had only been in love once, and Tom was the first man she'd been with since Jeff died.

Robin stripped off her clothes and watched Tom as he did the same. He had a runner's slender, muscular body that was so different from Jeff's. Robin moved against Tom and tried to block out thoughts of her lovemaking with Jeff. It was hard at first. Then Tom began to stroke her, and she let her body get lost in the sensations he created.

Robin felt a combination of pleasure and relief as they lay side by side, holding hands.

"Was that okay?" Tom asked when he was breathing normally again.

Robin turned to him and smiled. "It was more than okay."

"Will you promise not to laugh if I tell you something?" Tom asked.

"Cross my heart and hope to die," Robin answered.

"I was scared to death."

Robin burst into laughter, and Tom turned beet red.

"I guess I know who's a big liar," he said.

"I couldn't help it," Robin said. Then she grew serious. "I was terrified too. I haven't made love in . . . well, a while."

Tom turned toward Robin, and they moved against each other. Tom gently stroked Robin's face. "You didn't act like someone who was out of practice."

Robin kissed Tom, and they began to touch each other again.

Their first time had been fueled by adrenaline. This time, they were slower, and Robin felt wonderful when they were done and holding each other.

"I want to stay all night," Tom said, "but we can't risk anyone seeing us together. Will you think I'm awful if I go home?"

Robin smiled. "Nah. You always struck me as a guy who'd take advantage of a girl, then leave her."

Tom smiled. "You found me out. Will you let me take advantage of you again when the *Kerrigan* case is over?"

"I'm a glutton for punishment, so the answer is probably yes."

"Only probably?"

Robin flashed a mischievous grin. "You'll just have to wait and see."

Tom laughed and got out of bed. Then he stopped laughing and looked at Robin. "Thank you for tonight. It was wonderful."

"Ditto," Robin said.

CHAPTER THIRTY-EIGHT

It took a while for Robin to fall asleep after Tom left. Normally, she was off to the gym well before dawn, but the clock on her end table read 7:20 when she opened her eyes. She showered and checked her phone while she ate breakfast. There were texts from Amanda Jaffe and many others asking if she was okay.

Even though she'd skipped her workout at McGill's, she still walked into the offices of Barrister, Berman, and Lockwood much later than usual. It seemed like everyone in the office had heard about the incident at the Jazz Bar. The receptionist and her secretary asked if she was okay, and so did Robin's partner Mark Berman. Robin assured them that she was fine, but this was a half-truth. If she had been honest, she would have said that she felt terrific, only that would have required her to tell everyone how she'd spent the night, which could have had an impact on her ability to represent Mandy Kerrigan.

Mandy Kerrigan wasn't Robin's only client. When Mark left,

Robin hoped that she would be able to start work on an evidence issue in a tax fraud case. She had just turned on her computer when Loretta Washington walked into her office.

"I hope you aren't going to ask me about the shoot-out at the Jazz Bar," Robin said.

"That? No. I figured that you wouldn't be in today if you were dead."

"Then why are you bothering me? I have a ton of work, and I haven't been able to get to it because I've spent every minute since I came to work assuring people that I survived last night in one piece."

"This is about Kerrigan. You know Kim Sperling, right?"

"Yeah. She specializes in probate for the Bauer firm."

"I just found out that Harry Claypool, Margaret Finch's brother, has hired her to get him named as the heir to Margaret's estate."

"That was fast."

"And it's got to move him up a few spots on our list of possible suspects."

"That it does. Now, get lost so I can earn the money that pays your salary."

Robin hoped that she could start working on the tax case, but it was not to be. She had just brought up a Ninth Circuit case that she hoped would solve her problem when her receptionist told her that Alan Chen was in the waiting room.

Robin told her receptionist to bring Chen to her office. Chen's arm was in a sling, and he looked tired.

"How is the bullet wound?" Robin asked when Chen was seated across from her.

"I've had worse, but it's still no fun."

"When did you get out of the hospital?"

"Last night, around midnight. I got a cab home." Chen paused.

He looked sad. "I haven't been home since Kovalev sent his men after me and I had to disappear for a while. The house felt empty without Susan."

"I'm sorry about your wife. I lost my fiancé a few years ago. It was unexpected, and I'm still not over it, so I have some idea of what you're going through. But I don't know why you want to see me."

"I want to thank you for saving my life. Standish would have shot me if you hadn't stopped him."

"I just reacted when I saw him pull out his gun."

"Most people wouldn't have."

"Are you through playing vigilante?"

"Yes. You were right. Killing Kovalev wouldn't have brought Susan back, and it would have let Kovalev off the hook. I'd much rather see him rot in prison."

"Maybe you can help put him there."

"I hope so. Kovalev sent two men to kill Truman Alcott. I saved him and convinced him to tell the police about the auto accident insurance scam. The men are in police custody, so maybe they'll talk."

"Other than thanking me, did you have a reason to see me?"

Chen nodded. "Detective Marx came to the hospital and wanted to talk about what happened at Alcott's house and about two more men who were found in the trunk of a car on a logging road."

"What did you tell him?"

"Nothing. I said my head wasn't clear because of the pain meds I was given and that I wanted to get some legal advice before I saw him."

"Unfortunately, I can't represent you; it would create a possible conflict of interest. I'm representing Mandy Kerrigan, who is charged with killing the Finches. You threatened Margaret Finch on two occasions. I might have to tell the jurors about your threats at the trial in order to raise a reasonable doubt about Mandy's guilt."

Chen looked alarmed. "Are you going to do that? I didn't kill Margaret. I wasn't anywhere near the Finch home when they were killed."

"I believe you, but you can see why I can't be your lawyer."

Chen sighed. "Yeah, I get it."

"I can refer you to several good attorneys who can advise you. Give me a few moments and I'll get you some names and phone numbers. I'll even call the person you select, if you want me to."

"That's kind of you."

Ten minutes later, Chen left. Robin was glad he was okay. She hoped that the lawyer Chen chose would advise him to help Detective Marx put Kovalev and Standish away. They deserved to be locked up forever.

Thinking about Standish brought back Tom's warnings. Robin touched the gun she was carrying. She hoped she would never have to use it, but she knew that she had to be prepared in case Standish came after her.

As soon as Alan Chen left, Robin was able to get to work on the tax case. She ordered some rolls from her favorite sushi bar and ate lunch at her desk. By the time she wrapped up her research, it was after six.

She had left strict instructions that she was not to be disturbed even if the caller was the president offering her a spot on the Supreme Court, so she was not surprised that the red light on her phone was blinking like mad to tell her that she had several voice mail messages.

Robin deleted most of them, but one was from Mandy Kerrigan, asking Robin to visit her at the jail. Robin felt guilty that several days had passed since the last time she had talked to her client. She was too tired to go over this evening, but she vowed to go to the jail first thing in the morning to bring Kerrigan up to date on the investigation and to tell her what would happen once her trial started.

CHAPTER THIRTY-NINE

Mandy Kerrigan had been depressed every time Robin had visited her in the jail, so Robin was shocked when her client entered the contact visiting room with a huge grin on her face and a bounce to her step.

"Is it true?" Kerrigan asked in a rush. "Did you really shoot the head of the Russian mob and beat the shit out of his enforcer in the Jazz Bar?"

Robin sighed. "Where did you hear that?"

"Jungle telegraph, bitch. It's all over the jail. Everyone is talking about it."

"That's not exactly what happened. I did not shoot anyone. Someone else shot Jack Kovalev."

"What about beating up Kovalev's bodyguard? I heard he was a huge motherfucker."

"I did knock out another person who was in the room, but he was not a bodyguard and he was a normal-sized person."

Kerrigan dropped onto the chair on the other side of the table from Robin and leaned forward. "Tell me the gory details."

"I will not. There's an ongoing police investigation, so I can't talk about what happened."

"I can keep a secret."

"So can I, especially when telling you what happened could get me charged with obstruction of justice. So, let's drop this subject and talk about what's going to happen in your case."

Kerrigan leaned back. "You're no fun. I was hoping to get the facts so I could entertain everyone at lunch."

"I'm not talking, so feel free to continue spreading the fake news. Meanwhile, do you want to hear what's happening in the case where the DA is dying to see you get a lethal injection?"

Kerrigan sobered as Robin brought her back to Earth. "How is it looking?" Kerrigan asked.

"Your bio was very helpful. I've hired an investigator to help me work up a witness list for a sentencing-phase hearing. Hopefully, we'll never get there."

"Do you think you can clear me?"

"I can see why they charged you. You beat up Ryan Finch shortly before he was murdered, and you would have had a grudge against Nathan Finch because he made the drugs that got you suspended. Also, a witness saw you at the Finches' front door around the time everyone was killed. And there's something else we need to discuss."

"Oh?" Kerrigan asked.

"The Finches were shot with 9 mm ammunition. That's what a Glock 19 uses."

"So?"

"There was a police report in discovery about a domestic spat you had with a boyfriend. No charges were filed, but the report states that you had a Glock 19 with you."

"I had a license to carry," Kerrigan said, but she sounded defensive. "I was a world champ then, a celebrity. You were in the game. Didn't you have assholes wanting to fight you? I needed it for protection."

"That's not what's troubling me. Do you still have that gun?"

Kerrigan looked down at the tabletop.

"Mandy?"

Kerrigan looked up. "What I tell you, you can't tell anyone else, right?"

Robin looked Kerrigan in the eye. "Yes."

"Even if it's something I did that was stupid?"

"What did you do?"

"When I read about the murders, I . . . Look, I didn't shoot them, but I knew it would look bad if someone saw me at the house, so I got rid of the gun. It's in the Willamette River. I weighted it down. The cops won't be able to find it."

"Shit."

"I swear I didn't kill anyone. You have to believe me."

"You shouldn't have chucked the gun, Mandy. They can do tests to see if it's the murder weapon. Now that it's gone, the DA can tell the jury that you owned the same kind of gun that was used in the murders. If you testify, they can ask you about the gun. You'll have to admit you owned it and got rid of it."

"I didn't think about that."

Robin sighed. "What's done is done."

"Am I going to be convicted?"

"I don't know. The State has a good case. What I don't see, unless I'm missing something, is any evidence that puts you inside the Finches' home. There's no Kerrigan DNA or blood or footprints or fingerprints inside the house. And the police still don't have the murder weapon. So, I'm a little surprised that they didn't investigate more before arresting you. You've read through the copy of the discovery I gave you. Can you think of something they have on you that I've missed?"

"No. Have you found anything that will clear me?"

"We've uncovered a ton of evidence that we can put on to show that you aren't the only person in Oregon who had a motive to kill one or more of the Finches. I can tell you that they are one of the most dysfunctional families I have ever come across."

"What have you got?"

Robin told Kerrigan about Margaret Finch's involvement in the insurance scam and the murders of Otis Truax, the attempted murder of Dr. Alcott, and the disappearance of Dale Gibbs.

"It sounds like Kovalev was getting rid of everyone who could tie him to the insurance scam," Kerrigan said.

"And that would include Margaret Finch."

"What else have you got?"

Robin told Kerrigan about Alan Chen's threats to Margaret Finch, the debt Nathan Finch owed Mario Messina, how Harry Claypool might profit from the death of the Finch family, and the Fabers' lawsuit.

"Isn't there evidence that the killer came through the woods and the back door?" Kerrigan asked.

"Yes."

"There you are! That means anybody could have gotten into the house and killed everyone without being seen."

Robin and Kerrigan talked a little longer. When Robin left the jail, it was with mixed emotions. She was relieved to see that Mandy wasn't depressed, but she would have to think long and hard about putting her client on the stand after hearing what she had done with the gun.

Up until now, Robin had thought that there was a good chance that Kerrigan was innocent. Now she wasn't so sure. And Robin was nagged by the thought that Tom had a surprise he was going to spring that would send Mandy Kerrigan to death row.

CHAPTER FORTY

Harry Claypool was in a terrific mood when he left his lawyer's office. If his probate lawyer knew what she was talking about, his days of living in fleabag hotels and eating meals he could heat on a hot plate would soon be over, and he'd be sleeping in a king-sized bed at a Hilton and dining on the special at Applebee's or Olive Garden.

Mrs. Sperling had told him that he was his sister's next of kin and that Margaret was the only Finch with a next of kin. That meant he'd be inheriting the money, the house, and everything else the Finches owned—the whole enchilada!!! How great was that!!! The only other time he'd felt this high was the day he'd followed a drunk who had won big in a small-town casino to his car in the parking lot. He'd pistol-whipped the dumb bastard, taken his winnings, gone to another casino, and walked out with ten grand. That memory had helped him get through many nights during his four years at the Oregon State Penitentiary.

Claypool's great mood lasted for a period of twenty minutes after he was back in his room at the Excelsior Hotel, where you could pay by the week, the day, or the hour. That's when he answered a knock on his door and found a slender Black man and a large white woman standing in the hall holding warrant cards that identified them as Portland police detectives.

"Mr. Claypool?" the woman said.

"Yes?" Claypool answered warily.

The woman smiled a smile that Harry knew from experience was designed to get him to drop his guard.

"My name is Carrie Anders, and this is my partner, Roger Dillon. We'd like to talk to you."

"About what?"

"Your neighbors might overhear us if we talk out here. Can we step inside?"

Claypool was tempted to say no, but he was curious to find out what the detectives wanted to discuss. "Sure," he said as he stepped aside. "I'm afraid the accommodations ain't the best." He nodded toward Carrie. "You can have the armchair, and there's a chair at the desk. I'll take the bed." When everyone was seated, he asked, "So, how can I help you?"

"First off, let me offer condolences for the loss of your sister."

Claypool knew that he had to act sad, even though Margie had always treated him like something you'd scrape off the bottom of your shoe, so he bowed his head and pretended to choke up.

"I'm gonna miss Margie. She was always there for me, even when no one else was. You know what I mean?"

"We do. It's always tough losing someone you love," Carrie said.

"Amen to that. So, how can I help you?" Claypool asked, tired of the chitchat and anxious to know what the cops wanted.

"How does it feel to be a free man after four years inside?" Roger asked.

Claypool decided that it was best to act humble. "It's a little scary. In prison, you don't have choices. They tell you what to do, and you don't have to worry about room and board. Here in the world, you gotta think for yourself, if you know what I mean. But I'm trying to adjust."

"If what I hear is true, you might not have to worry about paying for food and lodging pretty soon."

"That's true, but it's not the way I'd have wanted to get financial security. Believe me, I'd rather have Margie and her family alive and well."

Roger and Carrie nodded as if they believed Claypool.

"And let me commend you on doing a great job of nailing Margie's killer so fast," Claypool said. "You might think that I distrust the police, being an ex-con and all. But I have great respect for the boys in blue, because they've always treated me with respect, even when they busted me. I mean, you guys have a tough job. So, like I said, how can I help?"

"We do have your sister's killer behind bars, but we want to shore up some gaps in our investigation so there's no wiggle room for the defense."

"Gotcha," Claypool said with a smile. "Ask away."

Roger told Claypool the date and time of the murders. "Do you remember where you were then?"

Claypool pretended to think. "You know," he answered finally, "I'm not really sure. At eight, I was probably back here watching TV."

"Any particular program?" Carrie asked.

"They're all new to me. This place is a dive, but they got cable, so I just channel-surf."

"It sounds like you and your sister were tight," Carrie said.

Claypool held up a hand with his fingers crossed. "We were like this, if you know what I mean." He shook his head. "I really miss her."

"Is there something that happened recently that changed the way you felt about Mrs. Finch?" Carrie asked.

"No. Why?"

"We talked to the receptionist at her firm. She told us that you visited her shortly before she was killed."

"Yeah, I did. I hadn't seen her in years, so I wanted to say hi."

"Didn't she visit you when you were in prison?" Carrie asked.

Claypool shrugged. "She's real busy." He laughed. "I always told her that she works too hard."

"Since you say you got on so well with Mrs. Finch, can you explain why her receptionist told us that she heard you calling your sister a bitch and saw you slam the door to her office when you, and I quote, 'stomped out'?"

"I . . . Uh, no . . . That ain't right."

"Then why did Mrs. Finch tell her receptionist to call security if you showed up again?"

"Okay, what's going on here? Do I need a lawyer? I thought you got Margie's killer, but it sounds like you're trying to pin her murder on me."

"Not at all," Carrie said. "We're just tying up some loose ends."

"Well, not with me you're not. I don't like where this is going, so I'm not answering any more questions without my lawyer."

"Okay, but that suggests that you have something to hide," Carrie said.

Claypool laughed. "You got some nerve trying to con me. I'm not some asshole fresh off the boat. I know all the little tricks you cops use to frame people, and I'm not falling for yours. Plus, I know that you can't ask me any more questions once I ask for a lawyer. Miranda, Miranda, Miranda! So, you can leave now."

The detectives stood up. "We're sorry you feel that way," Roger said.

"Thanks for your time," Carrie said on the way out.

"Motherfucker," Claypool muttered when the detectives were gone, taking his great mood with them. He didn't believe for one moment that those cops were "tying up loose ends." What they were doing was trying to tie a noose around his neck. Their case against that fighter must have been going south, Claypool decided, and they were looking for someone else to fry.

Claypool stood up and paced around his room. "What to do, what to do?" he asked himself, but he couldn't come up with an answer.

PART FIVE

The Door

CHAPTER FORTY-ONE

Robin had mixed feelings when she heard that Harold Wright had been assigned to preside over *State v. Kerrigan.* The judge would run a dignified trial and he would be fair to both sides, but he was so smart that his decisions on legal issues would probably be correct, which meant that Robin would have a limited or nonexistent possibility of getting a guilty verdict reversed on appeal if Mandy Kerrigan was convicted.

A week before the trial was to start, Robin walked into Judge Wright's courtroom. Tom McKee was sitting at one of the counsel tables. Robin hadn't been alone with Tom since the night of the shoot-out at the Jazz Bar, and the only time they had been together was when they had argued pretrial motions in front of Judge Wright in a packed courtroom, where their interactions had been overly polite and formal.

It required a lot of self-control to do no more than nod at Tom when she passed through the bar of the court. Tom nodded back, then looked down at the edited jury questionnaire Judge Wright planned to give to the citizens who had been specially selected for the jury pool in the *Kerrigan* case.

Moments after Robin took her seat, the guards led Mandy Kerrigan to Robin's table.

"How are you getting on in the jail?" Robin asked.

"An idiot tried me out when word got around that I was a professional fighter, but otherwise, no problems."

"How did the fight turn out?"

"Some lucky dentist is going to be paid a lot of money to restore the lady's smile."

Robin laughed. "So, no more challenges?"

"No, and, like I told you, all of the inmates know about the fight at the Jazz Bar and that you're my lawyer. You're a celebrity in there, and that makes me a celebrity too."

"Guilt by association, huh?" Robin said with a smile.

"Something like that. So, what's happening today?" Mandy asked.

"Not a lot. The procedure for picking a jury in every civil and criminal case is called *voir dire*. It's a French term that means 'to see, to say.' On the day of a trial in a normal criminal case, potential jurors are sent to the courtroom where the trial is being held. Then the prosecutor and defense attorney ask each juror questions in front of the other jurors to see if they want to keep a juror or reject her.

"Jury selection in a death case is different. In a death case, there is individual, sequestered voir dire, and the prosecutor and defense attorney question each potential juror out of the presence of the other potential jurors to avoid poisoning the entire jury pool."

"How would that happen?"

"Say you were arrested when you were a juvenile and your record was expunged. That means the judge would bar the DA from telling the jury about it. If a potential juror learned about the arrest from reading an article on the Internet and mentioned it in front of all the other jurors, the panel might have to be dismissed."

"Okay. I get it. Go on."

"The potential jurors in a capital case are summoned to a courtroom several days before the trial and are given a lengthy questionnaire that asks them about their education, military and work histories, the news channels they watch, their views on the death penalty, and other questions, the answers to which will help us decide who we want on the panel. After the questionnaires are filled out, both sides receive a copy.

"Last week, the DA and I submitted proposed questionnaires to Judge Wright. We got his proposed questionnaire on Friday. We're meeting today to ask for deletions or additions."

"Where are the jurors?"

"They're in another room. As soon as we finish, we'll leave, and the judge's clerk will hand out the questionnaires to the people in our specially selected jury pool."

Before Kerrigan could ask any more questions, Judge Wright's bailiff called the court to order, and Judge Wright took the bench. Both attorneys and Mandy Kerrigan stood, and the judge motioned them down. Since no jurors were present, the judge wasn't as formal as he would have been normally.

"So, gang, how upset with me are you?" the judge asked.

"No more than usual, Your Honor," Robin said. "And I have no objection to your revised questionnaire."

Judge Wright smiled. "Mr. McKee?"

"I'd like you to put back my question nineteen."

"The one about whether a professional fighter's hands are deadly weapons?"

"Yes, Your Honor."

"Miss Lockwood?"

"That question might be relevant if the Finches were beaten to death, but they were shot. So, the question isn't relevant to this case, and it's highly prejudicial because it's designed to make Miss Kerrigan seem like some super-dangerous person."

"I agree with Miss Lockwood. At trial, Miss Kerrigan's fighting skills might become relevant, and you can argue whether evidence about them is admissible then. But I'm not putting the question in the jury questionnaire. Anything else, Mr. McKee?"

"That's my only objection."

"Okay, then. I'll have copies made and handed out today, I'll send the completed questionnaires to you, and we'll start selecting a jury on Monday."

Court was dismissed, and the guards took Mandy back to the jail. Robin forced herself to avoid looking at Tom as she packed up. Then she pretended to check her phone to give Tom time to leave. When she was sure that Tom was out of the courtroom, Robin sighed and headed to her office.

CHAPTER FORTY-TWO

A week before Mandy Kerrigan's trial was set to start, Tom McKee sent over another batch of discovery. Robin had assigned Loretta Washington the task of going through it, but Loretta was writing a memo in support of a motion to suppress the statements that Mandy Kerrigan had made at her motel and the police station, which they expected Judge Wright to deny because their client had waived her right to have the advice of counsel and had answered all the detectives' questions voluntarily.

Loretta was also working on jury instructions, memos on some evidence issues that Robin thought might come up in the trial, and other assorted projects, so she didn't start going through the materials until four o'clock, two days before jury selection was going to start.

The techies had finally finished searching Annie Finch's laptop and Tom had sent over a log that indexed what was on the hard drive, and also on its external hard drive.

Loretta had been in the office since seven that morning. The only food she'd eaten all day was a sandwich that she'd wolfed down a little after noon, and she was starving and exhausted. She decided that there was no way she could slog through the new discovery in her condition, so she filled her backpack with it and headed home.

Loretta had met her boyfriend when they clerked for different justices at the Oregon Supreme Court. Sean Gabriel had gotten a job with one of the big civil firms in Portland at the same time Robin had hired Loretta, so they'd moved to Portland together and rented an apartment in an old three-story brick apartment house on a side street a few blocks from Twenty-Third Street Northwest, one of Portland's most vibrant thoroughfares.

Sean was cooking dinner when Loretta dragged herself into the apartment. He looked up from the salad he was creating.

"You look beat," he said.

"That is very perceptive of you."

"Go change, and I'll have dinner on the table when you return."

Loretta carried the discovery materials into the spare bedroom she and Sean used as an office. Then she swapped her dress for pajama bottoms and a T-shirt and splashed water on her face. When she walked into the dining area, there was a glass of wine, a steak, and a Caesar salad waiting for her.

"I knew there was some reason I put up with you," Loretta said as she took a long sip of her wine.

Sean smiled. "You look like you can use a few laughs. There's a comedy on Netflix one of the associates said was good. We can watch it when we finish dinner."

Loretta sighed. "If only I could, but the *Kerrigan* case is starting, and the DA sent over a truckload of discovery. I'll be in the spare bedroom reading a teenage girl's texts while you are chuckling away."

"Can't it wait?"

"It's a death case, Sean."

"You're right. I'll wait until we can watch the movie together."

Loretta topped off her glass of wine and carried it into their makeshift office. She plugged the hard drive into her laptop and found a file with texts Annie had sent to Donna. They were vile. Annie accused Donna of being a slut and a whore, and she taunted her, telling Donna, "He doesn't love you. You're his sex toy" and "He laughs at you and your sick, scrawny body." There were texts that told Donna that she would be better off dead and urged her to kill herself. Other texts suggested that she had engaged in perverted sex acts and that everyone in school knew how sick she was.

By the time she finished reading all the texts, Loretta felt so sorry for Donna. Beth and Steve Reynolds had described Annie as a normal teenage girl up until the end of seventh grade. What had turned her into a monster?

Loretta called Robin. When Robin picked up, Loretta gave her a summary of the texts.

"I'm sorry you had to read that stuff," Robin said.

"They are pretty hard to take. By the time I finished, I felt like I needed to take a bath to wash off the filth."

"So, who was having sex with Donna?" Robin asked.

"Annie never names him, but I'm betting on Annie's brother."

"You think he got her hooked on drugs and used that to get her to have sex with him?"

"Donna's autopsy report said that they didn't find drugs in her system. But Ryan was Donna's basketball coach, which put him in contact with her every day. If Ryan and Donna were in a sexual relationship, that might explain why Annie hated Donna."

"It's a possibility. Thanks for the update."

"I thought you'd want to know."

"See you tomorrow."

Loretta felt depressed as she packed up the discovery. She went into the living room. Sean was curled up on the couch, reading a book. Loretta sat next to Sean and put her arms around him.

"What's up?" Sean asked as he set the book on the coffee table.

"I need a hug really badly," Loretta said.

Sean smiled. "I can do that," he said, and he did.

The hugs led to passionate kisses. Loretta pulled away and tore off her pajama bottoms and T-shirt while Sean stripped. Then Loretta worked off all the bad vibes Annie's texts had created.

"You need to bring home your work more often," Sean joked when he was breathing normally.

Loretta didn't answer. Instead, she wrapped her arms around Sean and rested her head on his chest. While Sean stroked her back, she marveled at the parallel universes she inhabited. There was the now where she loved and was loved and life was fabulous, the way it was supposed to be. And there was her day job, where human beings did the most awful things imaginable to young girls like Donna Faber and slaughtered entire families. She wondered how long she could spend her days in the hell the images of the slaughtered Finch family invoked and the sadness Donna's autopsy photos evoked.

CHAPTER FORTY-THREE

"The West Hills Massacre," as the press kept calling it, had been front-page news since it happened, and almost everyone in the jury pool had heard about the mass murder. Many potential jurors also knew that Mandy Kerrigan, a professional fighter, had been charged with slaughtering a whole family. A smaller number had definite views of Mandy's guilt, and a larger number had negative and positive views on whether it was appropriate for the State to take the life of someone who had butchered an entire family. That was why it took three days to select a jury.

On the morning Robin and Tom were going to make opening statements, Robin dressed in a black pinstripe pants suit, white silk shirt, and comfortable black shoes. The morning was cool, but it wasn't raining, so Robin decided to walk to the courthouse so she could think about her opening statement.

When she left her condo, she noticed a man dressed in jeans and a black sweatshirt with a hoodie standing in a doorway across the street. He didn't make an impression on her, and she forgot about him and became absorbed in working on her opening statement.

The area around the courthouse was busy, and Robin had to wind her way through the pedestrians on their way to work at the courthouse or were going to appear there. When she was a block away, she saw the man in the hoodie again. This time, she thought there was something familiar about him. She stopped and stared. The man pushed back the hoodie. Lloyd Standish's once perfectly straight nose was slightly askew, and a fading black-and-blue hue still rimmed his eyes, reminders of the beating she had given him. Standish locked eyes with her for a moment before disappearing in the crowd.

Robin was surprised to see Standish so near a courthouse. A grand jury had handed down a multicount indictment charging him and Jack Kovalev with crimes ranging from murder to fraud after hearing testimony from Alan Chen, Dr. Alcott, Detective Chet Marx, and others about the auto accident insurance scam, the attacks on Alcott and Chen, the murder of Otis Truax, and the dead men in the trunk of the car that had been abandoned on the logging road.

Jack Kovalev's injuries had been serious, and he was recuperating in a secure wing in the hospital. After being treated by the EMTs at the Jazz Bar, Standish had disappeared, and no one knew where to find him.

Ken Breland was talking to Alan Chen when Robin entered the courthouse lobby.

"Hi, Alan. How are you doing?" Robin asked with real concern.

"I'm getting through each day," Chen answered with a sad smile.

"That's a start. Why are you here? I won't need you until we put on our case. That won't be for several days."

"I just wanted to watch the trial."

"The DA and I haven't asked the court to exclude witnesses, so that will probably be okay."

She turned to Ken. "I just saw Lloyd Standish," she said as the trio took the stairs to Judge Wright's courtroom.

Ken looked alarmed, and Chen turned toward Robin.

"Where did you see him?" Ken asked.

"He was watching my condo when I left for the courthouse. I didn't recognize him because he had a hood covering his face. Then I saw him again a block from here watching me from across the street. He must have followed me. When I stared at him, he flipped back the hood so I'd know who he was. Then he disappeared in the crowd."

"You're packing, right?"

"Always."

"Watch your back. Standish is a dangerous psychopath, and he'll go for you if he thinks he can get away with it."

When they reached the floor where Judge Wright held court, a herd of reporters stampeded toward Robin.

"Ready for your photo op?" Ken asked.

"I've practiced saying 'No comment' all morning."

The reporters attacked. Robin flashed a winning smile at the television cameras and repeated "No comment" ad nauseam as she worked her way toward the door to the courtroom. Mandy's case had received maximum exposure in the media, and the courtroom was packed. Alan Chen found a seat in the back. Ken followed Robin down the aisle toward the bar of the court before taking a seat beside Loretta behind Robin's counsel table, where Amanda Jaffe was waiting.

Amanda's long black hair fell across broad, muscular shoulders that had been formed by years of competitive swimming, which had brought her a college championship and a spot in the Olympic trials. She didn't have the slender figure of a runway model; she had an athlete's body, and her high cheekbones and clear blue eyes attracted male attention whenever she entered a room.

"Welcome to the circus," Amanda said just as the guards led Mandy Kerrigan out of the holding area to the defense table.

Robin had purchased a conservative dress for her client that made her look more like an elementary schoolteacher than a violent cage fighter.

"How are you feeling?" Robin asked as Kerrigan took a seat between her lawyers.

"Pretty nervous."

"If you weren't, I'd be worried," Robin said.

The bailiff rapped his gavel and told everyone to rise as Judge Wright took his seat on the dais. Moments later, twelve jurors and six alternates took their seats.

"Mr. McKee, are you ready to give your opening statement?" the judge asked.

"I am," Tom said. He consulted his notes one last time before walking to the jury box.

"Thank you for taking time from your busy lives to help us decide this very serious matter. The crime the defendant committed was horrific. I apologize in advance for having to show you pictures of the crime scene, but you can't appreciate how awful this crime is unless you see what the evidence will show the defendant did.

"During jury selection, I told you that four people were horribly murdered. Three were adults. They were Margaret Finch, Nathan Finch, and their son, Ryan. One was a fourteen-year-old girl. That's Annie, who was in eighth grade when the defendant snuffed out her life. An entire family wiped off the face of the earth, and the defendant is responsible.

"I'm guessing that you want to know why the State thinks we have found the person who massacred the Finch family, so let me tell you what the evidence will show.

"Mandy Kerrigan is a violent person. I'm not saying this because she is a professional fighter who earns her living practicing one of the most violent of sports, cage fighting. A person can be a professional fighter in the Octagon and a very nice person when they step back into society. We contend that the defendant is violent because shortly before Ryan Finch was murdered, the defendant beat him up in front of witnesses. When you see the crime scene photographs, you will see the results of that beating, which are still visible even though they are several days old.

"Why did the defendant beat up Ryan? We know why. The defendant's last fight was held at the Moda Center. She was a world champion many years ago, but she is at the end of her career now and she needed help to get through that fight. To give herself an edge, the defendant bought illegal performance-enhancing drugs from Ryan Finch, which she thought were untraceable. Then they were discovered when the defendant took a post-fight drug test. The defendant was facing suspension, the forfeiture of her purse, and the possible end of her career. In a rage, she went to the Gaslight, the bar on Naito Parkway where Ryan sold her the illegal drugs. When she found him, she took him into the alley behind the bar and beat the living daylights out of him.

"But that was not enough for the defendant. Shortly after beating Ryan, and still in a rage, she went to Ryan's home, entered it, and slaughtered an entire family.

"The medical examiner will tell you the estimated time of death.

A witness will tell you that she saw the defendant on the Finches' front porch during that time period. Annie's schoolteacher will tell you that he arrived at the house shortly after the defendant was seen leaving the scene of the crime and found the family murdered.

"If you watch television lawyer or cop shows or read mysteries and thrillers, you know that the police move in on a suspect when that suspect has the means, motive, and opportunity to commit a crime.

"Can we prove means? The Finches were shot to death with 9 mm ammunition. That's the kind of ammunition a Glock 19 uses. To date, we haven't found the murder weapon. But it's easy to get rid of a gun, and the defendant was not arrested until a day after the murders. More important, you are going to learn that the defendant had a permit to carry a Glock 19. The gun was not found during a search of the defendant's motel room and car.

"The judge will tell you that we don't have to prove a defendant's motive. In this case, it is easy to prove. The defendant hated Ryan Finch because she believed that he sold her drugs that Nathan Finch made that were responsible for destroying her career.

"What was her motive to kill the rest of the Finch family? That's easy. They were witnesses who could tell the police who had murdered Ryan Finch.

"Finally, there is plenty of evidence of opportunity. The defendant was at the Finch house at the time the medical examiner will testify they were murdered.

"So, that's a preview of our case, and I believe that when you have heard all the evidence, you will not have any doubt that Mandy Kerrigan is a quadruple murderer. Thank you."

Amanda leaned over and whispered to Robin, "I don't get it. I've read through the discovery, and the case is very skinny. There's no gun, no evidence Mandy was inside the house. How did they get an indictment?"

"I'm with you. Since I got the case, I've had this uneasy feeling that I'm missing something. I just don't know what it is."

"Miss Lockwood," Judge Wright said.

"Thank you, Your Honor," Robin said as she stood and walked toward the jurors.

"After all the evidence is in, Judge Wright will read instructions to you that will explain the law and how you have to apply it in this case. One of the most important things the judge will explain is the burden that the State must meet before you can find Mandy Kerrigan guilty. He will tell you that the State has the burden of convincing you beyond a reasonable doubt that Miss Kerrigan committed these murders.

"What does that mean? There are two big differences between the way you make a decision in a criminal case and the way you make a decision in day-to-day life. If you and I were arguing to one of our friends about whether the Trail Blazers are better than the Lakers, our friend wouldn't start listening with a presumption that one of us was one hundred percent correct and the other person was one hundred percent wrong.

"Now, after you and I told our friend about our teams' win-loss record, team stats, and individual stars, the friend we were trying to convince would vote for one side or the other if he or she was convinced fifty-one percent to forty-nine percent by one of us.

"The judge is going to tell you that in all criminal cases, the accused person is presumed to be innocent. So, right now, you have to start the trial believing that the police made a mistake when they arrested Mandy Kerrigan.

"So, here's the first difference between a debate over which is the better team, the Blazers or the Lakers, and a trial for murder. In a criminal case, the burden of proving that Miss Kerrigan committed these murders is one hundred percent on the State. That makes sense. If the police accused you of robbing me, wouldn't you expect them to bear the complete burden of convincing a judge that was true, especially if you didn't know anything about the robbery? During this trial, Miss Kerrigan and I could go to a movie and just come back for the verdict, because we don't have any duty to cross-examine witnesses or produce evidence or do anything, period. The burden of proof is on the State one hundred percent.

"Here's the second difference. To get a guilty verdict, the State has to do more than convince you fifty-one percent to forty-nine percent that Miss Kerrigan is guilty. Their burden is incredibly high.

"You've heard the term 'beyond a reasonable doubt.' What does that mean? Let's say that at the end of this case, in your heart, emotionally, you feel Miss Kerrigan is guilty, and in your head, unemotionally using logic, you think she committed these crimes, but one single piece of evidence—a photograph, a single sentence a police officer said, some little thing—makes you doubt her guilt, and this doubt is not silly, like Martians used a death ray to commit the crime, but it is a doubt based on reason and evidence. In that case, no matter what your heart and your brain tell you, it is your patriotic duty as a citizen of the United States to vote to acquit.

"Why do we place such a high standard on the State? What is the worst, most horrible thing that you can do? I will tell you. The most horrible result at the end of this trial would be sending an innocent woman to prison or death row.

"In this country, we believe that it is far better for the guilty to go free than to send one innocent person to prison. How do you feel when you pick up the newspaper and learn that an innocent person who has been locked up in prison for twenty years has just been set free when it was learned that someone else had committed the crime for which she was sent to jail? Believe me, you don't want to be a member of a jury who is responsible for sentencing an innocent woman to prison or death.

"What will the evidence show? The State will be able to prove that Miss Kerrigan did hate Ryan Finch and did beat him up. They will be able to show that she was at the Finch house around the time of the murders. What they will not be able to prove beyond a reasonable doubt is that she was ever inside that house. There is no DNA, fingerprints, footprints, or blood belonging to Mandy Kerrigan inside the Finch home. What's more, when the police searched the motel room where Miss Kerrigan was staying and searched her car, they did not find anything connecting her to these murders.

"Now, there is something else Mr. McKee did not tell you in his opening statement. Other people had a motive to murder members of the Finch family. Margaret Finch was a criminal defense lawyer, and one of her clients was Jack Kovalev, whom the police believe is the head of the Russian mob in Oregon. Mr. Kovalev was engaged in fraud. He would pay a driver to drive into the car of an innocent person, then the criminal driver would claim to be injured. Mrs. Finch would represent the driver and send him to Dr. Truman Alcott, who would write a report stating that the driver had suffered injuries, even if he had not. Dale Gibbs, an insurance agent who was on the take, would process the claim and authorize payment to the driver. All or most of the payment would go to Kovalev.

"This scam was very successful until a driver named Otis Truax killed Susan Chen, an innocent woman, during one of these staged accidents. Truax was arrested and charged with manslaughter. Mrs. Finch represented him. The district attorney offered Truax a deal if he would testify against Kovalev. Next thing you know, Truax is tortured and murdered. Then Dale Gibbs disappears, and two men who are part of Kovalev's criminal organization tried to murder Dr. Alcott. Who is left who can expose Kovalev's scheme? That's right. Is it any surprise that Margaret Finch was murdered and her family, who witnessed her murder, were killed?

"Then there is Harry Claypool, a man who was recently released from the Oregon State Penitentiary where he was serving time for armed robbery. The Finch children have no heirs, Nathan Finch has no next of kin. Who does? Margaret Finch. Who inherits everything now that the Finch family is dead? Mrs. Finch's brother, the ex-convict Harry Claypool.

"Then there is Nathan Finch, who is addicted to gambling and owes money to a bookmaker whom he can't pay because he was recently fired from his job at King Pharmaceuticals for stealing money to pay his gambling debts.

"Mr. McKee has made a big deal out of the fact that Miss Kerrigan was seen on the Finches' front porch. What he didn't mention is the fact that there is evidence that the real killer came through the woods at the back of the Finch home and entered the house through the back door.

"I'm going to sit down now so you can hear the evidence. Thanks for serving on Miss Kerrigan's jury. She's counting on you to be fair and impartial. If you are, when all the evidence is in, you'll see that the State has not met its burden of proving that she is a murderer beyond a reasonable doubt."

Judge Wright waited until Robin was seated at the defense counsel table before calling a recess. Everyone stood. As soon as the judge left the courtroom, Amanda turned to Robin.

"Nicely done," Amanda said.

"Thanks," Robin said, but she thought that Tom had done a good job too.

"What happens now?" Kerrigan asked.

"The State puts on its case, the DA will ask his witnesses questions that will make you look bad, but I get to cross-examine those witnesses, and I'm hopeful that we can use those answers to clear your name."

CHAPTER FORTY-FOUR

The guards took Mandy back to the holding area so she could use the restroom. Amanda, Loretta, and Ken gave their thoughts about the opening statements. Robin stayed in the courtroom because she didn't want to have to answer the questions that the reporters would shout at her if she went into the hall. She also needed to review the questions she would ask the State's witnesses when it was her chance to examine them.

Tom McKee was reviewing his notes too, and Robin forced herself to keep her eyes on her trial book and not let them wander toward her opposing counsel.

Fifteen minutes after Judge Wright called a recess, the participants and spectators drifted back to their seats.

"The State calls Clayton Morehead," Tom McKee said when court reconvened.

Moments later, a slender, balding man with bifocals and a full beard walked to the witness stand and was sworn.

"Mr. Morehead, who employs you?"

"I am employed by the United States Anti-Doping Agency, a nonprofit and nongovernment program that controls the drug-testing programs for the United States Olympic team."

"Do you also have a relationship with the Ultimate Fighting Championship, which is popularly known as the UFC?"

"Yes."

"Do you conduct post-fight tests to determine if a fighter in a UFC match has used performance-enhancing drugs?"

"Yes."

"What happens if you determine that a fighter has violated the anti-doping policy?"

"The fighter is suspended."

"In other words, they cannot fight in a UFC event?"

"Yes."

"How long is the suspension?"

"It varies. It can be months or years."

"Did your organization test the defendant, Mandy Kerrigan, after her recent fight at the Moda Center with Kerrie Clark?"

"Yes."

"What was the result?"

"We determined that she had used a drug that was designed to enhance her performance in violation of our guidelines."

"Was the defendant told the result of the test and the consequences of cheating?"

"Yes."

"So, she knew that she would not be able to earn a living in her chosen profession for the length of the suspension?"

"Yes."

"No further questions, Your Honor."

"Miss Lockwood?"

"No questions."

"The State calls Brenda Fairmont," McKee told the judge as soon as Clayton Morehead left the witness stand. A woman in her twenties walked toward the bar of the court.

"Who is she?" Mandy Kerrigan asked.

"She was in the alley behind the Gaslight when you beat up Ryan Finch. So are the next two witnesses Mr. McKee is going to call. Then he's going to call the police officers who came to the alley in response to the 911 call."

"Miss Fairmont, were you at the Gaslight with friends on the evening that an incident occurred in the alley behind the tavern?" McKee asked.

"Yes."

"Did you witness that incident?"

"Yes."

"Can you tell the jury what you saw?"

Fairmont gave the jurors a blow-by-blow description of the beating that Kerrigan had administered. Then she told them that her friends had pulled Kerrigan off Finch.

"Did the defendant say anything that let you know why she was mad at Ryan Finch?"

"Yes."

"What did you hear her say?"

"I don't remember the exact words, but she said something about being suspended and not paid because he'd sold her PEDs and they'd showed up in a test."

"Did someone call 911?"

"I did."

"Did two police officers respond to your call?"

"Yes."

"How did Mr. Finch look after he was beaten?"

"Not good. There was blood all over his face, and his nose might have been broken."

"Thank you. No further questions."

"Miss Lockwood?" Judge Wright said.

"Thank you, Your Honor. I just have one question for you, Miss Fairmont. Was Miss Kerrigan wearing gloves when she struck Mr. Finch?"

Fairmont thought for a moment. Then she nodded. "I think she was."

"And there was blood on Ryan Finch's face when she hit him?"

"Yes."

"No further questions."

The next witnesses that Tom called were the men who had pulled Kerrigan off Ryan Finch and the officers who responded to the 911 call. Except for eliciting the fact that Ryan Finch had not pressed charges, Robin asked no questions.

Tom McKee followed the testimony of the witnesses to the incident at the Gaslight with the testimony of the first responder to the Finch home. Then he called Sally Grace, the medical examiner, who testified that the four members of the Finch family had been shot to death with 9 mm ammunition. After Dr. Grace testified, a forensic expert from the crime lab showed the jury photographs of the crime scene and testified that Mandy Kerrigan's fingerprints had been lifted from the knob of the Finches' front door. He also testified that a Glock 19 used 9 mm ammunition.

During her cross-examination, Robin brought out the fact that the lab had not discovered any trace evidence like DNA, blood, fingerprints, or footprints belonging to Mandy Kerrigan inside the

Finch home. She also introduced photographs of the damaged back door.

"It's almost noon," Judge Wright said. "I have a few matters in other cases on my docket for one. Let's take our lunch break and reconvene at two."

Robin waited for the courtroom to empty. Then she, surrounded by Ken, Loretta, and Amanda, powered through the reporters and headed to Barrister, Berman, and Lockwood. Sandwiches and drinks awaited them in the conference room so they could chow down while they did a postmortem on the morning session. During the walk to her office and the return trip to the courthouse, Robin searched the crowds on the street for Lloyd Standish.

CHAPTER FORTY-FIVE

"The State calls Megan Radcliffe," Tom McKee said.

Mrs. Radcliffe looked nervous when she walked through the bar of the court, and she stared straight ahead so she would not have to look at Mandy Kerrigan.

"Mrs. Radcliffe, do you live across the street from the Finch home?" the DA asked when Mrs. Radcliffe was sworn and had taken her seat in the witness-box.

"Yes."

McKee pointed at Mandy Kerrigan. "Have you ever seen the defendant at the Finch home?"

Radcliffe's hands were clasped in her lap in a death grip, and she looked frightened when she turned her head toward the defense table. She looked at Kerrigan for a moment before looking away quickly. Her voice shook when she answered.

"Yes."

"Please tell the members of the jury when you saw the defendant at the Finch home and what she was doing when you saw her."

"It was the night that they—the Finches—when they were killed. I was going to watch a show on my television, and I wanted to get a snack. I walked to the kitchen."

"About what time was this?" McKee asked.

"It must have been around seven fifty, because the show hadn't started."

"Okay. Go ahead."

"On the way to the kitchen, I looked out a window and saw her, the . . . the defendant."

"Where was she?"

"She was standing in front of the Finches' front door."

"What was the defendant doing?"

"She was yelling something. I couldn't hear the words. And she was pounding on the front door."

"What did you do next?"

"I went into the kitchen and fixed a snack. Then I went back to the living room."

"What time was this?" Tom asked.

"I'd taped my show so I wouldn't miss any of it. It started at eight. I'm guessing I walked back to the living room somewhere between eight oh five and eight ten. I can't be sure of the exact time."

"Did you see the defendant again?"

"Yes. She walked down to the sidewalk and left."

"Did you get a good look at her?"

"Yes. There's a streetlight, and she was under it long enough for me to see her."

"While you were watching your show, did you look out the living room window?"

"Yes."

"About what time was this?"

"Eight fifteen. Eight twenty. I'm not sure."

"Did you see anyone at the Finch house?"

"No."

"Did anything else happen at the Finch house shortly after?"

"Yes. My show ended at eight thirty. Just around the time it ended, I heard a car driving up across the street. So, because of what I saw before, I looked out the window to see if the woman, the defendant, had come back."

"What did you see?"

"A man got out of his car and went to the front door of the Finches' house."

"Did you recognize this man?"

"Yes. My boys went to Marie Curie Middle School, and the man was Arthur Proctor, who taught them English."

"What did you see?"

"It looked like he rang the bell. Then he went inside. Shortly after, Mr. Proctor came running out. He left the front door wide open, and he looked very upset. I walked across the street. He was calling 911, and he told me to go back to my house. I did. Shortly after, police cars drove up to the Finch home."

"Thank you, Mrs. Radcliffe. Your witness, Miss Lockwood."

"You said that Miss Kerrigan was standing at the front door of the Finch home."

"Yes."

"Did you ever see her go into the Finch home?"

"No."

"Did you ever see her walk out of the Finch home?"

"No."

"Did Miss Kerrigan appear to be frustrated?"

"Objection," McKee said. "The witness would have no way to determine the defendant's emotional state."

"Sustained. Don't answer that question, Mrs. Radcliffe."

Robin had a whispered conversation with Amanda. Then she told the judge that she had no further questions.

"Mrs. Radcliffe, you only saw the defendant outside the front door?" the prosecutor asked.

"Yes."

"So, you don't know where she was before you saw her?"

"No."

"She could have been inside the Finch home?"

"Objection," Robin said. "Calls for speculation."

"I agree," Judge Wright said. "Sustained."

"No further questions. If Miss Lockwood has none, the State will call Arthur Proctor."

When Annie's teacher sat in the witness box, he looked grim.

"Mr. Proctor, what do you do for a living?" McKee asked.

"I am an English teacher at Marie Curie Middle School in Portland."

"Was Annie Finch one of your students?"

"Yes."

"Did you go to the Finch home on the night the Finch family was murdered?"

"Yes."

"Why did you go to their home?"

"Annie had been an excellent student when she was in my seventh-grade class, and I had her again in eighth grade in my honors English class. She was still doing well in my class, but her grades in her other classes had dropped precipitously, and she was truant a few times. She also seemed depressed or angry. It was obvious to me that she was having emotional problems, and there were conflicts with other students.

"I scheduled a parent-teacher conference with Mr. and Mrs. Finch, and I suggested that they think about taking her out of Marie Curie and placing her in a private school. I thought a change of scenery might solve some of her problems. Mrs. Finch seemed willing to consider the idea, but Mr. Finch was worried about the cost of a private school. They can be very spendy. I did some research, and I found out that there might be several ways to alleviate the pressure of paying for a private school, so I arranged to go over to the house that night to discuss what I'd found."

"What time did you arrive at the Finch home?"

"I don't have an exact time, but it was around eight thirty because the news had just started when I parked, and it starts on the half hour."

"Did you see anyone else near the Finches' house or on the street?"

"No."

"Did you go to the front door?"

"Yes."

"What did you do?"

"I rang the doorbell. No one came to let me in. I could hear a television. It was very loud. I thought it was possible that they couldn't hear me over the noise, so I rang again. When no one answered the bell, I tried the door. It was open, and I walked in."

"What did you see?"

Proctor took a deep breath. He didn't answer right away.

"Mr. Proctor?" Judge Wright said.

"I'm sorry, Your Honor. I find this difficult."

"Do you want some water?"

"Please."

The bailiff handed Proctor a glass, and he took a sip. Then Proctor returned his attention to Tom McKee.

"Annie was sprawled at the foot of the stairs, and her parents . . ." Proctor took another sip of water. "They were all covered in blood. I ran out of the house and called the police."

"Did the police arrive?"

"Shortly after I called."

"No further questions."

"Miss Lockwood?" Judge Wright said.

"Mr. Proctor, you testified that Annie Finch had conflicts with other Marie Curie students."

"Yes."

"Were you acquainted with another Marie Curie student, named Donna Faber?"

Proctor sighed and nodded.

"You have to answer *yes* or *no* so the court reporter can hear your answer," Judge Wright said.

"Sorry. Yes, I knew Donna."

"Was she in your class?"

"No. I'm also in charge of the drama club. We put on the school play, and Donna had a part in it."

"Donna Faber is dead, isn't she?"

"Yes," Proctor answered, his voice barely above a whisper.

"Was she the victim of cyberbullying?"

"Yes."

"Annie Finch started an online campaign of harassment against Donna, didn't she?"

"Yes."

"Did she tell Donna to kill herself?"

"That's what I've been told."

"Did Donna die by suicide?"

"Yes."

"Did Donna Faber's parents accuse Annie Finch of being responsible for the death of their daughter?"

"Yes."

"Did they file a lawsuit that named the Finch family and ask for damages in the millions of dollars?"

"I believe so."

"No further questions."

"The State calls Roger Dillon, Your Honor," said Tom.

Roger was sworn and took the witness stand.

"Mr. Dillon, how are you employed?"

"I'm a detective in the Portland Police Bureau."

"What unit are you in?"

"Homicide."

"Were you and your partner, Carrie Anders, given the responsibility of finding out who murdered the members of the Finch family?"

"Yes."

"At some point, did your investigation begin to focus on Mandy Kerrigan?"

"She became a person of interest fairly quickly."

"Why was that?"

"While we were at the crime scene, we learned that Miss Kerrigan had assaulted Ryan Finch, one of the victims, shortly before he was murdered. Then we interviewed Megan Radcliffe, who lives across the street from the Finches. She told us that she had seen the defendant at the Finches' front door shortly before Arthur Proctor discovered that the family had been murdered."

"What did you and Detective Anders do after receiving this information?"

"We learned that the defendant was staying at the Paris Motel and obtained a warrant to search her room and car."

"Did you go to the motel?"

"Yes."

"Tell the jury what happened when you got there."

The detective turned to the jurors and made eye contact with them, shifting from one juror to another as he related what happened at the motel.

"Miss Kerrigan opened the door when we knocked and invited us in."

"Did she ask to see your warrant?"

"No. She showed us the front page of a newspaper with a headline about what the press was calling 'The West Hills Massacre.' Then she said that she knew we would come for her because she had beaten up Ryan Finch and had been at the Finch house."

"Did you ask her if she murdered the Finches?"

"I did."

"What did she say?"

"The defendant admitted being at the house. She said that she rang the bell and knocked, but no one answered the door. She told us that she could hear a television with the volume turned up and decided that the Finches could not hear her, or Ryan had seen her and had told his parents that they should not answer the door. She said that she tried the door, but it was locked, so she left."

"What did you do next?"

"We were talking to the defendant on the landing outside her room so the room could be searched. It was cold, so we asked her if she would accompany us to the station, where it would be warmer."

"How did she respond to that suggestion?"

"She agreed to go. She said that she was bored sitting in her room."

"Did you continue questioning the defendant at the police station?"

"We did."

"What did you do when you concluded the questioning?"

"We arrested Miss Kerrigan."

"At some point, did you learn that the Finches had probably been killed with 9 mm bullets fired from a Glock 19?"

"Yes."

"Did you also learn that the defendant had owned a Glock 19?"

"Yes."

"Did you find the defendant's weapon?"

"No."

"Your witness, Miss Lockwood," Tom McKee said.

"Who is Jack Kovalev, Detective?"

"I'm not certain I understand the question."

"Let me make it easy for you. Is Jack Kovalev rumored to be the head of the Russian Mafia in Oregon?"

"He is involved in criminal activities."

"Hasn't he just been indicted for crimes ranging from murder to fraud?"

"Yes."

"Let's talk about the fraud case. Isn't it true that Mr. Kovalev has been charged with engineering a case of insurance fraud that involves hiring people to stage auto accidents?"

"Yes."

"Isn't it true that Margaret Finch represented members of Mr. Kovalev's crime family who were charged with crimes?"

"Yes."

"Did she also represent the people who staged these auto crashes when they sued an insurance company where a man named Dale Gibbs worked?"

"Yes."

"Did she refer these plaintiffs to a doctor named Truman Alcott?"

"Yes."

"Did Mr. Alcott write reports that stated that these plaintiffs had sustained injuries, even when they had no injuries?"

"Yes."

"Did Mr. Gibbs settle these claims based on the doctor's report?"

"Yes."

"Was Mr. Gibbs part of Mr. Kovalev's scam?"

"Yes."

"Did one of the staged accidents go horribly wrong when a man named Otis Truax rammed a car driven by Susan Chen and killed her?"

"Yes."

"Was Mr. Truax charged with manslaughter?"

"Yes."

"Did Mrs. Finch represent him?"

"Yes."

"Did the authorities offer Mr. Truax a deal after he was arrested that involved testifying against Mr. Kovalev and other members of his gang?"

"Yes."

"Was Mr. Truax tortured and murdered shortly after being released from jail on bail?"

"Yes."

"Has Dale Gibbs disappeared?"

"Yes."

"Did two men connected to the Kovalev crime organization try to murder Dr. Alcott?"

"Yes."

"Doesn't it appear that anyone who could connect Mr. Kovalev to this insurance scam is either dead, missing, or had an attempt on his life?"

"It would appear so."

"And now Margaret Finch is dead?"

"Yes."

"During your investigation, did you learn that Nathan Finch had a gambling addiction and owed money to an individual who ran an illegal bookmaking operation?"

"Yes."

"And you also learned that the family of Donna Faber was suing the Finch family because they believed that Annie Finch was responsible for their daughter's suicide?"

"Yes."

"Who inherits everything the Finches own?"

"Harry Claypool."

"Is he an ex-convict who was just released from prison, where he was serving a term for armed robbery?"

"Yes."

"Does he have an alibi for the time of the murders?"

"No."

"Detective Dillon, you examined the crime scene—the Finch home—didn't you?"

"Yes."

"Did you find evidence that suggests that the person who

murdered the Finch family broke out a pane of glass in the door at the back of the house that opens into the kitchen and entered the house through that door?"

"You could draw that conclusion."

"Isn't a section of Portland's urban forest right behind the Finch home and accessible through a gate?"

"Yes."

"So, their killer could have entered the forest through many trails, walked through the Finches' backyard, entered the house through the kitchen door, and committed the murders?"

"That's a possibility."

"Nothing was discovered connecting Miss Kerrigan to these murders during the search of her motel room and car, was there?"

"No."

"Did you ask Miss Kerrigan if she murdered the Finches?"

"Yes."

"What did she answer?"

"She said that she did not kill anyone."

"No further questions."

"Mr. McKee?" Judge Wright asked.

"Let's start with Nathan Finch. He had gambling debts. During your investigation, did you learn who his bookmaker was?"

"Yes."

"Did you find any evidence whatsoever that placed this person or anyone who worked for him at or near the Finch home at the time of the murders?"

"No. In fact, this person had several witnesses who placed him in a location far from the crime scene at the time of the killings, and, if he killed Mr. Finch, he wouldn't be able to get the money Finch owed him."

"Did the defendant have a motive to murder Nathan Finch?"

"Yes. He made the drugs that Ryan Finch sold her."

"Miss Lockwood spent a lot of time talking about Jack Kovalev and the insurance scam. She has implied that Mr. Kovalev had Mrs. Finch murdered because she could testify about the insurance scheme. Was Mrs. Finch the attorney who represented members of Mr. Kovalev's organization?"

"Yes."

"Had she been the organization's lawyer for a long time?"

"Almost ten years."

"So, presumably, she would know a lot of things that could incriminate Mr. Kovalev?"

"Probably."

"There is something called the attorney-client privilege, isn't there?"

"Yes."

"Doesn't that privilege make it impossible for an attorney to tell the police what a client like Mr. Kovalev, or anyone who works for him who was a client, told Mrs. Finch about crimes they have committed?"

"Yes."

"To your knowledge, during the ten years that Mrs. Finch presumably learned Mr. Kovalev's deepest and darkest secrets, has he ever tried to have her killed?"

"No."

"Have you discovered any evidence that Mr. Kovalev or anyone connected to him was anywhere near the Finch house when they were murdered?"

"No."

"What about the Fabers? Have you discovered any evidence that places them at the crime scene?"

"No, and they can prove that they were at a friend's house when the murders were committed."

"Which leaves us with the defendant, who was at the house when the Finches were killed, and had the motive to murder them. Nothing further, Your Honor."

"Any recross, Miss Lockwood?"

"No, Your Honor."

"Any other witnesses, Mr. McKee?"

"No, Your Honor. And the State rests."

"Then I think that this is a good time to adjourn for the day. Members of the jury, you can go home, but I don't want you reading anything about this case in the papers or the Internet, and you are forbidden to watch any news programs. Family and friends may ask you about the case. You must tell them that you can't discuss it until it has concluded."

When the jurors were gone, Judge Wright turned to Robin. "I assume you'll have motions you want to make. Let's take them up tomorrow."

The judge left the bench. Tom McKee made a brief statement to the reporters who were waiting in the corridor outside the courtroom before he returned to the district attorney's office. Robin talked to her client before the guards took her back to jail. Then she dealt with the reporters before she, Amanda, Ken, and Loretta left the courthouse.

"I think we got our ass kicked," Robin said when they were away from anyone who might overhear her. "What do you think?"

"McKee's cross of Roger killed us," Amanda agreed.

"Anything to add?" Robin asked Ken and Loretta.

"I agree with the ass-kicking comment," Loretta said.

Ken just shook his head.

"Are you going to put Mandy on the stand?" Loretta asked.

"I think that's a bad idea," Amanda said. "My rule is that you never put your client on if the case is going well or they have nothing to add, especially if you don't think they'll hold up well on cross."

"I agree," Robin said. "I only have a client testify if there is some piece of evidence that will kill us and the client can counter it. And Tom will grill her about the missing Glock on cross."

"Don't put her on," Ken said.

"So, what do we do?" Robin asked. "Do we have any witnesses who will help?"

"We can put Dr. Alcott on to beef up your argument that Kovalev had Margaret murdered," Ken said.

"You can argue that Kovalev's men came through the forest," Loretta said.

Robin sighed. "I guess that's better than nothing."

"Don't get discouraged," Amanda said. "McKee's case against Mandy is still thin."

"Yeah, but it's a better case than anything we can argue to the jury."

The discussion continued at Robin's office for a while, but everyone was tired, and Robin sent everyone home when it was clear that nothing was going to be accomplished without a good night's sleep.

Robin knew that Judge Wright would deny the motion for a judgment of acquittal she would make in the morning, but she had to make her record for an appeal in case Mandy was convicted. When she finished working on the motion, she left the office.

When she was in trial, adrenaline kept her going, but the effects wore off as soon as she left the courtroom. By the time she walked into her condo, she had trouble keeping her eyes open. She changed into a T-shirt and sweatpants, threw some rigatoni into a pot of boiling water, and covered it in the remains of a jar of marinara sauce she found in her refrigerator. She ate her meal without tasting a thing and tried to distract herself by watching a Trail Blazers game. At nine, she was overwhelmed by exhaustion. She switched off the set and crawled into bed, where she fell into a deep sleep.

CHAPTER FORTY-SIX

The next morning, Robin made her motion for a judgment of acquittal, which she delivered quickly and halfheartedly. To grant the motion, which would have led to a dismissal of the charges, Robin had to convince Judge Wright that taking the evidence in the light most favorable to the State, no reasonable juror could vote for conviction. As expected, the judge denied the motion and asked Robin if she was prepared to present the defense case.

Robin called Ken Breland as her witness. Ken played and narrated a video that showed the jurors the damage to the kitchen door, the path through the Finches' backyard that led to the forest behind the house, and traced the path along several trails that a person could take that ended in streets that bordered the urban forest.

Dr. Alcott was Robin's next witness. The doctor was living at a safe house and was brought into court with a plainclothes police escort. He told the jurors how the insurance scam worked, his, Margaret Finch's, and Dale Gibbs's parts in it, and concluded his testimony with an account of the attempt on his life and Alan Chen's rescue. When Tom said that he had no questions, Robin asked for a few minutes to confer with her client and cocounsel.

"We have to decide whether to put you on or rest," Robin told her client. "I don't want to give the DA an opportunity to cross-examine you about the gun. Plus, there's nothing you can say other than that you didn't kill the Finches. What do you think, Amanda?"

"I agree. Let's rest."

Kerrigan looked conflicted. "We haven't done much in our case," she said. "Maybe I can convince the jurors that I didn't do it."

"If you testify, you will have to tell the jury that you got rid of the gun, and that would be the nail in your coffin."

Kerrigan thought for a minute. Then she nodded. "Okay. If you think it's best, you can rest."

Judge Wright told the jurors that the presentation of evidence was over and it was time for the attorneys to make their closing arguments. Tom McKee checked his notes one last time. Then he walked to the jury box.

"I want to thank you again for taking time from your busy lives to help us decide this extremely serious matter. I am going to take this opportunity to explain why the defendant is guilty beyond a reasonable doubt of murdering three adults and a young girl at the beginning of her life.

"Did the defendant have a motive to kill one or more of the Finches? I think that has been established beyond any doubt. Nathan Finch had been fired from his job at King Pharmaceuticals because he had a gambling habit. He owed money to the people with whom he placed bets, and he had no income. So, he brewed up designer drugs in his basement that Ryan Finch sold.

"Some of these drugs were PEDs, or drugs designed to enhance athletic performance. The defendant purchased PEDs from Ryan, after being assured that they could not be detected in a post-fight drug test. When they were detected, the defendant's purse was held up, and her career was put in jeopardy. That provided her motive to kill Ryan and Nathan Finch.

"Means? The Finches were killed with 9 mm rounds. A Glock 19 fires 9 mm ammunition. The defendant owned a Glock 19. Where is it? Probably someplace she put it.

"Opportunity? Dr. Sally Grace, the medical examiner, told you that the Finches were murdered around eight o'clock. Megan Radcliffe told you that the defendant was on the porch of the Finch home during the time period when the Finches were murdered.

"Now, the defense will argue that there is no evidence that Mandy Kerrigan was inside the Finch home, but Miss Kerrigan made a fatal slip when she was questioned by Detectives Dillon and Anders, and her own words are going to convince you that she is guilty beyond a reasonable doubt."

Robin felt like she was going to throw up. There was something she'd missed, and Tom McKee was going to tell her what it was.

"The defendant is seen on the Finches' porch at a little before eight o'clock. The TV is blaring. She tells the detectives that she rang the bell and knocked but no one came to the door, so she tried the door. It was locked, and she left."

McKee paused and looked at the jurors.

"Let's see if her story holds up. It's eight oh five. Megan Radcliffe returns to her living room to watch her show. As she passes the window that gives her a view of the Finch home, she sees the defendant leaving the Finch home and walking away from it.

"Now it is around eight fifteen. Megan Radcliffe looks out her living room window and across the street. There is no one in front of the Finches' front door.

"Let's fast-forward to eight thirty. Arthur Proctor arrives to talk to the Finches about a private school scholarship for Annie. He doesn't see anyone near the Finch house or on the street. The TV is still blaring. We can guess that the killer turned up the set to cover the sound of the screams and shots, so the Finches were probably all dead at eight oh five.

"Mr. Proctor knocks and rings the bell. What does he do when no one answers? That's right. He opens the front door and goes inside the house."

McKee paused again.

"Ladies and gentlemen, the defendant lied when she said that she couldn't go into the Finches' house because the door was locked. We know that the Finches' front door was open at eight thirty; no one was at the Finches' front door between eight oh five and eight fifteen. Who opened the door? If the Finches were dead, they could not open the front door. If they were alive, someone would have to have appeared magically between eight fifteen and eight thirty, got the Finches to open the door, killed them, and left. All in fifteen minutes. It is highly, highly unlikely that happened.

"Do you have any doubt that the defendant lied when she said that she could not enter the Finch home at eight o'clock because the door was locked? The door was not locked when she said it was. Why would she lie? Because she went into the Finch home and murdered four innocent people. Thank you."

Robin's face did not display any of the turmoil she was experiencing, because trial lawyers learn to mask their emotions. A witness can die on the stand and a good trial lawyer won't blink.

The judge asked Robin if she was ready to make her argument. She asked for a brief recess. As soon as it was granted, Robin, Kerrigan, Loretta, Amanda, and Ken formed a huddle.

"I didn't see that coming," Loretta said.

"None of us did," Robin said.

"The door was locked!" Kerrigan insisted.

"Do you have any idea who opened it?" Robin asked.

"No."

"How do we counter McKee's argument?" Robin asked.

"The killer came in the kitchen door," Loretta said.

"What do we say when Tom argues that it was Mandy who came through the back door?" Robin asked. "There's no proof that anyone else was near the house when the Finches were murdered. Tom will argue that Ryan was the intended victim. His bedroom is very close to the kitchen. He'll say that Mandy found that out somehow and killed Ryan before looking for Nathan. Nathan was with Margaret, and Annie came down from her room, so she had to kill everyone. Then, since she was near the front door, she left through it."

"Maybe McKee won't think of that argument," Loretta said.

"And maybe the moon is made of green cheese," Robin answered.

CHAPTER FORTY-SEVEN

Robin argued that the jurors should have a reasonable doubt about Mandy Kerrigan's guilt because so many people had a motive to kill one of the Finches and no one knew who was the intended victim. She emphasized the fact that everyone connected to the auto insurance scam was dead, missing, or had an attempt made on their life. She told the jurors that someone working for Jack Kovalev could have come through the kitchen door and murdered the family, who, Robin argued, were dead when Mandy Kerrigan was at the front door.

Tom countered Robin's arguments exactly as predicted, and Robin was certain that her client was going to be convicted because she had missed the prosecution's key argument.

Judge Wright recessed the trial for lunch, and Robin, Ken, and Loretta went back to Barrister, Berman, and Lockwood, while Amanda went to her law office.

Robin grabbed a sandwich and retreated to her office. She didn't have an appetite, and she only pecked at the sandwich while she tried to think of what she could have done to save Mandy.

When she returned to court, she only half heard the judge's jury instructions as she continued to flagellate herself for failing Mandy Kerrigan. After finishing instructing the jurors at three o'clock, Judge Wright sent the jury out to deliberate.

Robin returned to her office, and Amanda went to hers. A little before six, Judge Wright called Tom and Robin back to the courtroom to tell them that the jurors had not reached a decision. He wanted to send them home for the night and have them return the next morning at nine, unless there was an objection.

"Is it a good sign that they haven't decided?" Kerrigan asked.

"I think so," Robin said. But she'd said that to keep up Kerrigan's spirits. She'd been in the business long enough to know that it was impossible to predict a jury's decision based on the length of time it took the jurors to reach it. One holdout could keep a jury working for days.

The emotional pain caused by her feeling that she had let down her client kept Robin up most of the night. When she woke up, she was groggy and depressed. She had worked so hard for Mandy, and she knew she was very smart, so how had she missed seeing Tom's argument about the door? A little voice reminded her that Amanda, Loretta, and Ken had not seen the problem with the door, but she was lead counsel. It was her responsibility to catch these things, and she had failed miserably.

She could not muster the energy to work out, and she walked to her office in a funk. She had a brief due in the Oregon Court of Appeals. She tried reading a case that she thought might have some good language for an argument she wanted to make, but her mind wandered.

The call telling her that the jury had reached a verdict came at four thirty. Robin alerted Amanda and gathered Ken and Loretta. No one spoke during the hike to the courthouse. When Robin walked into the courtroom, Tom was seated at his counsel table, looking toward the bench. She bet that he was as nervous as she was, because the most stressful part of a trial for all the participants is the time between learning that the jury has reached a verdict and learning what the jury has decided.

"What's happening?" Kerrigan asked when she was seated next to Robin.

"The jury has a verdict."

The bailiff rapped his gavel, and everyone stood. Judge Wright asked the bailiff to bring in the jury as soon as he was seated. Robin's heart was beating like a trip hammer, and her stomach was in a knot.

The jurors took their seats.

"Have you reached a verdict?" the judge asked.

Fredrick Manning, a retired schoolteacher, stood.

"Are you the foreperson, Mr. Manning?"

"Yes, sir."

"Very well. Miss Kerrigan, please stand."

Robin and Amanda stood with their client.

"Mr. Manning, how does the jury find on count one of the indictment, which charges Miss Kerrigan with the aggravated murder of Nathan Finch?"

"We find the defendant guilty as charged, Your Honor."

Robin felt light-headed, and she barely heard the rest of the guilty verdicts. Mandy stared straight ahead. When the foreperson was finished reading the verdicts, Mandy turned toward Robin.

"I didn't do it. I never hurt those people. The door was locked. I couldn't get in. I swear it."

"We'll appeal," Robin told her client, even though she could not think of one of the judge's rulings that was in error.

"I can't go to jail," Mandy said. "I didn't kill anyone."

"I know," Robin said, but her voice lacked conviction.

Kerrigan's face closed up, and she glared at her lawyer.

"I should never have let you represent me. You should have figured out what the DA was going to say about the door."

"You're right, Mandy. I fucked up."

Robin got through the rest of the court proceedings in a fog. She had failed Mandy Kerrigan. There was no way she could spin what had happened. The judge told the attorneys that he would begin the sentencing phase of the trial on Wednesday. Now Robin had the daunting task of convincing twelve people who believed that Mandy Kerrigan had slaughtered a whole family that she did not deserve to die.

CHAPTER FORTY-EIGHT

Robin went up to the jail to talk to Kerrigan about the sentencing phase of the case, but her client was so distracted and angry that Robin left without having accomplished much. Amanda was waiting for Robin at Robin's office with Loretta and Ken. They tried to console her, but she told them that the verdict was in and they had to concentrate on saving Mandy Kerrigan's life. The brainstorming session ended a little after seven. Amanda left, Ken started notifying the witnesses he had lined up for the sentencing phase of the case, and Loretta went home.

Mental fatigue and depression wore on Robin. She said goodbye to Ken and headed home. It was dark when she left her office and began the walk to her condo. A light rain had started to fall, so there weren't many people on the street. She should have noticed the man who was following her, but she was exhausted and her attention was focused on the sentencing hearing.

There was a park that took up a block on the way to her condo.

The park was bordered by some restaurants, art galleries, and other apartment buildings. No one was in the park, and Robin decided to cut through it. By the time the sound of the footsteps rushing toward her interrupted her thoughts, it was too late for her to grab her gun. She swiveled to face her attacker, but Lloyd Standish brought the butt of his gun down hard on her forehead. Robin staggered backward, stunned. Standish kicked her in the stomach. She doubled over, and he hit her in the head again. The blow knocked her to the ground and left her on the edge of consciousness.

Standish loomed over Robin. His gun was pointed at her face.

"Don't pass out on me, bitch. I want you awake and aware when I pull the trigger."

Blood ran down Robin's face. She willed herself to look Standish in the eye. The only chance she had was to bait him into doing something stupid that would give her a chance.

"Too bad you aren't man enough to fight me, but you always struck me as a pussy."

Standish laughed. "Good try. I've seen that movie. The hero and the bad guy throw down their weapons and go at each other mano a mano. It's not going to work, Robin. I'm not the least bit tempted to have a fair fight with you. My only regret is that I won't have time to—"

Standish's head exploded before he could finish his sentence. Robin's mouth gaped open as blood, skull fragments, and pieces of Standish's brain rained down on her.

Standish's body folded in on itself and collapsed in front of her.

"Holy shit!" was the best Robin could come up with. Then she looked for her savior, but she didn't see anyone in or near the park.

* * *

An EMT was working on Robin in the back of the ambulance that had been sent to the park along with a police car in answer to Robin's 911 call. Roger Dillon and Carrie Anders arrived shortly after the uniforms because Robin had asked the dispatcher to send them to the scene.

"This isn't some scam you thought up to get a mistrial, is it?" Carrie Anders joked when Robin had told the detectives what had happened and Anders was certain that Robin was okay.

Robin flashed a tired smile and gave Anders the finger.

"Any idea who saved your bacon?" Anders asked.

Robin did, but she wasn't going to do anything to endanger the person who had saved her life.

"I looked around the park when I got over the shock of seeing Standish's head explode, but I didn't see anyone. They were probably long gone."

"No guesses?" Carrie asked.

"I'm pretty woozy, Carrie, and I can't think straight right now."

"You don't look good. Are you going to ask for a postponement of the sentencing phase while you recuperate?"

"No. This isn't the first time I've had my bell rung. I've had concussions, and I'm not experiencing any of the symptoms. All I need is some painkillers and a good night's sleep."

"Don't be a hero," Dillon said. "Ask the judge to give you time to recover. We'll back you up."

"Tell McKee what happened; I'm certain he won't object," Carrie said.

Robin knew that Carrie knew that she and Tom had a relationship, and she studied Carrie for any signs of sexual innuendo. She saw none. What she did see was a friend who was concerned for her welfare.

"I'll call him and ask him to contact Judge Wright. If he has no objection, I'm sure the judge will give me a day or so to look human."

"Hell, a scar will improve your looks," Carrie said.

Robin started to laugh, but it hurt, and she grimaced instead.

Even though there were only a few blocks between the park and Robin's condo, Anders and Dillon insisted on driving her. Carrie went up with Robin and left when Robin assured her that she would be able to put herself to bed.

Robin phoned Tom as soon as Carrie left. It was only nine, but it felt like it was hours later.

"What's up?" Tom asked when he answered the phone. He sounded suspicious.

"Nothing good, Tom. Lloyd Standish tried to kill me an hour ago."

"What?!"

"I'm okay. A medic checked me out. I'm not concussed, and the damage is all superficial. I'll be good as new in a few days. And that's why I'm calling. I want to ask for a setover until Monday to start the sentencing phase so I don't look like the bride of Frankenstein when I'm back in court."

"Okay. Hold on. Tell me what happened."

Robin told Tom about the attack and her mysterious rescuer.

"Do you want me to come over?" Tom asked when Robin was through.

"Of course I do. But you can't come over while we're still in trial, and I wouldn't be much company. As soon as I hang up, I'm getting in my PJs and gobbling a few of the painkillers the medic dispensed. You'd be babysitting a corpse."

"If it's your corpse, I wouldn't mind."

"Ew! I had no idea I was dating a necrophiliac. Maybe I should stop seeing you."

Tom laughed. "If you can come up with a joke that quickly, I guess your brain is in one piece. You get to sleep. I'll call Judge Wright and get you the setover."

"Thank you, Tom."

"I'll think of a way for you to pay me back when this case is in our rearview mirror."

Robin disconnected and silenced her phone. When she was ready for bed, she swallowed two of the pain pills. While she waited for the medicine to kick in, she lay in the dark and thought about the person who had saved her life.

Alan Chen was a sniper, and he hated Lloyd Standish because Standish was responsible for killing his wife. Chen also knew that Standish had been stalking Robin.

It didn't take a genius to figure out who had saved her, but she was going to keep her deductions to herself. Alan Chen was grieving. Based on her personal experiences, Robin knew that he was going to keep grieving for a long time. If Dillon and Anders figured out who had saved Robin, more power to them. But she wasn't going to bring more trouble into Alan Chen's life.

CHAPTER FORTY-NINE

Robin was a little dizzy and in pain when she got up. She switched on her phone and checked it for messages. Loretta, Amanda, Ken, and several members of the press had left voice mails. An email, text, and a voice mail informed Robin that Judge Wright had scheduled a Zoom call between Robin, Mandy Kerrigan, and Tom for nine o'clock.

Robin punched in the number for Ken's cell phone.

"Are you okay?" Ken asked.

"I'm fine. A little dizzy, but I blame the pain pills for that."

"It's all over the news. They said Lloyd Standish almost killed you."

"Yeah, he did, but a good Samaritan shot him before he could finish what he started."

"Who came to the rescue?"

"I didn't see who it was, and I'm being truthful."

"You think it's Alan Chen, don't you?"

"I'm not going to guess."

"The police could go after him for shooting Standish," Ken said. "Everyone knows he blamed Standish for his wife's death, and he was a sniper."

"You're not telling me anything I don't already know."

At nine, Robin joined the Zoom call from her condo and explained what happened in the park. Then she got Mandy's consent to ask for a few days to recuperate. Tom didn't object. The judge asked Robin if she would be ready to go on Monday, and she said she would be.

The attempt on Robin's life was front-page news and the lead story on all the local television newscasts. Judge Wright hoped that the jurors had obeyed his instructions about not watching or reading anything about the case. If any of the jurors learned about the attack on Robin, there could be a mistrial.

While Robin, Tom, and Mandy Kerrigan listened, the judge had the jury brought into the courtroom and told the jurors that something had come up that had nothing to do with the case but made it necessary to recess until Monday. Then he told them again that they had to avoid television news, the Internet, and newspapers and warned them against discussing anything about the case with anyone, including family.

Robin was glad that she'd taken Carrie's advice and not played the hero by trying the sentencing phase right away. She was in a lot of pain in the morning, and one look in the mirror told her that she could get a role in any zombie movie without even auditioning. Besides the stitches, she had a black eye and a bad cut where her head had hit the ground when she fell.

She didn't have any material from her cases at home. She could have asked her secretary to bring files to her condo, but she had a headache and decided that would not be a good idea. Jeff had gotten her hooked on black-and-white movies from the forties, and she watched *The Maltese Falcon* and *Casablanca* on a channel that was showing Humphrey Bogart movies all day.

She ate an early dinner and watched a football game. The game ended at eight thirty. She tried to watch another movie, but the pain from her injuries was acting up, so she took two painkillers and drifted into a deep and disturbing sleep.

In her nightmare, she was trapped in a dark place with damp, cobwebbed corridors that stretched forever and refused to stay straight, curving when they should have ended before sending her back to a place she had just been.

She was lost and terrified and desperate to escape. The dark, wood-paneled walls of the hallways hemmed her in, and she tried every door she passed. Some doors were locked, and some opened into other hallways.

She ran harder, frantic to find a way out. She grabbed a doorknob and pulled. The door swung out, then it swung in, locking and unlocking.

Robin jerked awake, her heart racing and her thoughts racing even faster. She walked into the living room and looked at the lights on one of the bridges that crossed the river as she tried to piece together the idea her nightmare had prompted. When she'd worked out everything, she looked at her clock. It was twelve thirty. Ken was probably asleep, but she couldn't wait until the morning.

"We got it all wrong," Robin said as soon as Ken picked up.

"What time is it?" Ken asked, groggy from being awakened.

"Mandy is innocent, and I think I know what happened."

"Talk to me," Ken said, suddenly wide awake.

Robin told him what she had worked out.

"You might be right," Ken said when she finished.

"It's the only way to explain how the door could have been locked when Mandy tried it at eight oh five and open when Proctor tried it at eight thirty."

"The hard part will be finding a way to prove that you're right."

"We've got the weekend to do that," Robin said before she told Ken a few ideas she had for getting the evidence she would need to convince Tom to dismiss the case against Kerrigan.

"It's a stretch, but I'll get to it first thing."

"Go door-to-door and pray that someone saw something. Meanwhile, I'll check the dates when Annie started cyberbullying Donna Faber and call Carrie Anders."

It took Robin a long time to get back to sleep, and her dreams weren't peaceful. When she woke up at a quarter to six, she lay in bed, fighting for a few more hours of rest and losing the battle.

Robin knew that it was too early to call Carrie Anders, and she didn't have the energy to work out, so she dressed, scarfed down a bagel, and walked to Barrister, Berman, and Lockwood. The office was dark and deserted. She turned on some lights and made a pot of coffee. Then she found the log of the texts that had been pulled from Annie's phone and computer. When she found the date of the first cyberbullying text, she went on the Marie Curie Middle School website. A surge of adrenaline shot through her when she found what she'd been looking for. She'd been right!

Over the years, Robin had become friends with Carrie Anders, and there had been a few occasions when they had met off the grid to work together when they were both convinced that cooperation would lead to the solution to a case. Robin had Carrie's number in the contacts on her phone.

"How are you doing?" Carrie asked, concerned about Robin's injuries and her mental state after losing the trial.

"You've always had an open mind, Carrie," Robin said, going straight to the reason for her call and jumping over the small talk. "I think Mandy is innocent, and I think I know who killed the Finches and why. Will you listen to me? If I'm right, I'll need your help to prove it."

"Your client is definitely guilty, Robin. You're grasping at straws."

"You might be right, but what if you're not? As it stands now, I'm convinced that the jury is going to send Mandy to death row. Please listen to what I have to say. I know you. You couldn't live with yourself if you knew you'd been responsible for sending an innocent person to her death when you could have saved her."

There was dead air for what seemed forever. Then Carrie said, "I'm listening."

Robin laid everything out for the detective. She told Carrie what she needed from her.

"Okay, Robin. You've got me thinking."

"Will you do it?"

There was a long pause. Then Carrie said, "Yes."

"There's one more thing. When I visited the Finches' house, I walked through Annie Finch's room. There's a gym bag in her closet. Inside the gym bag, there is a pair of black thong underwear in a ziplock bag. You should see if there's semen on it. If there is, you should test it for DNA."

As soon as her call to Carrie ended, Robin called Amanda.

"We have to meet," Robin said. "I know who killed the Finches."

As soon as Robin finished talking, Amanda said she would be at Robin's office at nine.

Robin's door was open, and she heard voices in the corridor. She walked down the hall to Loretta's office.

"What's got you so excited, boss?" Loretta asked when she saw the big grin on Robin's face.

"War counsel at nine. We're going to save Mandy Kerrigan's life."

CHAPTER FIFTY

The sentencing phase of Mandy Kerrigan's trial was scheduled to start at nine on Monday morning. When Robin entered the courthouse, only Amanda was with her. Ken Breland was hard at work on the tasks Robin had assigned him, and Loretta was in the office working on legal issues Robin was worried Tom might raise. Robin had not heard back from Carrie, and that worried her, as her chance of saving Mandy's life might hinge on what Carrie discovered.

Robin had covered her wounds as best she could with makeup, but the damage was still visible. Reporters bombarded her with questions about the attack when she walked toward the courtroom. She said that there was an ongoing police investigation and she could not discuss what had happened. Several reporters asked her if the attempt on her life was connected to the trial, given that Lloyd Standish was an enforcer for the Russian mob. Robin hid behind her "no comment" mantra until she was safely in the courtroom.

Ken had served several subpoenas over the weekend. Arthur

Proctor was chatting with Beth Wrigley and her mother on a bench in the hall outside the courtroom.

Proctor stood up when he saw Robin. "I read that you were attacked. Are you okay?" he asked.

"Yes. Rattled and a little sore, but I'm fine otherwise. Thank you for asking."

"Can you tell me why I'm here?"

Robin smiled. "I don't have time right now. I'll be calling you this morning, and it will become clear."

Robin escaped the press by going into the courtroom. Tom McKee was already at his counsel table, and it took all of his self-restraint to keep from rushing over to Robin.

As soon as the guards brought Mandy Kerrigan into court, the bailiff told the attorneys that Judge Wright wanted to see them in his chambers. When the judge was satisfied that Robin was competent to continue with the trial, he ushered the parties into the courtroom and had the bailiff summon the jury.

Judge Wright knew that the jurors would see Robin's injuries. As soon as the jurors were seated, he asked them if they had followed his instructions about avoiding news coverage on television, the Internet, and radio. When the jurors assured the judge that they had followed his instructions, he told them that the case had been set over because Robin had been in an accident from which she had fully recovered.

After polling the jurors to see if Robin's accident would have any effect on their ability to be fair and impartial, Judge Wright moved on to the rules governing the sentencing hearing. He told the jurors that there were three possible sentences that could be imposed on Mandy Kerrigan now that she had been convicted of aggravated murder. They were life with the possibility of parole, life without the possibility of parole, and death.

After hearing evidence from the parties, the jurors would have to answer three questions: first, whether the conduct of the defendant that caused the death of the deceased was committed deliberately and with the reasonable expectation that death of the deceased or another would result; second, if raised by the evidence, whether the conduct of the defendant in killing the deceased was unreasonable in response to the provocation, if any, of the deceased; and third, whether the defendant should receive a death sentence. Judge Wright instructed the jurors that each of them must vote yes or no on the questions and that a death sentence would not be imposed if there was a single no vote on any of the questions.

Tom was not allowed to put on evidence that repeated evidence that had been presented during the guilt phase of the trial. Robin suspected that he would rest his argument for death on the horrifying nature of a mass murder. She was right, and the State's case was very short.

"Miss Lockwood, are you going to present any evidence?" Judge Wright asked.

Before Robin could answer, Ken Breland walked into court.

"May I have a moment to talk to my associate?" Robin asked.

Ken walked through the bar of the court. He looked excited, and Robin was equally excited when he told her what he had found. When they finished talking, Ken left the courtroom, and Robin turned to Judge Wright.

"We have several witnesses, Your Honor. Miss Kerrigan calls Beth Wrigley to the stand."

Beth and her mother entered the courtroom. Beth looked very

nervous when she was sworn, and Robin smiled at her in hopes of calming her.

"Where do you go to school, Beth?" Robin asked.

"Marie Curie Middle School."

"What year are you in?"

"Eighth grade."

"Were two of your friends Donna Faber and Annie Finch?"

"Yes."

"How long had you known them?"

"Since elementary school. Third grade, I think."

"Were you all on a basketball team together starting in fourth grade?"

"Yes."

"Besides basketball, did Donna like acting?"

"Yes."

"Was she in the school play?"

Tom McKee stood up. "Objection, Your Honor. I can't see how this information is relevant to the questions the jurors have to answer."

"Miss Lockwood?" Judge Wright asked.

"They are relevant to the third question, which asks whether Miss Kerrigan should receive a death sentence. Why this evidence is relevant will become clear after some of our other witnesses have testified."

"Based on that assurance, I will overrule the objection. Please continue, Miss Lockwood."

"Was Donna involved in the school play in seventh grade?"

"Yes."

"What teacher runs the drama club?"

"Mr. Proctor."

"That's Arthur Proctor?"

"Yes."

"Did you notice a change in Donna's personality after she tried out for the play?"

"Yes."

"What change did you observe?"

"Donna was always quiet and shy, but she stopped hanging with us, her friends. We'd ask her to do stuff, and she'd make excuses. And she seemed, I don't know, scared."

"You said that Annie Finch was on the basketball team?"

"Yeah. She was our best player."

"Did her personality change toward the end of seventh grade?"

"Yes. She stopped hanging with us too. And she started being really mean to Donna."

"Did she start cyberbullying Donna? Did she call her names like *slut* and *whore*?"

"Yes."

"Did the cyberbullying begin after Donna got involved with the school play?"

"Yes. About a month after Donna auditioned."

"Was Annie involved in the school play?"

"No."

"Was she in Mr. Proctor's seventh- and eighth-grade honors English class?"

"Yes."

"No further questions," Robin said.

Tom cast a confused look at Robin.

"I don't have any questions," McKee said.

"Thank you for your testimony," Judge Wright said to Beth. "You're all done, and you can leave."

The courtroom door opened, and Ken came in again. Robin asked the judge for a moment to talk to her investigator.

"Carrie got a hit," he whispered.

"What did she find?"

"The car shows up on a feed from a private security camera. You can read the license on one of the shots."

"Tell her to come to the courthouse."

"Will do."

"Is Mr. Simms here?"

"He's in the hall."

"Tell him to come into the courtroom."

Ken went into the hall, and Robin addressed the judge.

"Miss Kerrigan calls Mitchell Simms."

Moments later, a stoop-shouldered man in a business suit with a slight paunch and brown hair took the oath.

"Mr. Simms, how are you employed?" Robin asked after Simms was sworn.

"I'm a financial advisor with Arthur and Krieger."

"Where do you live?"

"My wife and I have a house in the West Hills on Azalea Terrace."

"Is your house across the street from a trail that leads into a section of Portland's urban forest?"

"Yes."

"Have you heard about the murder of the Finch family?"

"They lived fairly close to us in the West Hills, and everyone has been talking about it."

Robin addressed the court. "I am handing Mr. Simms a photograph of a car that I would like marked Defense Exhibit 7. Does this car look familiar?"

"I saw a car like it parked across from my house somewhere between seven thirty and eight thirty on the night that the Finches were murdered."

"How can you be so certain that was the night and time you saw the car?"

"I remember the night because I mentioned seeing the car to my wife when we heard about the murders on the morning TV news. It stood out because our house is on a dead end. It didn't belong to any of our neighbors, and we don't get a lot of visitors."

"And the time?"

"I heard the car park when a show I was watching started at seven thirty. I looked outside and saw the car. A person was out of the car and walking into the woods."

"Could you identify him?"

"No. I'm not even certain it was a man. I just saw the person's back."

"Did you see the car again?"

"No. The show was an hour. The car wasn't there when I looked at eight thirty."

"No further questions."

"No questions," Tom said.

"Miss Kerrigan calls Ken Breland."

"Mr. Breland, how are you employed?" Robin asked when Ken was sworn.

"I'm your investigator."

Robin handed Ken Defense Exhibit 7. "Did you take this photograph?"

"Yes."

"When did you take it?"

"At two o'clock yesterday."

"Who owns this car?"

"Arthur Proctor."

"No further questions."

Tom stood. "May we have a sidebar, Your Honor?"

"Why don't we take the morning recess? I'll see counsel in my chambers."

"What's happening?" Mandy Kerrigan asked.

"A lot. I'm hoping to put evidence before the jury that will convince them that you didn't kill anyone. Sit tight while I see the judge."

Robin and Amanda entered Judge Wright's chambers moments after Tom McKee.

"What's going on, Robin?" Tom asked when the door was shut. It was clear that he was upset.

"Let's keep this civilized, Tom. I'm as curious as you are. Let me ask the questions. Well, Robin, what is going on?"

"I have concrete evidence that will prove that Arthur Proctor killed the Finches."

"Kerrigan has been convicted. You can't retry the case," Tom said.

"No, but one of the questions the jury has to decide is whether Mandy should be put to death. I don't think the jurors will vote for a death sentence if I convince them that she's innocent."

Judge Wright smiled. "That's a pretty powerful argument, Tom."

Robin turned to Tom. "You put on a hell of a case. I never saw that argument about the door coming. But I think I've figured out how the door could have been locked at eight oh five and open at eight thirty, and I'm almost certain that Proctor killed the Finches and why he did it. If I'm right, do you really want to put obstacles in my way?"

Tom looked sick. Then he thought about what Robin had said.

Robin waited to hear Tom's answer, because what he answered would decide whether she would ever see him again.

Tom took a deep breath. "Go ahead. I don't want an innocent woman on death row. But that is where I'll argue she belongs if you can't convince me that I made a mistake when I charged her."

Robin let out the breath she'd been holding. "Thank you."

Judge Wright stood up. "Let's get to it, Miss *Mason*. Do you plan on getting your suspect to confess on the stand, like Perry always did?"

"You'll find out soon enough. I've subpoenaed him, and he's waiting in the hall. I'm going to call him after Carrie Anders testifies."

Tom's mouth gaped open. "What's she going to say?" he asked.

Robin smiled. "Carrie's here for show-and-tell."

CHAPTER FIFTY-ONE

While the judge and the attorneys were in Judge Wright's chambers, Carrie had set up her laptop and the bailiff had put up a screen so the jurors could see what the detective was going to project.

As soon as everyone was back in the courtroom, Robin started her direct examination.

"Detective Anders, as part of your investigation into the murder of the Finch family, did the Portland Police Bureau collect footage from traffic cameras and private security cameras?"

"Yes."

"Early this morning, did I tell you about a car and identify its owner?"

"Yes."

"Did I ask you to see if you could find any footage that showed this car on a traffic camera or any other camera between seven thirty and eight thirty on the evening the Finches were murdered?"

"Yes."

"Did you know where the car was at eight thirty?"

"It was parked outside the Finch home."

"Is that because Arthur Proctor owned the car in question and was at the Finch home calling 911 to report that the family was dead?"

"Yes."

"After I called, did you receive a call from Ken Breland, my investigator, during which he told you that a car similar to Mr. Proctor's had been seen parked on Azalea Terrace at seven thirty on the evening that the Finches were murdered, near a forest trail that could be taken to the rear of the Finch home?"

"Yes."

"Did you narrow your search?"

"I did."

"Do you know where Arthur Proctor lives and where Marie Curie Middle School is situated?"

"Yes."

"Mr. Proctor has testified that he drove to the Finches' house to discuss the possibility of sending Annie Finch to a private school. If you drove from Mr. Proctor's house or the middle school to the Finches' home, would you drive anywhere near Azalea Terrace?"

"No."

"Did you find any film that showed the car around the time of the murders?"

"Yes."

"Please tell the jurors what you found. Then show them the footage."

Carrie turned to the jury. "You can drive from Azalea Terrace to the Finch home in five minutes, give or take a few minutes depending on traffic. Azalea Terrace is a dead end. You go to the end of the street and make a right on Pine Way. Then you drive on Pine past the entrance to Elk Meadow, a gated community, for a few miles before turning up Cotton Lane and making a right on the Finches' street."

"Did you find any film footage that showed Mr. Proctor's car on the route from Azalea Terrace to the Finch home that you related to the jury?"

"Yes. Elk Meadow has security cameras on the gate that is situated on Pine Way. Film from the security camera shows Mr. Proctor's car driving past the gate at eight twenty-seven."

"How do you know that the car depicted in the security footage belongs to Mr. Proctor?"

"The license plate shows up in one of the shots."

"Please show the footage that shows Mr. Proctor's car to the jury."

Carrie did. The film was only a few seconds long and it was grainy, but the license plate was visible, if unreadable. Next, Carrie showed a blowup of the license plate that was readable. Then she told the jury that the license was registered to Arthur Proctor.

When Tom said that he did not have any questions for the detective, Robin called Arthur Proctor to the stand. Since he had been waiting in the hall, he didn't know what Mr. Simms, Carrie Anders, and Beth Wrigley had said.

"Thank you for coming to court again," Robin said. "I know this is a school day, and I'm sorry I've inconvenienced you."

"That's all right. I know how important this hearing is."

"Was Annie Finch one of your students?"

"Yes. She was in my eighth-grade honors English class."

"Did you tell her parents to take Annie out of Marie Curie Middle School and put her in a private school because you felt that she was underperforming?"

"Yes."

"Why did you go to the Finch home on the night they were killed?"

"Mr. and Mrs. Finch were worried about the cost of sending Annie to a private school. I had discovered a number of ways they could ease the financial burden. I had a file with information about scholarships and student loans. I showed it to the detectives."

Robin put a map up on the screen that showed Proctor's house and the Finches' home. She used a pointer to trace a route between the two homes.

"Is this the route you took to get to the Finches' house?"

Proctor studied the map. Then he nodded.

"Yes."

"Did you direct a seventh grader named Donna Faber in the school play?"

"Yes."

"Did you learn that Annie Finch had cyberbullied Donna and Donna had died by suicide?"

"Yes. It was very sad."

"Donna's parents had filed a lawsuit against the Finches because of Annie's actions, hadn't they?"

"Yes."

"Did you tell the police about the cyberbullying or the lawsuit?"

"No. I was very upset. I had discovered the bodies, and I wasn't thinking clearly. When I did remember the lawsuit, I assumed that the police would find out about it during their investigation."

"Are you aware that Annie began her campaign of harassment against Donna shortly after she started acting in the school play?"

"No."

Robin picked up the log of the files on Annie's computer and the printout of several files the lab had discovered.

"I'd like these printouts marked Defense Exhibits 17 through 35."

"No objection," Tom said.

Robin turned back to Proctor. "I've just entered into evidence printouts of files from Annie Finch's laptop and phone in which she calls Donna a whore and a slut and other foul names that suggest that Donna was having sex with someone. Do you have any idea who her lover might be?"

Proctor shifted in his seat, but his expression did not change.

"No. I had no idea that Donna was engaged in that kind of activity."

"You are aware that it is illegal for an adult to have sex with a fourteen-year-old girl?"

"Of course."

"Is your car a black Volvo with the license number 671RGK?"

"Yes."

"That's the car you drove from your house to the Finches' house on the night they were murdered?"

"Yes."

"Your route didn't take you anywhere near Pine Way, did it?"

Proctor hesitated for a fraction of a second before answering, "No."

"If you drove to the Finches' house the way you said you did, how do you explain passing the entrance to the Elk Meadow estate at eight twenty-seven?"

"I didn't."

Robin had the bailiff play the footage Carrie Anders had discovered.

"That's your car, isn't it?"

Proctor peered at the grainy photograph. "It looks like my car, but it's someone else's vehicle."

Robin showed the teacher the blowup that showed Proctor's license plate. "Does the Department of Motor Vehicles usually issue two drivers identical license plates?"

Proctor stared at the screen and didn't answer.

"A witness testified that he saw a car very similar to your car parked on Azalea Terrace at seven thirty on the night the Finches were killed. Did you know that there's a trail that a person can follow to the Finches' backyard that starts next to that car?"

"No," Proctor answered. Robin noticed that his answer was not as confident as some of his early responses.

"One of the key pieces of evidence against Mandy Kerrigan was her statement that she could not enter the Finch home around eight o'clock because the door was locked and your statement that the door was open when you arrived at eight thirty. Mr. McKee argued that the door had to be open when Miss Kerrigan was on the Finches' porch because the Finches were dead then and no one went to the front door between the time Miss Kerrigan was on the porch and your arrival.

"Let me ask you what you think of a possible explanation of the events of that night that would explain how the door was locked around eight o'clock and open when you arrived.

"I had my investigator walk the trail between Azalea Terrace and the Finch home. It took him fifteen minutes at a quick walk. If someone parked his car on Azalea Terrace at seven thirty and took the trail to the Finches' backyard, he would have arrived at seven forty-five. The killer enters the Finch home through the back door. Then he murders the Finches and is set to leave through the back door when he hears Miss Kerrigan pounding on the locked front door. He waits until she leaves, then unlocks the door. Then he walks or jogs back to his car and drives to the Finch home, arriving at eight thirty, and gains entrance to the house through the door that he has unlocked, so he can report the murders and avoid suspicion. What do you think?"

"I . . . I'm not going to speculate."

Robin took out the ziplock bag with the black thong panties she had discovered in Annie's gym bag. "Did Annie Finch wear a pair of panties that looked like this when you had sex with her?"

"I never had sex with Annie or any of my students."

"A forensic expert at the crime lab is running a DNA test on semen found on these panties. Was Annie Finch furious with you for sleeping with Donna Faber?"

"I never slept with Donna Faber."

"Was Annie using these panties with your semen on them to blackmail you? Is that why you killed her?"

"I did not have sex with Annie Finch, and I did not kill her."

"If I'm wrong, the lab won't find your DNA when they get the results of their test. Would you be willing to give a DNA sample to the lab for comparison purposes?"

Proctor stared at the ziplock bag.

"Mr. Proctor," Judge Wright said. "You have to answer the question, unless you want to assert your right to have a lawyer advise you of your Fifth Amendment right to refuse to answer the question on the grounds that it might incriminate you. What do you want to do?"

"I . . . I . . ."

"Yes?" the judge asked.

Proctor collected himself and sat up straight. "I believe I should discuss this matter with an attorney."

Carrie Anders had been sitting in the back of the courtroom with Roger Dillon. The detectives walked through the gate that opened into the bar of the court and up to the witness stand.

"Arthur Proctor," Carrie said, "I am placing you under arrest for the murders of Annie, Nathan, Ryan, and Margaret Finch."

Then she read Proctor his Miranda rights and led him out of the courtroom.

Robin had been watching the jurors and Tom McKee during her examination of Arthur Proctor. They looked stunned.

"Your Honor," Robin said, "I think there are grounds for dismissing the case against my client, and I move for a dismissal with prejudice so she can get out of jail."

"Mr. McKee?" the judge said.

"What has just happened . . . It's unprecedented. I'm leaning toward agreeing with Miss Lockwood, but I'm going to have to talk to my supervisor."

"That sounds reasonable," the judge said. "We'll recess while you go to your office, and we'll reconvene when I hear from you."

"What just happened?" Mandy asked.

"Robin just pulled a rabbit out of a hat," Amanda said. "And you might be going home very soon."

CHAPTER FIFTY-TWO

Half an hour after Tom McKee had gone to his office to brief Mike Greene, he returned to the courtroom and moved to dismiss all the charges against Mandy Kerrigan with prejudice. Mandy, her face stained with tears, hugged Robin before being led to the jail by the guards to wait for the paperwork that would officially set her free.

"You don't look happy," Amanda said to Robin as several reporters surrounded Tom, asking for comments.

"Mandy's criminal case is over, but her career might be over too. She's still suspended for using PEDs."

"Are you going to help her get her career back on track?"

"I said I would. I'm hoping that the UFC will consider what she's gone through as an adequate punishment, but I don't have high hopes that they will."

Amanda put her hand on Robin's shoulder. "If anyone can do it, you will."

Robin smiled. "Thanks for the vote of confidence."

Ken and Loretta had already left, and Amanda followed them. A group of reporters walked over to Robin, and she told them how happy she was that justice had been served, before using her injuries as an excuse to stop answering questions.

When Robin was alone, Tom walked over.

"Okay, Sherlock. Tell me how you figured out that Proctor killed the Finches."

"It was the door. If Mandy was telling the truth, the door had to be locked at eight o'clock and unlocked at eight thirty. That meant that someone inside the house—the killer—had unlocked the door after Mandy left. So, the killer was inside at eight o'clock. The killer would not have left through the front door, because someone might see him, and there would be no reason to, since entry had been made through the kitchen door. That meant he had come through the forest on one of the trails.

"I had Ken go to all the trailheads and ask people in those neighborhoods if they had seen anything unusual around the time the Finches were murdered. We got lucky with Mr. Simms. Once we had our suspicious car on Azalea Terrace, I asked Carrie to check surveillance cameras in the area, and we got lucky again.

"I was already suspicious of Proctor. I checked the Marie Curie website. Annie started cyberbullying Donna shortly after rehearsals for the play started. I was certain that the girls were sleeping with the same man, and Proctor was the link between the two."

"Why did he go back to the house after the murders? If he'd stayed away, no one would have suspected him."

"It was the panties. She kept those panties in that ziplock bag for a reason. I'm guessing Annie was using them for blackmail. I don't know if she forced Proctor to try to convince her parents to send her to a private school or if she was asking for money, but I bet she told him that she had a pair of panties with his semen on them and threatened to give them to the police so she could prove he'd had sex with a minor if he didn't do what she wanted.

"I'm guessing that Proctor killed the rest of the Finches first and planned to kill Annie after she told him where she'd hidden the panties, but something went wrong and he killed her before she could tell him where they were hidden. Mandy said that she might have heard a scream and a shot when she was pounding on the door. Maybe Annie screamed for help when she heard Mandy, and Proctor shot her to keep her quiet. Proctor must have panicked and run back to his car. Then he realized that he could get one more chance to search for the panties if he went back to the house before the police came. Of course, he had to call 911 for cover because his car was parked in front of the house."

Tom laughed and shook his head. "Have I ever told you that you are very, very smart?"

"Not that I remember."

"Well, you are, and I think we need to celebrate."

"You want to celebrate losing a case you'd already won?"

"I want to celebrate being saved from making a horrific mistake. And I think the proper way to do that would be a candlelight dinner at Portland's best French restaurant."

"Or we could go to my condo. I still feel funny about going out in public looking like the bride of Frankenstein."

"I think you look like the bride of Frankenstein's cute sister."

Robin laughed. Then she stopped smiling. "Have you heard anything about who the police are looking at for killing Lloyd Standish?"

"You know they're looking for Alan Chen."

"He saved my life."

"And I am very glad he did. I doubt he'll be charged with a crime, because he saved your life. Now, do you feel better?"

Robin smiled. "Yeah, I do. My place at six?"

"Sounds good."

Tom took a step toward Robin. She knew he wanted to kiss her, so she turned away and started collecting her files and laptop.

"Later, stud." She pointed toward the courtroom door. "The press is watching."

Tom laughed and went back to his table.

Robin was pressed against Tom before the door to her condo had swung shut, and they covered the distance between the door and Robin's bed in record time.

"Whoa," was all Tom could manage when they were lying side by side.

"Ditto," Robin said as she squeezed Tom's hand.

"I think I'm going to throw more of our cases."

Robin released Tom's hand and punched his arm. "You didn't throw Mandy's case. I won it fair and square."

"Nah, I knew she was innocent all along. I just wanted to make you look good so you'd get more clients."

"That was very nice of you. Can you think of a way I can thank you?" Robin said as she rolled on top of Tom.

"Let me think about that while I recuperate."

Robin pressed her head against Tom's chest. Things had looked so bleak a few days ago, but tonight there was only sunshine. She felt proud of herself for not giving up in Mandy Kerrigan's case. Mandy might still be in a bad place, but any place was better than a tiny cell where she would have waited to be put down like a dog.

As Robin listened to Tom's heartbeat, she couldn't help thinking about Jeff. She knew he would be happy for her if he was watching. And she was happy. She hadn't known Tom long, but she believed that he was decent and good, the type of man she could see herself spending a lifetime with. Relationships can end for a dozen reasons, but she thought that the signs were good that this one would last.

ACKNOWLEDGMENTS

I want to thank the team at St. Martin's, starting, as usual, with my editor, Keith Kahla, who makes my dull prose into something Shakespeare would be proud of; Chris Ensey and Sara Robb, my copy editors, who clean up my mistakes so I sound halfway intelligent; Hector DeJean and Martin Quinn, who help my books reach the public; and the rest of the people who help me tell my story: Grace Gay, Jonathan Bush for his great jacket designs, Paul Hochman, Ken Silver, Omar Chapa, Benjamin Allen, Katy Robitzski, Sally Richardson, Catherine Turiano, and Thérèse Plummer, the voice of Robin Lockwood.

I want to thank my agent, Jennifer Weltz, and everyone at the Jean V. Naggar Literary Agency; Marissa Margolin, my fabulous, talented granddaughter, without whom I would never have been able to describe a teenage girl's room; and my extraordinary spouse, Melanie Nelson. I am also grateful for the support I get from my daughter, Ami Stamm Margolin, my son, Daniel Margolin, his wife, Amanda, and my talented grandson, Loots, who puts up with my teasing. I am a lucky guy!